THE WIDOW'S REDEEMER

PHILIPPA JANE KEYWORTH

ISBN (eBook): 978-1-9998652-2-1

ISBN (Print): 978-1-9998652-4-5

ALSO BY
PHILIPPA JANE KEYWORTH

LADIES OF WORTH SERIES

Fool Me Twice

A Dangerous Deal

Lord of Worth

REGENCY ROMANCES

The Widow's Redeemer

The Unexpected Earl

MULTI-AUTHOR SERIES

Finding Miss Giles

FANTASY

The Edict

There are several people I want to thank for helping me with my writing over the years:

First, thank you to Clare Hughes. You were the first person to read my stories, and your praise and encouragement was why I continued to write, so thank you.

Second, thank you to M.M. Bennetts. You have given me boatloads of advice, both literary and historical, and you have proofread my work more than once. Without your advice and encouragement, I would not be in print today, so thank you.

Third, thank you to my Mum and Dad. Thank you Dad for spurring me on whenever I've been flagging in my writing journey, thank you Mum for actually reading it, and thank you both for who you are and how you love and support me.

CHAPTER ONE

Everything has beauty, but not everyone sees it.
– Confucius

"I don't understand your meaning, sir." A little crinkle appeared between Letty's brows. She folded and unfolded her stitchery, her hands becoming more agitated with every second that passed.

She cast the sewing onto a small side table and began teasing the frayed cuffs of her muslin day dress before standing abruptly. Leaving the doctor behind, she walked over to the small window set deeply into the farmhouse wall. Silence followed. She stared at the rugged slabs of stone that made up the thick wall and kept the winter winds at bay.

The beginning of the week had brought her husband back from the gaming hells of London. He had been sickening from exposure to rain and cold on his journey home and had fallen from his horse. Could life be so ready to change? Were the cards being dealt as she stood here?

The physician was packing up instruments into his old leather bag. There was the clink of draught bottles as they slotted into place, the creak of un-oiled leather, and the click of a stiff clasp.

Letty swung back round to face the retreating doctor. "But surely there is something more that may be done?"

His small white head shook in a well-acted sadness. Perhaps he had given this news a dozen times, perhaps he had given it a hundred times over. His headshake was so perfected and his eyes so full of sympathy. It was a slow and definite last retreat.

"It is merely a matter of nursing him until his time comes." He paused, wetting his bottom lip before taking a long breath. "Has he drawn up a will?"

Letty's thoughts scattered everywhere at once. She had not thought about a will. Even the mention of one but two days ago would have seemed unwarranted, almost absurd. Yet here John lay, with waxy skin and red-rimmed eyes, the smell of fever on him. The scent was curious; body odours were mingling with the wood smoke and damp, producing a rank and stale smell.

A will, was that what the doctor had said? John had been in charge of business matters, and he would not have had the forethought to write a will at seven and twenty, or at least not the care.

"I am not sure." She reached a hand up, unconsciously checking her hair. These were not things she had expected to confront in her second year of marriage.

"I suggest you summon your lawyer as soon as possible. It is hard to estimate how much time your husband has left."

She nodded dumbly, blinking quickly in a last, vain attempt to understand the enormity of what was happening. A sad smile marked his lips, as though that settled the business. With no more to be done, he took up his case and descended the tight spiral staircase.

Letty followed behind, grappling with the feeling of shock

but still aware of her obligation to see the doctor out. In front of the house, the small boy who looked after the farm's horses waited with the doctor's animal. Letty watched the physician mount the small Dartmoor pony. The animal shook his head in impatience for his hay and stable and was only happy once his hooves were falling in a steady beat. John's wife waited at the door until the creature disappeared from sight.

For a moment she stood silently, contemplating the sentence which had just this evening been hung over her life. The gathering gloom descended upon her still figure, leaving her a lonesome silhouette in the evening farmyard. Dew settled unbidden upon the landscape, the droplets disturbed a little by a sea breeze. The sky was dark—hues of blue, grey, red, and purple all slowly merging into one as night formed above her. In a far off pasture the soft lowing of a cow could be heard. The familiar sound brought her back to the problems at hand. She shook off the desire to sleep and, turning on her wooden heel, walked hastily inside.

A small fire, which had been lit early in the evening, was glowing sluggishly in the grate. The scent of it had gradually penetrated everything in the room. Objects surrounding the bed were cast in an unusual light. Several rapidly drawn up letters scattered a small desk in the corner of the room, the wax on each one looking like a small arachnid in the dim light. A bowl of tepid water reflected a little of the firelight, giving the depths an eerie luminescence. A rag hung over the side of the basin, like a lone shipwreck survivor crawling to safety.

The moonlight was firmly in control of the rugged landscape outside the window when she finally drifted off. The large winged armchair in her husband's room had become her home in the past week, ever since he had been taken ill. The heavy woollen blanket, which was now draped across her unconscious frame, had become the roof over her head.

Letty was awakened by nightmares only half an hour

after she fell asleep. Too many worries consumed her mind which, until settled, would prevent her from further rest. Soon, realizing the cold had frozen her aching joints, she rose to dab her husband's brow. He made no indication of consciousness.

The farmhands had brought John back after finding him unhorsed and drenched on one of the farm tracks. After all, a drunk man was no horseman. Letty had not heard from him while he had been in Town and even his return had been a surprise.

Pausing a moment, she watched the knitting and un-knitting of his feverish brow before turning and making her way to the desk. She shuffled the letters that lay there into some kind of order and gingerly placed another log on the fire.

"Lettice?"

She spun on her heel at the sound of the rasping voice. Small feet bore her swiftly from the fireplace to John's side. She knelt on the wooden floor to better look into his weary eyes. He was groggy, his eyes roving about the room, though Letty could see lucidness as they settled upon her.

"Yes, John? How do you feel?" She dunked the cloth in the basin and made to wipe his beaded brow.

"No, no more of that. You have made me cold enough." He turned his head from her.

She nodded slightly, placing the rag back into the basin.

"Why has this come upon me?" he cried out suddenly. "I am in such pain!" He writhed on the bed and upset the soiled bed linens.

"How can I make you more comfortable? Your pillows, do you wish to sit up?"

"That's the last thing I want to do, Lettice. My back, it aches terribly." He paused. So little strength was left to him; it was an exertion even to speak a single sentence—especially a sentence filled with anger. "My mother was right. We should never have left Town. None of this would have come upon us."

Her eyes dropped to the disordered bedcovers. "We would never have met."

He made no response and turned his head away once again. Letty could not stand the feeling of ineptness. She stood up, pausing by the chair, and then made her way to the fire. There was an old loaf of bread left on a cutting board by its side. She was hungry; it was early morning, a long time since she had had her frugal dinner. She started sawing off a piece to toast over the fire.

"Will you not ask if your sick husband wants something to eat?"

"Do you?"

"No, but you could at least act the caring wife."

Letty did not answer. It was best she refrained while John was in this mood. Then, with a sobering feeling, she realised that perhaps there would not be many more of his moods to bear.

"The doctor said...well, he said the fever is not abating. He was worried. You are weakening rather than strengthening."

"And so I expect he thinks I should call the lawyer." John coughed, a wracking sound that clawed at his lungs and rattled his core.

"He did mention it, yes." She did not mean it as an attack, but John took it to be one.

"So quick to make me sign over my fortune. I have been ill but a week." The well-known scowl lines of his face deepened in a sneer.

"John?" She turned to face him. Despite their differences, to tell a man he was dying could never be an easy thing. How could she approach it? How could she say it?

As it was, she would not have to bear the discomfort of speaking it. He had turned his head away again, and he would not turn it back now. He had read it in her anxious eyes all too clearly. Death was inevitable to all men, and to him it would come sooner than to most.

She stayed by his bed, quiet, trying hard to clear her mind of all the thoughts that clamoured for attention. It was still dark beyond the walls of the house, dark like her mind which was filled with a hundred worries. She would go on through the night worrying, waiting by his side and watching his pain.

Dawn came slowly. She rose from the chair she had been waiting in and walked round the bed to face him. As her gaze fell on his face, the cockerel crowed. His eyes were cold, distant, and lifeless. His body was pale and hard, the worries of a lifetime written in the lines of his harsh, heavy face. She left him there. She did not close his eyes but walked through the cold house in search of her shawl so that she could go to the village and fetch the funeral men. The lawyer never came and neither did her tears.

John's body was made ready for burial, and the farm's tenants were duly informed. Letty would be the only one following the coffin to the graveyard on that bleak walk. No friends came; even family, it appeared, were unable to attend. Letty wondered that John's mother did not come to bury her son, to see the last trace of his earthly self disappear into the ground. It would not be until later that she would receive a letter explaining that, upon hearing of her son's death, the mother had locked herself in her room and was refusing to eat or come out. To lose a husband had been the first trial for that mother to overcome, but now a son also within two years was more than she could bear. So Letty was left to walk behind her husband's coffin alone.

The last of the rich brown earth was tossed carelessly by the gravedigger. The soil sprayed across the grave that contained a body that was once a man. Feeling a cold northerly breeze spring up, Letty clasped the material of her thin pelisse closer. She looked around the deserted graveyard, sighed quietly, and then turned to make the lonely walk home.

Letty's mind was absent. Her body, however, was seated in a large leather armchair, the springs of which were becoming rather too obtrusive, while the stuffing was half there and half missing. The chair was in a tiny room at the back of a building that constituted the solicitors' offices. The rambling structure was situated in the village, a little set back from the other buildings, and was condemned by many to be in a worse state of repair than the infamous blacksmith's. This was partly due to the age and personality of the main law-working occupants, but it was also because their clientele possessed a low standing and, therefore, a deficient income.

Despite the building's exterior and the general tattiness of the objects within, it was a tidy little office. Nothing seemed out of place, and, unlike most solicitors' desks, this one did not have paperwork scattered across it. Letty was alone in the room for a long while. The faint mutterings and voices, muffled by the wall, floated in to her. The noises all washed over her, and she did not pay them much attention. How could she be interested in the chit-chat of persons she had never met when her future was being located, shuffled, and glanced over?

The man who would be the bearer of all news concerning her future eventually opened the door. He paused on the threshold. Letty could hear his steady breathing though she did not look round. Her head remained perfectly still, her eyes forward, and she had a politeness about her carriage. She clasped her hands loosely in her lap, ready for whatever would be thrown into them. She may not have had a governess who had taught her fine languages or clever mathematics but, thanks to her parson scholar of a father, she was no fool. That pause upon the threshold was one small thing which warned her of what was to come.

Why would a solicitor pause on the threshold, run a handkerchief over the perspiration that had suddenly beaded on his brow, give four brisk sniffs, and then straighten his plain cravat before facing his client? The answer was plain and it was simple. It whispered itself into Letty's mind. It said: fear.

She smiled faintly as the solicitor took his seat. He was a short, wiry old man and rather outmatched by the much too large wooden desk. He managed a small, polite smile before he placed his stack of papers carefully out before him. With all of them equally spaced and perfectly straight, he cleared his throat and began.

"Now, Mrs. Burton, ah, here we are, ah, yes. Now I have drawn up and put together all the estate's values and assets including the farm and the house." He refrained from using the term "your house", and that was when she began to realise her true predicament. "I have then compared them to repayments needing to be made, yes, um, now...." He readjusted his wire-rimmed spectacles while the small tuft of white hair in the centre of his head quivered. "Yes, ah...."

Letty's heart was tugged a little by the awkward situation this man had been placed in. She rested a tentative hand on the desk but took care to distance it from the solicitor's own hands. She captured his gaze with her frank brown eyes. "Mr. Glenville, I am led to believe that sometimes husbands have little to leave to their wives due to unfortunate business circumstances leading up to a sudden death. I understand that this cannot be helped." She kept her eyes on his, speaking far more with them than with her mouth.

"Yes, yes, of course. So glad you understand, Mrs. Burton. It can cause such upset, you see, when the value of the estate and assets comparative to various debts is read out. That is why—well, never mind that." He reshuffled the papers then took them up again and read on in a calm, precise voice. When he had finished, Letty remained poised for a few moments longer, allowing the information to take its rightful place in her mind. She had been completely unaware of the debts and the precarious position John had been in before he died.

"I see," she said finally, with far more firmness than Mr. Glenville had expected. "And now, tell me truthfully, can the assets fulfil the repayments in their entirety with anything left over?" Her eyes fell back into focus as she spoke, containing a hardness that had not been there before.

"Well, Mrs. Burton, this is where it gets rather more complex. You see, your husband's affairs had fallen into, well, how shall I say? Difficult times. Therefore, through my calculations of his estate and the debts he accrued from purchases, as well as the debts from ah...several respectable establishments in London."

Letty's neck could not help but tense at the reference to her husband's regular appearance at some of London's most fashionable gaming hells. It had not been unusual for him to be away from Cornwall for weeks at a time while he entertained himself in London. She remembered the look of disgust and the lack of farewell as he journeyed away from their house each time he went to the metropolis. How could he, a bred gentlemen, stand to be in the country with little or no entertainment? Coupled with this was the severe lack of society that had attended him ever since his marriage to Letty. So severe were the consequences of his disadvantageous marriage that to spend only moments in his wife's presence was too much for him to bear.

He would be off, of course, entertaining himself in some club or another, chasing days of past glory in the far-gone Seasons. He met his friends, the ones she was never permitted to see, the ones in front of whom she could only prove an embarrassment. She had often wondered what those friends had heard of her. If it were spoken from John's lips, then it would not be praise. There had been a few times when his words had stung more than his hand upon her—not many, but a few.

"Oh, I beg your pardon, Mr. Glenville. Could you please repeat what you just said?" Letty's back straightened and her mind returned from that far off place.

"Have no fear, Mrs. Burton." Mr. Glenville smiled slightly. He liked Lettice Burton, even if she had married above her station. She seemed a sweet girl, and yet, as he saw her sitting there, he reflected that she was much changed from the girl he had seen on her wedding day. She no longer looked an innocent, fresh-faced child; she was a woman now, at least about the eyes. There was a sort of wisdom there, a lack of that childlike naivety she had once borne. "I understand this is a difficult time. Losing a spouse is a terrible thing, especially at so young an age."

Letty bowed her head in assent, but behind the eyes that Mr. Glenville had deemed wise, there was no grieving heart. Was that wrong? Letty felt pangs of guilt, and yet, as she raised her head again and felt the slight bruising at the back of her neck, the guilt bled away.

"What I was beginning to explain was the financial plan for Highfield. In order to cover the debts owed, I am afraid that the only way is to sell the house and the farm along with it."

Letty, after several days of widowhood, felt the first tears pricking her eyes. The guilt came back, but it was overcome with sadness. She thought with fondness—and bitterness—of the home she had shared with John and for a moment could not bear the thought of its inevitable loss.

"I understand, Mr. Glenville. I give you all the authority to see to the matter. I shall prepare the house and farm for a new owner and take my leave of the tenants."

"Madam, I know this is outside of my authority, but I just wish to inquire—have you anywhere to go? I would not go about selling this property for you if you have no safety."

Letty smiled at him, his kindness a surprise yet fitting with his winsome face. "It is quite all right, Mr. Glenville. I am sure that my family will take me in." She said it with a certainty she was far from feeling. "In the meantime, the debts must be paid. Please sell Highfield, and before other debts are settled, take your own wages out of the sum. I do not wish to see you underpaid."

Mr. Glenville looked down at the desk, shuffling papers in a brisk fashion. He pulled a handkerchief out of his pocket and fluffed it about his nose. He was trying his hardest to smile his thanks without seeming impertinent. When he looked up, he saw a large smile brightening Letty's mouth, and it instantly put him at his ease. The smile remained, covering the anxiety inhabiting her mind and protecting her from further sentiment or questions. She rose to exit.

Mr. Glenville came out from behind his desk and made to take her hand. The sudden movement caused Letty to shrink back instinctively, her arms moving to protect her body. Mr. Glenville's owl-like eyebrows rose and crinkled in confusion. Letty, her wide eyes taking in what she had just done unconsciously and the harmless gesture of the man which she had misread, dropped her hands to her sides in embarrassment.

"Thank you, Mr. Glenville," she said, trying to speak as though nothing unusual had just occurred. "You have been exceedingly helpful. If you could send me a missive here and there, to update me on the sale's progress and debt repayments, I would greatly appreciate it." She made no move to give him her hand.

The small man, willing to ignore the strange episode,

bowed deeply before straightening again. Something flashed in his eyes, but Letty missed the look of admiration he bestowed upon her. She was already crossing the threshold, planning in her mind what needed to be done next.

Letty had barely eaten a thing at lunch, and now, as she was walking to the farm tenants' houses, a feeling of weakness came over her. She would not be eating until the leave-taking was done, however long it took. The sky was overcast though it was not likely to rain. Letty observed the sun-whitened clouds that threw everything into an oddly naked light.

The dirt track, which she had walked down so many times to oversee the farm work while John was away, was slightly damp thanks to last night's rain. Her black widow's garb had been bought at the cheapest price, so if a little mud spattered the hemline she did not much care. She was too used to walking in the country to be bothered about hemlines or complexion.

Her small figure went in and out of the few cottages on the farm. She bade farewell to the many families, the familiar smell of animals and earth in her nose. She was touched by the few words of condolences that were uttered, even if the tenants cared little for the loss of John. She saw their many concerned eyes and knew their feelings were for her.

To them she was the kindly parson's daughter who came and asked after each and every one of them, never forgetting a name. Yes, they would be sorry to see her go, yet the promise of a new master who might not be as tyrannical as the last was something that gave them hope. Why had the gentleman come from Town to a small piece of Cornwall in the first place? It was a piece of the country scorned by the modish, and clearly it had been scorned by him as well.

Letty knew of the many questions that her union with John had raised. They had been worlds apart in station, and they would never have married had it not been for one indiscretion. That one incident, which had been so easily misread, was the reason she had been married for two years to a man who did not love her. If only John had not led her into a compromising situation because of his own desires; if only she had not so easily mistaken his lust for love. He had been a man whom she had thought she loved, and it had taken time for that naivety to fade after their hasty marriage. She had slowly realised his resentment of her, and it was a resentment that had in two years grown savage.

Yet, as she spoke to each tenant she felt a slight loss, a slight sense of pain at the parting she was making from the place that had been her home, no matter the circumstances. She remembered that she needed to write a letter to her parents asking their shelter. Would they be able to take her back into their parsonage? Somehow, it seemed impossible to go back to her childhood home—that place where her father had once tutored John, where they had met, where the unfortunate incident had happened which forced them to marry.

Too much had happened to her, had been inflicted upon her, for her to return to that place where she had once been so innocent. She felt as though the innocence she had worn in her youth had become polluted. She could not return to live the life of someone she would never be again. As the last tenant closed the door behind her, she turned toward her home, and as she walked back in the twilight, she knew that tonight, at least, it was too late to think upon the future.

THE FOLLOWING MORNING BROUGHT A letter from Theodora Burton, Letty's sister-in-law, who resided in Truro.

The small, pretty hand, familiar to Letty, brought a little smile to the young widow's lips. What had her relative been up to now?

17 October 1815

Dearest Lettice,

How are you? I am so sad to hear of John's passing away. It was such a dreadful shock! I actually said to Mrs. Grockel, my housekeeper, how sudden it was. I even dropped my paintbrush when I read the letter you sent me about it. (I was in the midst of decorating a small cabinet and now it is totally ruined as I dropped a black paintbrush right in the middle. I have no idea what to do about it. Mrs. Grockel said to paint it one colour again. I told her if she wished to spend hours repainting the pattern she is welcome to it!)

Anyway, I am getting quite beside the point! Mr. Burton— well, David to you, I suppose, since you are family—has become quite ill, and as I thought you may be in need of some company and so shall I, I am inviting you to come and stay with us a while. Would you like to? Please say yes, for if I only have Mrs. Grockel to speak to I may fall ill myself, though I do not wish to exaggerate, of course.

I hope everything is well with you, dear sister, and I look forward to seeing you soon. I send my love—

Your dearest sister-in-law,
Theodora Burton

Letty folded the letter and laid it in her lap. She turned to gaze out of the parlour window onto green fields that heaved up and fell away outside. Her thumb stroked the thick paper; perhaps it would be good to visit Theo. It had been a long time since she had seen her, and it would be a way to save her parents any expense. Her father had been graced with a decent parish, but that did not mean money had ever been plentiful. The thought of her father only brought her mind back to John. If only money had not been so scarce when she had been young! Her father would not have had to take on gentlemen to tutor. She would never have met John, and they would never have married in a desperate attempt to avert the scandal.

She suddenly shook herself. What was she doing? Self-pity would help nothing. The past was set in stone and ultimately unchangeable. She must think of the future. If she could not change past actions, she could at least try to survive the present. She reprimanded herself and then, flicking the long plait of hair she had been fiddling with back over her shoulder, she rose, clasping the letter. She sat in John's old chair at the large wooden desk, the high back overshadowing her, and took out a sheet of paper. Once the letter to Theo was finished, sealed, and sent, Letty went about packing the few dresses she owned into a small trunk. She saw to the business of the farm, and finally coming back to Highfield, she began saying goodbye to her home.

And so the farm, the house, and all the possessions therein were left to the debt collectors. Letty took her final leave with only a small trunk and a portmanteau to her widowed name. She removed to her sister-in-law's house in Truro. While Theodora's husband remained sick, Letty would be the young wife's comforter and companion.

The widow remembered with such clarity the day on which she left: the crisp morning air that pinched at her cheeks before she stepped up into the carriage; the sweet smell of earth that was laced with traces of briny sea air; the wind that flung her long hair back and forth, loosing it from the contraptions imprisoning it; the sky that was thick shades of iron grey and layers of towering clouds building above; the heath and shrub- covered landscape in all its unruly beauty she knew so well—all was left to the elements behind her. The animals were hidden away in warm homes together, the only farewell being the natural blow of westerly winds.

The harshly sprung carriage afforded a small view through a murky pane of glass of the country which she loved. This view she engraved in her mind's eye. She would keep it for a time when she needed to know there was a place like heaven, a paradise somewhere.

CHAPTER TWO

Honour thy father and thy mother.
The Good Old Book

25 October 1815

Dear Papa,
      I hope my letter finds you and Mama in good health. Since John's passing, I understand my place is at home with you and dear Mama. However, my sister-in-law, Mrs. Theodora Burton, has requested my coming to visit her. Her husband is sick, and I feel it only right to help her in this time.

I know what you would say, Papa: "Help the sick and needy." And so I find myself preparing to go and stay with her. I do miss you both very much, but I know that you have plenty of occupation and shall do just as well without me. No doubt you are busy in your garden, Papa, and Mama is busy planning meals and gift baskets for needy parishioners.

The funeral has taken place, and please do not feel uncaring for not coming. It was perhaps best I was on my own, and, Papa, please tell Mama not to worry over me for I know she shall. I am quite well actually, and being in the company of my sister-in-law can only improve my spirits. I shall write to you again in a few weeks to arrange my coming home.

You may cross the letter with news from home though please do not add another sheet as I shall be out of pocket for a short while. Give my love to Mama.

Your affectionate daughter,
Lettice Burton

"Letty?"

Her sister-in-law was calling her. She could hear her now, her small feet thumping on the thick staircase carpet.

"Coming, Theodora."

"How many times must I tell you to call me Theo? It is so unnatural to be called by one's full name unless one is being scolded." The plump girl had entered the room without permission, an impish grin on her face and her feet skipping, with no consideration of that fact that her husband was knocking at death's door. Her fresh-faced enthusiasm was proof of her only lately coming out of the schoolroom. She blew a few golden curls out of her eyes before peering rather obviously over Letty's shoulder.

"I am merely writing to my papa. I think they expected me home once I told them of the sale of Highfield." Better to just tell Theo than wait for her to read the entire letter.

"Oh, pish!" She flailed a small hand under Letty's nose. "They do not need you half as much as I do. Now I am come to ask if you will not walk with me in the garden, for it is too tedious to be cooped up in here all day." The young girl looked about her as though the room had just turned into a dungeon.

Letty had to admit that she could do with a little fresh air in her lungs. Before she could accept the proposal, however, Theo had already slipped a hand through her arm and was dragging her away from the writing desk. She scarce had time to blot her paper before being forced from the room.

"But Theo, should you not stay with David?" Letty's voice of concern was only a source of irritation to the young girl, emphasizing the difference between the two of them. Letty tried persuasion, asking the young girl about David and his condition but could only extract a begrudging, "He's fine!" from the child-like wife. The loveless match was only too evident.

Letty and Theo's differences were vast, and yet somehow, through their sisterly connection, there was an odd—if sometimes grinding—rapport between the characters. Letty derived amusement from Theo's mad antics although she did, on occasion, intervene to subdue her wilder flights of fancy.

Theo was, however, in Letty's mind, still a child. At only seventeen she had married David, and, despite the lack of love between the two, the couple was what was considered happy in their good looks and wealth. Of this, thank goodness, Letty had never been envious.

How much did their loveless marriage differ from what her own union had been? It was true she had seen violence and felt pain, but she simply could not believe that Theo and David's union could provide contentment. How could any person be content in a marriage without love? Money and looks were all very well, but they did not fulfil. This, at least, she had learned from her own marriage. Perhaps it was her father's sermons, speaking against the love of money, that had given her a lack of belief in its providing happiness.

Letty tried another of her persuasive questions, but this time her hostess was less tolerant.

"Oh, do not plague me with questions of him! Have I not been tormented enough having a sick husband who prevents me from joining any of my important social engagements?"

This selfish statement shocked Letty for a moment, even knowing Theodora as she did.

The girl's small plump frame stood squarely, and one fine hand rested on her hip. "Besides, Mrs. Grockel is with him. I think I can leave him quite safe!" She rolled her large blue eyes as Letty sighed. The girl then crossed her arms in ultimate defiance. There was no more argument from the older sister-in-law and so Theo grabbed her arm and dragged a beaten Letty downstairs.

As they neared the garden, the scent of lavender hung lightly on the air, mingled with that of rosemary and thyme. They made good their escape through the French windows. Letty's searching feet found soft grass that sprung under her pumps. The herb beds that lined the lawn contained small, furry shrubs in a hundred different shades of green.

She walked on behind her sister who skipped ahead like a young filly, free of her stable at last. Although the guilt of leaving David did not abate, Letty had to admit she was happier for the fresh air, and perhaps Theo needed time away from the sickbed. The coolness outside brought roses out on Letty's cheeks and pricked the end of her nose. Soon the morning dew was wicking its way up her black mourning dress and wetting her ankles.

"See? This is lovely! A hundred times more agreeable than staying indoors. And I know how much you love to walk, sister."

Letty reprimanded herself for writing Theodora off as completely selfish. She was like a cloudy day; rays of sunshine sometimes battled their way through.

"And I know your love of novels, which is why I have decided to take a trip to town today in order to browse the lending library. No, no, do not protest! Even if you will not go, I shall. I swear I will collapse from boredom if I do not have a wonderful love story to read! I declare I was ready to elope with Vincentio after reading *The Italian*."

Letty simply could not let Theo go out alone. They returned to the house, and as they sat eating sweetmeats, Letty desperately tried to distract Theo from her plans.

"Surely, David would wish you to sit with him a while?"

"Oh, Letty! I did not ask you to stay so that you should make me feel guilty." Theo toyed with the food on her plate, managing to look beautiful even in her petulance.

Letty bit back the first remark that sprang to mind, praying for patience.

"I know it is hard." She paused, but Theo made no move to recollect that Letty had only recently lost her husband. "I do not mean to make you feel worse. It is only that David may be wishing for company. He must be bored in that room all alone."

"Yes, I suppose you are right." Theo rested her chin in one hand, taking on a pose of dejection. Then, quite suddenly, she sprang to life again. "But you must see, dear sister? I shall be far more inclined to stay with David should I have a book to read. Indeed, he may even wish me to read to him. Oh, we must go, we must!" she cried, her eyes bright with enthusiasm.

And with that, Letty knew she had lost the war. She considered arguing that David would not wish to hear of swooning heroines and haunted castles but decided, wisely, against trying. She agreed to lend Theo her countenance against her better judgment. Once they had finished their repast, they both pulled bonnets over their hair and placed cloaks about their shoulders. They set out from the house at a quarter past two in the direction of the lending library.

As they made their way down the cobbled street, people milled about them. Some cast curious or even offended glances at the sight of Letty in her blacks. It was but human nature to think the worst of people. She knew she should already be in lavender if she was out walking. She should not have come out like this; it was worthy of causing talk among the idle gossipers, but how could she help it?

As she walked beside Theo, the happy female stepping out gaily, she knew she could not make her feelings known to the girl. That would only cause more trouble. Theo was not like her, and this she must remember. She came from a family of four girls, herself the youngest. She was not used to her plans being denied. No, it would be better for all concerned if Letty said nothing. Besides, she could barely catch breath it was so hard to keep up with the eagerly progressing girl.

"Come, come, Letty! I know for a fact there are several novels just in, and I do not wish to miss them. That naughty friend of mine, Miss Jessica Linton, borrowed two books I wanted last time."

"I hardly think all the books shall have gone by the time we get there." A chuckle escaped Letty and was rewarded by a bright smile from her sister.

"At least you show some happiness. Perhaps you shall be a pleasant companion after all, though do not settle on a book I want for I shall not forgive you easily!"

When they had finally reached the desired building, both the girls had lost their breath and stood panting a little to catch it before entering. The flagstone steps in front of the library had not eased their journey one bit. Theo put a hand to the wall as she drank in air.

"Proprietor, Mr. Vickers." Theo read from the well-polished brass plaque. She brushed her fingers over the lettering. "What a boring name. I hope I shall not have to speak to him!" She giggled recklessly and jibed further at this man's name. She was dithering all over the place when a pair of ladies exited the establishment.

"Oh, I am sorry," gasped the euphoric girl after bumping into the first of the women.

"That's quite all right," the lady replied in brisk tones, but the deep wrinkle-line about the woman's mouth did not move nor the frown she wore above it. She proceeded to usher her staid-looking daughter before her and marched away down the busy street.

Letty spoke as soon as the lady was safely out of earshot. "Theo, you really must be more careful." Theo's face turned sour but Letty remained firm. Turning away, she started to enter the building only to meet with a collision herself.

Books took flight as though given life, their covers flapping like wings. A tall gentleman was knocked back into the doorway only just managing to maintain his balance.

"Oh, I am so dreadfully sorry!" Bending down with no care for clean skirts, Letty retrieved as many books as possible —until her frantically scrambling hand brushed the hand of the gentleman in question. She flinched, her arm jolting away from the contact.

"Lady, you are a curse!"

She directed her anxious eyes to his face. "I do beg your pardon, sir." Her voice wavered as her eyes came into contact with his. They were dark under the brim of his tall hat and singularly peeved. He stared directly into her eyes for a second and then rose.

As they both stood up straight, she found herself dwarfed by his size. The top of her head was confronted by a cravat, the perfect example of a Gordian knot. A crisp white shirt, a silk waistcoat, and a stunning blue coat that expertly followed the lines of his figure accompanied the carefully folded linen.

"Out of my way, if you please!" The tall man did not bother to bow; he snatched the offered books from her frozen hands and strode off without a backward glance.

Letty frowned, too shocked by his rudeness to speak at first. She had not met many distinguished gentlemen, excepting those few who had been students under her father.

This man was obviously a gentleman, and judging by the self-assured air of his walk, he was one who bore rank. It did not take the brains of a bluestocking to see he was probably a member of the ton. The dress was fashionable down to the last covered button. She had only seen a few men of that calibre, and walking in public in Truro was not an activity usually undertaken by his species. He was surely not at home here, his usual surroundings almost definitely being the metropolis with its style and distractions. Perhaps such rudeness was his way; people with the world at their fingertips cared little for others. She was glad she had not met many like him although she knew some would scorn her for thinking it. However, Letty knew that even a farm worker would possess more courtesy than that man. She felt herself fill with sudden anger. Give her the country and burn London!

She realised she was shaking from the encounter but could not decide whether it was from alarm or indignation. Thankfully, Theo did not notice. All this time she had been staring after the gentleman like a goldfish, her mouth gaping in a most unladylike fashion. Then, while he was still quite within earshot, she cried, "I do believe that's the Viscount Beauford. What an odious gentleman he has turned out to be! It is just as the gossip says." She beamed in triumph.

"Theo, hush!" whispered Letty, her sense overtaking her umbrage. She was relieved, however, to see his step did not falter. Perhaps she could hope he had not heard—though she did not know why she should entertain that hope.

"Well, honestly! He bumped you as much as you bumped him. One would expect him to act more politely. Though I must admit he had the dreamiest eyes, did you see? Anyway," —the girl's tone turned mocking—"perhaps you should take your own advice and be careful, Lettice, or you might bump into somebody!" Theo winked naughtily at her sister-in-law before prancing through the door.

They weaved between the library shelves for quite some time before Theo's mischievous spirits got the better of her again. Using the cover of a Mrs. Radcliffe novel, she whispered, or rather, spoke, to Letty. "I simply must tell you about the Viscount. Oh, there is so much to say...."

"My dear sister," Letty murmured to the excited chatterer. "A book cover does not shield your voice from others' ears as you seem to believe." She tapped the cover with her fingertip. The widow then turned and smiled politely at an obviously upset Mr. Vickers whose large, grey eyebrows were twitching disapprovingly from behind his librarian's desk.

"Yes, but I do not care for being quiet when I am telling you of the most delightful gossip!" Theo's eyes sparkled and despite Letty's protestations she carried on merrily. "Lord Beauford came here not a week before you, and he is said to be quite the rake! I've heard he keeps an opera dancer in Paris, would you believe! I heard of it through Mrs. Wimley, who spoke to Mrs. Reddison about it, who had it from her own maid's sister, no less." Theo said this in all seriousness as though the gossip chain of village women was as important as the informants in France.

"I met him at the assembly three evenings ago—you know, the night David took ill? Well, he was quite dashing. Only asked the prettiest girls to dance and stood and looked half bored, half miserable for the rest of the evening. But that is not the best of it." Theo's pitch grew higher. "He is supposed to be hiding in the country for calling out a man in London. Don't you realise? It is illegal. He had his seconds and everything sorted, apparently, before it was called off. Some scandal about a woman. He actually wanted to kill the other man until the law came down on the whole thing!"

"Indeed, he sounds truly delightful." Letty smiled falsely at the librarian in an attempt to mollify him from a distance.

"Yes, well, no, he was not when he bumped you, though I

have to say those eyes were unforgettable." She clasped a novel to her bosom and sighed. "How can one forget such dark eyes? Last Season in London he was the rage, you know. So wealthy and so very handsome. Everybody was setting their cap at him."

"Fascinating," replied Letty, still smiling and beginning to steer Theo quite forcefully out of the library and away from a very aggravated Mr. Vickers.

"Oh, what a delight! Mrs. Radcliffe, I declare, is one of the best people alive for writing such glorious stories. I swear all women should build an altar on which to worship her!"

"Theo, you are shocking! Though I agree her writing is rather diverting." Letty's eyes twinkled ever so slightly.

"Not just diverting. You must learn to be more passionate, Letty. It is delicious, sumptuous and ooh!" She wriggled on the seat of the hackney they had hired.

Letty's face broke into a smile; her sister was, as always, the entertainment of the day. Soon the young widow could see the familiar architecture of Theo's home. The hackney drew to a stop and a footman, smelling suspiciously like ale, opened the door and handed the ladies down.

They made their way quickly up the path through the dusk light. Entering the well-lit doorway, Theo immediately began teasing the ribbon knot beneath her chin to remove her fetching bonnet.

"Mrs. Grockel?" She pulled hatpins out, scattering them across the hall table. "Mrs. Grockel?" She drew the soft ribbons out of their embrace and let the hat fall from her head. "Mrs. Grockel? Where is she? I am absolutely famished and simply must eat! I want at least a little tea before I sit down to read."

Theo was turned the other way when the housekeeper appeared from a doorway to the side. Letty took one look at the woman and her stomach dropped. The housekeeper was crying, great, rolling tears navigating their way down the wrinkles of her old cheeks. Mrs. Grockel could not face her mistress and Letty guessed why. She spoke in quiet undertones to the young widow, but the explanation was not really needed.

"Master has been taken most ill, miss, much more so than before. I've sent for Doctor Cotton but...but he's suffering so, miss. Been asking for me to get pen and paper to write his will —that's 'twixt his delirious states, miss. You must send Mrs. Burton to him. He has to see his wife if he's goin' to go."

Letty nodded, offering a small handkerchief that the old lady accepted gratefully. The young widow thanked the old retainer who then retreated.

"Theo?" Letty's voice was strangled by sorrow. She came quickly across the hall floor to take the hand of her sister-in-law. "Theo, dear?"

The girl was discarding her soft kid gloves on the hall table.

"You must go to David now, Theo. Mrs. Grockel has informed me he is very ill. Theo, you must go to him." Letty's voice was gentle and yet contained real urgency. Theo, whose first answer would have been less than pleasant, saw the look of fear in Letty's eyes and said nothing. She snatched her hand away, picked up her skirts, and bounded up the stairs like a wild thing.

Letty was left in the hall to listen to the screaming as Theo tried to decipher Mrs. Grockel's verdict on the patient. She could hear the moans of a man in too much pain and the wails of a girl who would be widowed too young, like herself.

The house entered a state of limbo, a state that most would experience sometime in life and one that Letty was now experiencing for the second time in as many months. Cold water was brought up to soothe the invalid and dirty water brought back. Broth was cooked, spooned into a bowl, and sent up, only to be refused by both husband and wife.

Letty almost believed Theo was truly upset about her husband's dying, an inevitability which had now been confirmed by Doctor Cotton. He had an acute case of pneumonia. Yet, after her initial outburst, Theo was not in fact spending her time with her ailing husband but with her books in her own rooms. Letty's first thoughts were of anger, but, as the days slipped slowly by, she realised that a child like Theo should never have to face death.

Alas! As much as Letty prayed and wished it, it was not for Theo to be spared. David died three days later at a quarter past one in the morning. Theo had not been with him; neither had Letty. It had been Mrs. Grockel who witnessed the last will and testament of Mr. David Burton and she who saw him breathe his last. She said to Theo that he had gone peacefully, as though to sleep.

Yet, as Letty held the wailing girl, she knew Mrs. Grockel's words could offer no consolation. What could, when Theo had lost a husband, her only security in the world? The widow comforted Theo like a child, and the girl's tears ran like the rain in the autumn. Her eyes grew red and swollen, and the salty taste seeped in and swirled in her mouth. She clutched at the back of Letty's gown and stayed sobbing for some time before allowing her thoughts to collect and express themselves.

"What is to become of me? Oh, sister, I am alone. I have no home, I have nothing! I shall be cast upon the world and die!"

"Hush now. Nothing bad will happen to you." David's cold face appeared in Letty's water-coloured memory. At the least, she knew Theo would be provided for. David, unlike his brother, had never been reckless with money. "It will all be well, I promise." She carried on rhythmically rubbing Theo's back as one would a newborn.

The conversation carried on in much the same soothing way. Theo's ravings became worse and more fantastic until she succumbed quite suddenly to sleep. She had not accepted even a little gruel at suppertime. Letty would have to be sure she ate tomorrow.

She gently pulled the clasps from the golden hair and took off the young girl's slippers before drawing a cover over her on the bed. Theo looked frail and weak as she lay against the covers and Letty did not want to leave her. It had been a long day, however, and Letty felt in need of a break before she saw the night through.

Letty left Mrs. Grockel watching over Theo while she made her way to her own room. She was standing silently at its centre, contemplating the tumultuous events of recent days, when a maid entered. She looked young and a little scared, and Letty was sure her own startled expression did not help matters.

"Hello?" said the widow questioningly. She looked over the girl, unsure of why the young servant had come.

"I brought this, ma'am. It's warm." The maid proffered a jug of water that she had been clutching to her chest.

"Ah, did Mrs. Grockel send for that?" Letty relaxed a little.

"No, ma'am, she was busy, but I thought you would be wanting a wash, for the day has been long." The young maid walked to the washstand and poured water into the floral bowl. Licks of steam curled up above the flat surface of the clean water, making the bowl look more than inviting to Letty.

"The lady's maid is with the mistress now, but if there is anything you need you can just call me, ma'am."

"What is your name?" Letty's eyes were full of gratitude as she looked from the bowl to the thoughtful maid. She was a pretty, fairy-like sort of girl with blonde curls and unusually dark brown eyes for such a fair complexion. Looking at her open and honest face, Letty could not help but take to the young girl.

"Maria, ma'am."

"Well, thank you, Maria, you have been most kind." Letty found herself wanting to reward the maid. "But I do not think I shall need any more help this evening, and you should most certainly make your way home to your family. It is late and there is no more to be done tonight."

The maid's face glowed with appreciation as she curtseyed and then left Letty alone in the room.

The widow walked to the steaming bowl of water and washed her face. She felt rejuvenated as the fresh water hit her tired skin. She cupped her hands and splashed the water on her face several times before patting her skin dry once again. Finally, after another few moments in silent contemplation, she took up a shawl from the back of a chair and returned to Theo's room.

"It is all right," Letty said to the housekeeper. "I shall stay with her. Go and rest. You nursed David ceaselessly, and you must be exhausted."

The woman smiled a little in agreement. "Thank you, ma'am."

Mrs. Grockel left Letty and Theo alone. Letty took her place in a chair beside the bed to watch over the sleeping girl. Through the night the elder sister sat beside the younger that slept. From the chair she stroked Theo's hair and gently sung to help her sleep. In the morning the elder sister was still there.

Letty stood, pausing a moment to brush back the hair from Theo's sleeping face. She smoothed the creases of her dress, picked up Theo's slippers and put them away, then walked over to the window to draw the curtains back. She gazed out the window into the clear blue sky of morning, thoughts crowding her mind.

Her hand unconsciously rose up and felt the hair that had gone into disarray during the night. As she looked out onto the street at the comings and goings of the passersby, she pulled the clasps and clips from her hair. She untangled it as best she could with her fingers, teasing and gently tugging the locks apart. She swung the thick length of it around to her back and put her hands to her cheeks. It had been cold last night, and the faint reflection on the glass showed how pale her skin was.

Her fingers traced the sill as she thought upon her father's words: "Man makes plans in his heart, but God determines the steps he makes." How much her plans had been upset! The family she had wanted and the home she longed for seemed so far away. Now Theo would suffer the same fate as her—though Letty did hope that Theo, with her beauty and fortune, would be able to start again. An eligible match was, for her, at least, still very probable even if it did not come about overnight.

Sunlight flooded the room. She heard a small moan from the bed and turned back to Theo. Enough of that thinking—it was time to see to what needed doing. The sunlight gave the dreary atmosphere of the house a firm push out of the door. It was bright in this room, a haven from the truth that lay behind the doors, a haven from the future that was unjust and yet inevitable.

"Good morning, Theo," Letty said, as the girl still blinked sleep from her eyes. "Shall I call for some breakfast? Do you think you can manage it today?" She pulled the bed curtains back just as a maid would do.

Theo did not speak, but that meant nothing. The young

girl needed food, and whether she liked it or not she was going to be fed. Letty made her way to the door and called Maria to bring up some breakfast for her mistress—nothing too heavy. As she came back into the room, Theo sat up a little, batting at the irksome covers that enveloped her.

"I shall hate having to wear black. It is such a sombre colour and does nothing at all for one's complexion." Her blue eyes scrutinized Letty and clearly did not approve of what they saw.

"There are many pretty mourning dress designs to choose from now. The lace work can be quite beautiful," replied Letty, thinking her sister enough recovered to be up and dressed. If she could manage it, she would make sure that Theo dealt with this situation herself. She needed to grow up a little and this would do just that for her. There were the mourning clothes to order, the funeral to be arranged, and Theo's future to be decided. Letty would help, but she did not want to allow her sister-in-law to do nothing.

Despite Letty's desires, it would be she who decided everything. She called on the coroner, spoke to the funeral directors, and decided the date of the interment. She composed letters and sent an urgent message to David and John's mother hoping she would not shut herself away again.

Next, Letty started about the house, ordering things to be packed away, moved, or sold. She was in the attic of the house one afternoon when Maria offered her services. They sat among piles of boxes, deciding what Theo would want to take with her from this house and what needed to be simply discarded. Maria had been packing a box of things that Theo would want to keep. After half an hour of working, she stopped what she was doing and made to speak.

"Shall we...." She stopped in nervousness.

"Yes?" encouraged Letty.

"I know it may be wrong to ask but shall we...shall we be needed much longer, by the mistress, I mean?"

Letty placed another ornament in a box. "I cannot say, but I am sure you shall be given another situation."

The maid nodded silently.

"You have been most diligent in your work these past days. How long have you been in this house?" Letty was fully aware of what social boundaries she was crossing.

The maid's youth ensured her naivety, however, and she did not notice the unusual question.

"Just six months. It was a great position when I was offered it. My ma was so pleased."

"And your mother, is she a maid too?"

"No, no, my mother is blind. That's why she was so pleased for me. Work is hard to come by for her, and I was not old enough to be in service until now."

Letty nodded, understanding Maria's earlier question and the anxiety that had been clear in her face. The widow reflected that it had been only one death and yet so many lives were being affected by it.

Over the following days Letty continued to pack and order whilst also consoling the widow who could not get over her distaste for the dresses she would have to wear. Theo went about the house, tugging at uncomfortable sleeves and neck-lines, whimpering like a spoiled pup. Letty bore her work silently though not without the occasional biting of her tongue. As long as she could gain at least a few hours' sleep each night, she could bear Theodora well enough. However, it was not until her mother-in-law arrived at the house that she realised just how much she was able to withstand.

CHAPTER THREE

Can I see another's woe, and not be in sorrow too?
Can I see another's grief, and not seek for kind relief?
– WILLIAM BLAKE

"Woe is me! My children have left me along with my husband. God has cursed me!" The echoes of Clarissa Burton's lament threw themselves into the house before her plump foot had even settled on the threshold. They were enough to make any servant's spine quiver.

"Mrs. Burton?" Letty, having been packing in the attic once again, came down the stairs to greet the new arrival.

"Ah, my dear Lettice, how my heart aches for both our sakes. Come to me." Clarissa held out her plump arms; they stretched towards her daughter-in-law and embraced her firmly. Letty could feel the warmth of her mother-in-law through the black silks.

"But tell me, where is Theo? No, wait! Do not speak. She is crying alone in her room, no doubt? I thought as much, so in love with David was she." The short woman's head bobbed, making the ostrich plume that projected from her hat duck and weave furiously at least a foot above where her person ended.

Letty, whose mouth was beginning to twitch and quiver, firmly pushed the smile away before answering. "Well, not exactly, Mrs. Burton." Then her brow furrowed. She was trying to think of an acceptable reason for Theo reading another of Mrs. Radcliffe's novels in her room and eating some, if not all, of the confectionary brought to her in her time of need.

"It is of no matter. I shall be with her directly. Or at least as soon as this buffoon manages to carry my cases in without smashing them into the door frame!" Picking up an umbrella from the stand, Clarissa soundly whacked the footman on the head. "Have a care, Tibbs!" Her shrill voice rang out through the hallway, causing the very bricks to reverberate.

"Yes, ma'am," said the gruff footman who had served this lady faithfully for many years. Despite his muttering and general grumblings, he did as he was bade and did not seem at all abashed by her treatment of him. Letty's smile came back with a vengeance, and she was glad her mother-in-law did not turn directly back to see her grinning.

"Anything else, ma'am?" The manservant caught a clear picture of Letty's rebellious smile and, although his face remained unmoved, his eyes twinkled in answer.

"No, no, Tibbs! Now leave us be and attend to the horses, will you? The poor creatures have had you hounding them all day. Give them some straw or hay or whatever you feed them."

Tibbs nodded, his mischievous eyes holding an unspoken joke, though it was well camouflaged by the constant scowl that marked his unkempt face. He put his tattered hat back on his head and walked out of the hall. This was not before Letty heard him mutter something about the horses having to pull their mistress' large behind about the country.

As she turned away to cover the ever-irritating smile, she

felt something rise inside of her, something long forgotten—laughter. The muscles that worked while she smiled seemed unused and rusty. The realization of laughter and happiness only encouraged the smile on her face to become larger and wider. It was as though some magical potion was at work, and Letty found it quite a job to suppress its effect before her mother-in-law mistook it for rudeness.

Clarissa ignored Tibbs' comment, if she had heard it, and marched imperiously through the hall, her large bottom wiggling this way and that as she bore down upon Letty.

"Now tell me, my dear, what have you been doing? I've missed you so. My nerves have been dreadful, you know? I have barely eaten a thing." She failed to count the cream tea she had had on the journey, and the breakfast before that, and the extra toast. "It is very lonely being in the country all by myself. I have made plans to remedy that, but never mind that now." She dabbed her rosy cheeks with a lace handkerchief.

The scent of lilac overwhelmed Letty's nostrils.

"I am just glad to see you, though I must say you are not looking your best. You have lost your bloom, my dear. No doubt because you are missing dear John. Oh, life is cruel!"

The mention of her husband's name did nothing to her. Not one emotion stirred. She thought it odd that there was no anger, frustration, or sadness anymore. Perhaps the organ that allowed humans to feel pain had broken inside her. There was no misery. There was nothing.

"Yes," she said simply. She loved her mother-in-law; she was a caring woman, and Letty knew the lady never wanted to hurt her.

The old woman clasped her hand tight and squeezed it reassuringly. No matter this woman's faults, Letty would forgive her. She had lost a husband and her only two children in the space of two years. Of all the people that Letty had met in her short life, this woman was the one that deserved the most grace. "I've been helping Theo manage the house as well. David did everything so she has been quite lost without him." Letty tried to guide her mother-in-law upstairs in vain; the woman stood her ground and nodded her head in understanding.

"Ah, and she is so young, so newly married, I expect she understands little of business and household management matters! My dear husband did all the business side of things too. When he died, I was thrown into that violent sea without someone sensible like you to guide me. You were far too busy with John at the time. I was left alone and desolate, much as I am now and probably ever shall be. I miss my dear Percy!" She dabbed a handkerchief at her eyes which were welling with tears, not for Theo but for herself. "Let me see dear Theo. I must console her."

The rest of the afternoon drifted by slowly with the scent of lavender water, the application of smooth chocolates, and the pungent smell of hartshorn every time one of the ladies felt faint from grief—though perhaps the faintness was more often caused by overindulgence.

Letty popped in and out of the upstairs bedchamber throughout the day, checking on the two grievers residing within. Apart from that task, she busied her mind with the ordering of the objects that had been found in the attic and, once finished, began the choosing and overseeing of dinner. She did not expect the ladies to want to eat anything publicly in the dining room and ordered ample portions of the acceptable supper to be taken to each of their rooms.

Letty entered old Mrs. Burton's room holding her supper tray, which she had insisted on taking up instead of allowing Mrs. Grockel to do it. She placed the tray on the small table and turned to see Mrs. Burton asleep in a chair by the fire. The young woman picked up the Mrs. Radcliffe novel, which lay on Clarissa's chest, glancing at it and smiling before placing it on the table. Theo would not be happy until she had converted the entire world. Letty removed the old lady's spectacles and placed a warm blanket over her sleeping frame.

"Oh!" Mrs. Burton woke slowly. "Oh, my dear." She glanced at the supper tray and looked up at Letty. "Life is such a hardship, but you are the sweetest of creatures." She spoke in saddened tones while she took her daughter's hand. "And look at us both. Cast upon the world, alone and yet together." The soft blue eyes smiled up at her.

"Now get to bed, you silly girl. You are up far too late. I could not bear another relative falling ill." The woman patted her hand and released it and, without waiting for an answer, fell promptly to sleep again.

For Letty it was hard to fall asleep that night. All the activity of the day had not given her mind time to calm. Dust from rearranging the attic still irritated her nose, and her eyes had begun to ache after examining so many documents. The excitement of Clarissa Burton arriving was another happening that had taken over her thoughts for most of the day. Her mind was still quite awake, tripping and tumbling over the messy jumble of her thoughts even at this late hour.

The house had not been quiet since Clarissa's arrival, but now, as the church clock in the town struck midnight, the house was wrapped up in its four walls and slumbering peacefully.

The widow put a shawl about her shoulders, and her soft slippers padded over the cold floorboards making them creak here and there. It was a relief to be walking; it put off the certainty of lying awake in anxiety for at least another hour.

She heard a faint scratching as a mouse ran terrified from her presence into the kitchen. She smiled a little while the furry creature made good its escape—a creature so small and scorned by humans, and yet it had the free will to roam the house right under the owners' noses, heedless of rules that did not apply.

The floorboards were marked with lengths of dark grey moonlight which had managed to make its way in between the blinds and shutters. It was the only light to guide her on her ghostly walk. As she moved onwards, she began to plait her hair. The rhythmic pulling and twisting always settled Letty. It occupied her for a while as she made her reluctant retreat back upstairs.

If the servants should find her down here in the dark of night, it might cause them to talk. Clarissa would not leave it alone if she heard of it. She had already commented on her daughter-in-law's lack of bloom. Who knew what woeful laments and wild remonstrations Letty would be subjected to? Clarissa would, at the very least, insist on sleeping in the same bed just to be sure her daughter-in-law was resting properly.

Letty finished the plait, secured it, and swung it gently over her shoulder to rest on her back. Trouble sleeping was not something new to Letty. She had had trouble sleeping since becoming a married woman, but there were reasons for that she wished never to remember. There were nights too dark to recall, too painful to ever recount. That, however, was in the past. She was safe from that now, even if she did not always feel so. Besides, it was not just fear of John that had created her insomnia. Now that she was free—and alone—there was, in a way, far more to fear. She paused as she came upon her own room. The bedroom door stood in front of her, and as her cold hand touched the brass door-handle, she felt despair creep into her bones. The night stretched ahead like an unwelcome journey, a journey that did not wish to end.

"You will see, my dear. We shall be happy once again! That is if the Lord decides to stop cursing us. I told my husband we should never have left Society. To leave Town is an awful thing. Perhaps that was our sin. But never matter, we shall be back soon enough. Perhaps if we pay penance by attending enough parties and throwing parties of our own, we may make the Lord happy again and be happy ourselves. Though I shall not fully believe it."

Clarissa's theology and maudlin tones across the breakfast table could not help but amuse Letty as she sipped her tea.

"Ah, at last! I was waiting to see that smile upon your face again, my dear. It is too long since I have seen you happy. I have been vindicated in my choice—London it is! Now bring a message to Tibbs"—she turned her plump body with some effort to the one serving girl—"that I want the horses ready by nine o'clock and no later."

"Will that be the carriage too, madam?" asked the simple Maria with an obvious awe in her eyes at the prophesying and imperious older lady. Her hands twisted and turned themselves over behind her back. She had obviously never encountered a mistress like this before.

"Well, of course, you daft child! I do not intend to ride myself! Although, once I was noted to have a fine seat." The woman wore a look of far off memories. Then, quite suddenly, she was back in the present with a vengeance as she swatted at the poor maid. "Now be off with you!"

"And thank you, Maria," said Letty, conscious of the girl's fear. The young maid threw a pair of grateful eyes at Letty before scampering out of the room like a smacked child.

"I was quite a rider in the day, you know? That is how I first caught Percy's eye." Clarissa had dropped back into her delightful daydream and was patting Theo's hand affectionately.

"Mrs. Burton? Excuse me for saying so, but if we are to

leave today, that will surely be problematic for the sale of this house and the moving or sale of the furniture?"

Letty could not be more happy to be leaving with Clarissa. She was spared, yet again, from burdening her parents with her presence. Yet, as ever, her practical mind took the lead firmly away from her happiness.

"Letty, you must call me Clarissa; you are family, dear. And do not worry your head about this place. Mr. Pottle, my solicitor, shall be in charge. He is rather stuffy, but I am sure he will be adequate. He shall come tomorrow, so all we need do is shut up the house."

"And the servants, Clarissa?" Letty obeyed her superior but eyed her carefully.

"Pottle shall pay them all handsomely. I assure you, they shall be taken care of. Which reminds me, dear, you could do with a maid. We shall find you one in London. The agencies are quite good now, particularly...oh now, what was the name? Percy and I used a good agency once, but I cannot remember it. Never mind—we shall find you a good little maid." She tapped her dimpled chin with one finger before picking up a cake and performing a meditative chew.

"If it is no trouble to you, I would love to take Maria with me," Letty said, referring to the frightened maid who, only a moment ago, had fled the room. It was now no secret to Letty that the maid had been supporting her relatives with her wages. Any length of unemployment could prove devastating to her family, and Letty could not bear the thought of child or mother starving.

"Are you sure, my dear? She is not at all bright." Clarissa shook her head disapprovingly.

"Oh yes, I am quite certain, Clarissa. She has proven herself to be very hard working and efficient whilst helping me set the house to rights. She really is a most charming girl."

"I am astonished you pay so much attention to a little housemaid."

"She has been very useful to me," Letty replied with a mild shrug of her narrow shoulders.

"Yes, but can she dress hair? Or you for that matter?"

"She will do well with perhaps a little help from your own maid. It will not inconvenience you, I think."

"Very well, if it pleases you. And what about you, Theo? Shall we wait until Town to find your maid?"

"I shall answer that after I have told you the most fascinating gossip." The young girl was all excitement and joy as she spoke. "It had quite slipped my mind earlier, but now I remember it. Have you heard the Viscount Beauford is in Truro?"

"No! I had not!"

"And Letty and I saw him."

"You did? Tremendous! I remember him as a youth. I knew his mother a little in Town and saw him, though most of the time he was studying at Eton. He was quite a handsome young man and very charming. I wonder if he still is?" The old woman began to muse.

Theo began to giggle at Clarissa's dreamy face, and she would have explained the entire story of Letty walking straight into one of England's most eligible bachelors had not Mrs. Grockel come in with the morning's post. Among all the envelopes was a letter for Theo.

The girl paused in her repast, opened it, and read the contents.

"You look pale, dear. What is the matter?" Clarissa peered closer in a concerned way only to be shocked when Theo burst into a fit of great sobs before throwing the letter in her direction.

"Oh, my!" Clarissa cried, taking the letter and shouting for Maria. The maid came scuttling in.

"Hartshorn! Hartshorn, girl, and be quick about it!"

Maria returned almost immediately with the needed antidote; Letty was thankful that the girl had done well in front of Clarissa. With the drama over, Theo was put to bed to recover from her hysterics, and the maid was sent away. All was calm again. Clarissa finally read the letter that had so upset Theo and passed it to Letty soon after.

"Refusing to let a young girl go to Town—how foolish! They say that they cannot entrust her into the care of a person whom they know nothing about! Has not my son been married to their daughter for the last year? Of all the effrontery! I am shocked. Shocked, I tell you!"

Despite Clarissa's various outbursts, Letty finally managed to read the whole letter. She refolded it and put it slowly down in front of her. She placed her hands on top of each other in her lap and stared at the table for a moment.

"Do not tell me your parents shall do the same?" cried Clarissa, a little uncertain and filled with foreboding.

"No, indeed, Clarissa. I am independent now. I shall most certainly come with you." Letty would send a letter to her parents when she arrived in Town to tell them where she was residing. They would surely breathe a sigh of relief to have one less mouth to feed. At the same time, she felt guilt about the implications of calling herself independent. She was not financially independent by any means; she had no money from her marriage and must rely entirely on the mercy of this woman. Her only independence was in her not having ties or responsibilities to anyone.

Only a few seconds passed before her guilt became too much. "Though you know I do not have money...."

"Do not speak of it, my dear. I want your company." Clarissa clung to her like a vine. "And I feel awful, for I know the predicament that John left you in. Mr. Glenville wrote to me—do not be angry with him, for it was at my request. All was as I had dreaded. But have no fear." Her expression took on a triumphal note that wiped the smile from Letty's face. What was her mother-in-law planning now? "We shall merely have to find you a dashingly rich husband in Town, and everything will be well. I can, in a manner of speaking, bring you out, I dare say. Though it cannot be quite the same, otherwise people would talk, you realise, since you have been married before."

"But Clarissa, I cannot. I am in mourning, and so are you for that matter. We shall have to keep to our own company until we can come back into Society." Letty's common sense dampened Clarissa's excitement.

"Oh, fiddlesticks! That is most unhelpful. Not that I wish you to forget John straight away, of course." She patted Letty's hand melancholically. "The Lord knows I still miss my dear Percy dreadfully. And John was such a dear boy. I certainly do not wish to hurry you out of mourning for him."

"Of course not."

"But you have so much more time, you see? And you are quite eligible for another match. I fear the Lord will not bless us, but never mind that. Let us content ourselves with your beautification. That bloom must come back before I introduce you into Society."

Clarissa's next fear was that those friends she had left behind would not be there when they arrived back in Town. Once she had worried about this for an appropriate amount of time, she occupied herself with planning chance meetings for Letty to have with gentlemen. For she must meet some eligible men before the end of her mourning, no matter what she said!

CHAPTER FOUR

*Be courteous to all, but intimate with few, and let those few be
well tried before you give them your confidence.*
– GEORGE WASHINGTON

L ondon was going to bed as they arrived. Shops were
being shut up for the night, the lamps were being lit,
and people were wandering home as darkness crept in. But, as
with most cities, when some went to bed others awoke.

Letty stared with a little interest from the small, grimy
window of the carriage. She could see a dim haze of light from
the windows they passed. She could make out hundreds of
residences, too many front doors to count. There were gentlemen, walking in pairs or threes, making their way to their
favourite clubs. They looked forward to drinks with friends,
cards, or perhaps the chance to witness a bet. The respectable
would be abed by three but the dissolute would still be drunk
while the rest of London breakfasted.

The country widow admired the clothing of the men they
passed. They were so painstakingly attired in beautifully cut
garments, perfectly arranged neckties, with hair cropped and

combed forward into the popular romantic styles. As the carriage rolled by, they faded like phantoms into the night. Then, as the carriage made its way through the fashionable part of Town and out the other side, these men appeared no more.

Here the streets seemed darker and more sinister. Less people walked abroad and the roads and alleyways surrendered to the shadowy darkness. When the creaking carriage finally drew to a halt, Letty was relieved to see a warm doorway open upon them. The rich smell of smoke from blazing fires hit her like a cry of welcome.

"Oh, how I do ache after long journeys!" Clarissa sighed. "The Lord has never been kind to me when travelling. Well, at least we are here. Perhaps we can expect a little more happiness now we are in Town. For now though, I think it would be best to have a little something to drink and then go straight off to bed. I am not sure about you, my dear, but I am absolutely exhausted." So tired was Clarissa that she did not even give Tibbs the customary beating with her umbrella.

Letty could not dispute the plan, for they had been travelling for several days and she really was tired. Although the journey was uneventful, the parting from Theo had been emotionally draining. She had cried and screamed and then become silent as a statue, all things that only emphasized her childish propensities. The young girl may not have wanted to leave the small party bound for London, but Letty could see it would be best for her. She was glad that Theo would not have the opportunity to get herself into trouble in the capital. Letty could already see the strain the young girl had put on Clarissa's nerves and was happy, when the time came, to release her into her parents' care.

They had left her at midday on the second day of the journey. Clarissa had said her farewell and retreated back inside the carriage, not wanting to converse with the people who had snubbed her chaperonage. Letty had been left with Theo. She had taken up her hand and squeezed it gently while they stood on the gravel driveway.

"Goodbye, sister. I hope you become...happy here after a time. Who knows what life will bring?"

The girl had scowled and pulled her hand away. "You are wrong. We are no longer sisters. There is nothing binding us together anymore."

"Very well, then shall we at least part friends?" Even this last attempt at peace had failed. Theo had simply turned on her heel and vanished into the house without another word.

One more familiar face had disappeared from Letty's short life. Perhaps she and Theo would meet again and with time the girl would mature. And yet, as the carriage passed over the driveway and left Theo's house behind, Letty had looked back through the avenue of oaks with a sinking suspicion that this hope was unfounded.

With the journey finished, Letty sat sipping a warm drink in the London house, her first activity in the metropolis. Despite the excitement of a new place, her weariness began closing in. After finishing the beverage, she made her way upstairs. Maria had already unpacked her things, eager to please her new mistress. She came straight over to Letty as she entered the bedroom and took her gloves and hat.

"Will you want to be undressed now, ma'am?"

How could this maid look so bright-eyed and full of energy?

"Yes, please, Maria," replied Letty, though the idea of a maid undressing her was about as alien to her as it would have been to Maria.

Maria, so happy with the prospect of living in Town and still being able to support her family, did not notice Letty's inexperience. She hummed enthusiastically in spite of the tiring journey, and went about her work quickly and efficiently. She was about to plait her mistress' hair when Letty stopped her.

"No, thank you, Maria. I...I would like to plait my own hair, if I may?"

"Of course, ma'am," said the maid, picking up discarded garments and putting them away.

Although Letty had tried to dissuade her mother-in-law, the woman had insisted on buying her some new travelling clothes and a new day dress and had promised to order several more day and evening gowns. Letty assured her it was quite unnecessary, to which Clarissa replied, "My dear! Although I have been in the country away from the oasis of Town, I have kept up to date with the new fashions, and—I say this with love, my dear—your dresses are not quite right for Town." A charitable smile formed on the old lady's face.

Letty had not really bothered about the fashions when buying her mourning dresses. It was more her money being in scant supply and her need of the garments quickly that had spurred her on. If truth be told, Letty had never bothered with the fashions at all. It was not to be supposed that she did not like a fine dress, expertly made and beautiful when worn. She had a few times traced a finger over the fashion plates and magazines in the library. Yet, she could never justify spending such sums of money on an item of clothing, no matter how much it enticed her. In hindsight, perhaps it was a blessing that she had never ordered elegant gowns. For where would she be now if even more money had been spent during her marriage?

As Letty lay in bed, her tired mind wandered over these thoughts, becoming more confused and jumbled. She felt a kind of happiness now she had arrived in Town, or perhaps it was more a contented feeling. For now, Clarissa would look after her, and despite Clarissa's eccentricities, Letty enjoyed the company of her mother-in-law. Letty had a certain amount of anticipation about life in Town; after all, who of her acquaintance had not been excited by the thought and delights of Town? Perhaps it was something that was bred into you as a woman—to be excited about this place and to have as your ambition in life regular visits throughout the Season. Even Clarissa had been lifted out of the doldrums by coming back to Town and her old home.

Now Letty was in the fortunate—although some would say unfortunate—position of not knowing what would happen tomorrow. The anxiety that she felt at that unknown presented itself as a gentle thudding of her heart, but she wondered whether she was mistaking excitement for anxiety. It was a pleasure not to know what tomorrow would bring for she knew, at the very least, that she was secure in Clarissa's care.

The next morning did not bring anything specific—at least, not at first. The house was being put to rights, Tibbs was assaulted several times by his loving mistress on the matter of the bill for the carriage hire, and Letty was left to read one of her favourite books. This was a leisure she had not been afforded for several months as Theo had not left her alone to read. She therefore took to her old pleasure with relish. Although she felt a little guilty about not being occupied more fruitfully, she did manage a truly enjoyable escape into the world of *Waverly*. Scott's descriptions held Letty captivated and Plain Rose, Waverly's final choice for a bride, was always her favourite despite the beauty of Flora.

She was lost to the world until, quite suddenly, she realised she had not written to her parents since the letter she had sent after arriving at Theo's. She jumped up from the sofa and made her way rapidly to the writing desk in the corner of the room. Clarissa would not mind; she had given Letty free rein of the house while they were in London. Besides, her mother-in-law was busy refreshing herself with sleep and many varieties of food in another part of the house. It had been too long since she had eaten almonds, raisins, and other foreign delicacies. She had truly missed all of the pleasures and amenities that only London could afford.

Letty pulled a sheet from the desk and picked up a quill that had been newly tipped. The paper was thick and the ink left the thinnest lines of writing upon the page.

20 December 1815

Dear Papa and Mama,

I am sorry that I have not written to you since staying with Theodora Burton. I have been remiss in my contact, but things seem to have happened so quickly. How to start? I am so sad whilst writing this for remembering what has happened. Theodora's husband David has passed away. It was quite unexpected and happened only a week or so after I arrived at their residence.

Though Theodora was obviously distressed, she managed to recover well enough to travel after the funeral to her father's home. I believe she will stay with her parents for the foreseeable future....

This sentence reminded Letty about her awkward parting with Theo. One thing that was easy to foresee was that Theo would not stay a single woman for long. Those full and petulant lips, the easy curves, and shiny guinea curls combined to form an undeniably beautiful, young widow. Her character was both selfish and ignorant, but her looks more than made up for those shortcomings. She would grieve David's loss quickly, and a gentleman wanting a wife who was game for amusements, laughter, and expensive living—which did not exactly narrow the field—would marry her soon.

Marriage was a circumstance that Letty knew was out of her own reach, and should it present itself she did not know what her reaction would be. True, she was still of a marriageable age, but her prospects had never been good. Her father was a poor vicar, and her mother shared in his lack of connections.

I know that when last I wrote, I spoke of coming home to you and Mama. Since then, however, my mother-in-law, Mrs. Clarissa Burton, has asked me to come up to London with her to stay in the Town house she has rented out for the Season and, when we are out of blacks, to attend some of the Season's amusements.

Although I wish to see you both, I do not know when I will— I have accepted my mother-in-law's invitation and we arrived in London yesterday. Do not worry over me, and once again, I am sorry I did not write to you sooner. I am sure that you shall not miss me. I do not know when I shall write to you again, but I do not think I will be coming back to live at home in the near future.

I believe I am to act as Clarissa Burton's unofficial companion. I know this will make things easier for you without the worry of having another person to support. It will also be of benefit to Mrs. Burton who, I believe, would become lonely without another for company. This will give me an independence of sorts which I should also like.

Do not worry if you do not hear from me. I shall be well looked after in Mrs. Burton's house. I send my love to both of you.

Your ever-affectionate daughter,
Lettice Burton

. . .

Now that the letter was complete, Letty went in search of Tibbs. She passed the sealed paper into his capable hands and asked him to send it.

"Aye, ma'am."

"Thank you, Tibbs, you are so kind." She smiled at the footman, whose aged face she could not help but like.

"You're welcome, ma'am, and may I say, you're a lovely addition to the 'ousehold." He grinned, revealing a missing tooth and a soft side to his usually gruff exterior.

Letty returned to the morning room and resumed her place on the window seat. Her book, however, lay unattended in her lap as she pondered. It was odd to feel sad about not returning home when she had already been away for several years. Perhaps she had been looking forward to the maternal and paternal care, but then, she knew there was still a part of her that did not want to go back there. She did not think she would be strong enough to face that place of childhood joy. She could not go back to the place where she had left her innocence, where she had left her happiness and excitement about future life. It would be too hard to return there. She had strength enough to come to new places, but going to old ones would only leave her thinking about the changes in her life and how different it could have been and how different she had become.

She did not like to think of it, for she was sure she would not like what she saw in herself. It was better not to think of it. She knew that dwelling on the past would do no good for her contentment or character. She did not wish to sit idly by and contemplate what she could have had and could now never obtain.

No, she must look ahead. There might not be happiness in her future, but there could maybe be contentment. She sighed, smiling faintly at the empty room. She picked up *Waverly* to resume her reading but stopped when she caught sight of a figure approaching the house. She leant closer to the window, her seat the perfect vantage point. Through the pane of rain-spattered glass, she could see the visitor was tall and that he was striding quite purposefully towards the building, his greatcoat flying out behind him. No doubt he was anxious to escape the bullying of heavy raindrops that had been falling intermittently throughout the morning. The book was forgotten in her lap as she placed a hand on the cold windowsill to gain the longest look. Surely, he did not intend to visit here?

Moments later her question was answered when she heard noises in the hall. Letty glanced at the clock on the mantelpiece. It read half past eleven. Abandoning the window, she quickly checked that the ribbon marking her place was tucked firmly between the pages before laying the book on the table beside her. She reached the doorway onto the landing in a few seconds, her black silks swishing with her. Then she paused to listen.

How could somebody already be calling on them? They had not announced their arrival in Town, and if anyone had heard about it, then surely they must know they were in mourning. It had only been a short while since her own husband's death and though Clarissa had finished the mourning period that society demanded, she had not yet donned any dress past the colour of lavender. Perhaps this person was one of Clarissa's family paying his condolences. Letty scrambled at any explanation that did not put either herself or Clarissa in an awkward position.

She heard a deep voice echoing off the marble floor of the entrance hall. The sound of a man's voice made Letty's body unconsciously tense. The melancholy tones suggested that he had come to pay his respects. There was a jingle. What was that? Perhaps some loose coins? Then a scraping sound. Was that his cane on the floor? Clarissa's unusually loud voice then assailed her ears, a voice she could hear perfectly well, though it was coming from two floors below.

"Oh, thank you, dear Edward! It is such a comfort you have come." Clarissa's podgy feet drummed across the floor to him. There was a moment of quietly spoken words—a volume that Letty had no idea her mother-in-law was capable of—and then that jingling again.

"You must come and meet my daughter-in-law who has come up to Town with me. She has been quite wonderful, dear Major, despite her saddened state."

"Ah, would this be the delightful Theo again?"

"No, my other daughter-in-law, Lettice. I do not suppose you have met her."

"I cannot say that I have, Mrs. Burton."

Letty discerned a drop in his friendly tones making her fingertips tighten around the doorframe.

"She is quite charming, though a little out of sorts as you can imagine. She misses John dreadfully, methinks. But no matter, I intend to launch her into Society as soon as is acceptable. Though I cannot contain my patience much longer with this pesky mourning period business. Honestly, dear Edward, there is an eligible girl just wasting away upstairs, and she has been so faithful—I would see her comfortably settled. She must have her chance at love again. The Lord knows I would love a chance of my own, yet how could I forget a lifetime with dear Percy? I am cursed."

Letty did not have to see her mother-in-law's face to know the expression which must mark it, but that was not what was occupying her thoughts. As the conversation below continued, her body and mind were filling with anxiety.

"Now come and meet her. I daresay she will enjoy meeting

somebody new while she is confined within these four walls, especially someone who knew John so well!"

"It would be a pleasure, Mrs. Burton." Still the cool tone lingered.

A friend of John's? The man's tone had been so cold when he had spoken of her. She felt numb inside. Who was this bosom beau of Clarissa's who knew John and would now meet her? She supposed that her anxieties were groundless, but she could not control them. She was frozen numb inside, and whether she was capable of conversing she did not know. Just what could his arrival mean?

She did not have much time to ponder. Still listening, she could hear them mounting the stairs. A brisk walk back to the sofa allowed her to resume the pose of intent reading, but she did not take in a single thing from the page while she waited for her mother-in-law's acquaintance to reach the top of the stairs. Her curiosity was dampened by the unknown, and she felt mortified that Clarissa had said so much to him on her account.

Her heart raced a little. What did that change in his tone mean? How could he contain negative feelings towards her when they had never met? Perhaps she would be mistaken in him. It would be like her to overthink the situation, but the fact that he had known John put peace firmly out of her reach.

After a few minutes of trepidation, her mother-in-law appeared in the doorway on the arm of a most handsome military gentleman. Letty put her book down but remained where she was, her eyes wide, taking in every part of the man and her surroundings. If she had realised she was not smiling, she might have attempted to rectify that, but as it was, her mind was far too engaged to think of politeness.

The gentleman came closer and that made Letty stand, not to greet him but rather to move away. She placed herself half behind the side table.

"This is my dearest daughter." Clarissa stood back, allowing the visitor to hold his hand out in a request for Letty's. "And Lettice, this is Major Deveril, one of my lost John's dearest friends."

The gentleman let a half-smile lift his countenance. This lasted as long as fair weather in England. Too soon did a look of deep sympathy become etched onto his expressive face. Was this one of the men who had patronized gaming hells with her husband on his visits to London?

"Pleased to meet you, Mrs. Burton. I am so sorry for your loss." His hand still waited for hers.

Letty's hand balled into a fist at her side. She had watched his changing expressions, and now she could see he was returning the scrutiny and judging her, just as thoroughly as she was him. Finally, not wanting to embarrass Clarissa, Letty stretched out a trembling hand. He took it. Whether or not he noticed the shaking, the coldness, or the perspiration that had broken out across her palm, she did not know. He bent over it and she flinched at the action.

He stood upright once again, releasing her hand. When she snatched it back too quickly, he raised an eyebrow. She heard that jingle again as he stood straight and noticed the medals falling into place on his crimson coat.

"Thank you. I am pleased to make your acquaintance, sir." She managed a calm voice. She was still wondering at the propriety of this gentleman's visit, but, more than that, she was wondering at the gentleman himself. He had a boyishly handsome face, but she could not begin to trust him for that. She inhaled, realizing that she had not been breathing for the past few minutes.

Her mother-in-law must have read the question in her eyes.

"Edward is a dear family friend, Lettice. He has been known to us for—well, it must be decades!"

"Indeed, madam. Though I am afraid I've never had the pleasure of meeting you before, Mrs. Burton."

Letty nodded but continued her silence. Now that he had turned to converse with Clarissa, she studied him from a safe distance. The level set of his jaw and the drawn-back shoulders left no doubt as to the confidence of his air. His hair was a light brown, and the curls were pushed back away from his face leaving the tanned skin exposed. His green eyes held a light, and his mouth was broad and full of emotions. Yet it was the eyes she came back to, the eyes that were filled with coldness when they rested upon her.

"Shall I ring for some tea? Please be seated." Clarissa took up her role of hostess with ease despite the long gap since her last visitor.

The Major, now seated on the divan, stretched his long legs out before him but stayed quite upright, attentively leaning in to the ladies. Clarissa began a frivolous conversation with the gentleman, who responded playfully to her musings on the social life in London and filled her to the brim with the Season's gossip.

"And the Viscount Beauford, what of him?" Clarissa's eyes were as large as soup plates by this point.

To Letty the name sounded familiar. Was that the odious man in Truro whom she had collided with at the door of the library?

"Beauford?" The Major's mouth curved up into a rueful grin. "He is back here in London apparently, madam. Though I believe the man Beauford challenged has taken his wife away to his country seat for a few weeks. Everyone says he was afraid of the Viscount, and it was he who called the law down on the whole shady situation."

"Indeed? Well, the Viscount has certainly grown up much since I last saw him. Causing his own scandals, I never would have thought it, such a sweet woman his mama was."

As they carried on, Letty's interest faded. She listened only a little to the conversation but watched the two speakers, still unsure of what she thought of this Major Deveril. He seemed charming and gay enough company, but a depth to those green eyes hid something. The fact that he never once looked towards her was also peculiar.

Despite his attitude towards Letty, he seemed to know just what to say to Clarissa—every anecdote or bit of information that would titillate and please her. His way with words was both smooth and sharp. This was particularly clear in his description of a hideous dress that Lady Frenshaw had been wearing last Friday at the theatre.

Clarissa was called away after about twenty minutes of social chitchat to oversee a problem with the dinner menu and a screaming cook. This left Letty and Major Deveril alone. When the click of the door sounded, his green eyes rested upon her with a finality which was intended to scare her. In some ways it did. Her body unconsciously tensed; her eyes darted around the room, ensuring she was ready for whatever followed.

"Are you missing John?"

The direct question put her on her guard. After a moment she answered, "Yes, sir." The lie did not sound completely convincing, even to herself.

"Indeed. I expect the lack of a husband's status and connections makes the grieving of a widow more acute?"

Letty's hands twitched a little in her lap. "I do not understand your meaning, sir." She was finding it hard to keep his gaze, and with every passing second, she wanted to put more distance between them.

"Simply that without John's connections, which must have been a convenient elevation for you, life is, no doubt, much more of a struggle." His voice did not falter, and neither did his eyes. He spoke in an innocent voice, but there was hardness beneath the surface.

"Sir!" She stood up suddenly. "If you imply what I think, then you are not honourable. I may have been unconnected before I met John, but if I had ever thought his status would be gain to me, then I was a fool."

"Madam, please. I am simply curious to know more about my lost friend's wife." He could see the wild innocence in her eyes and softened a little in response.

She bent down to retrieve the book that had flown from her lap during her outburst.

Unfortunately, the well-bred Major had bent down himself to retrieve the book. The sudden motion and proximity of the man caused Letty's instincts to take over. She leapt back, her hands and arms raised, ready to block blows from her face.

The attack never came. The Major had retrieved the book and was holding it out to her. He took in what just happened and frowned, his eyes full of bewilderment and his cheeks blushing slightly.

Letty's eyes, which were screwed shut, opened a little, and she saw his harmless posture and the boyish blush. It took some moments to relax, but she eventually accepted the book in a jerky movement before resuming her seat.

"I did not mean to alarm you."

"It was nothing." Letty's voice was small. She could not feel her humiliation yet. The fear which had overtaken her body was still tangible.

"John never mentioned you read." He tried to change the conversation, and his voice had suddenly become gentle and friendly, though he watched her carefully as if trying to figure out the answer to a puzzle.

She nodded, still unable to look him in the eye. She turned her head away, exposing the side of her neck.

"Ah, Mrs. Burton," said the Major, still gently but with determination. "You seem to have something on your neck." He came forward slightly, drawing a handkerchief from one of his deep pockets and offering it to her. He watched her as though it were a test.

She frowned at him, not wanting to come into contact with his hand. Before she had a chance to take the proffered material, he leant forward, attempting to remove the mark from her neck himself. It was a gesture most improper, but he never intended to actually touch her. The mark was a phantom invented by him; he only wished to see her reaction.

She immediately fell back on the divan and then shuffled along the length of it to get away from him. He retracted his hand but continued to regard her, now with a look of sorrow creeping into his eyes. He dropped his hands by his sides and slowly took a seat at the opposite end of the divan where, just a moment ago, she had been sitting. The widow's strange behaviour was bringing back many memories, most of them unwelcome.

It had been a year since he had come back from the war. The Glorious Emperor was what Napoleon had dubbed himself. Well, there had been nothing glorious about the Corsican's war. That was why Deveril had been overjoyed when he had been offered a post training recruits on English soil away from the front line. Death had been just one part of the war. After all, there was more than one way to create terror in your conquered subjects.

Deveril had thought himself a brave and intelligent officer, but what could any officer do for the Portuguese women who had been abused by the French troops? What good had his intelligence been to him then? What good was his bravery when bravery was not what they needed?

Now, here, sitting before him, or rather cowering before him, was an Englishwoman with the same fear in her eyes, reacting to him the same way that those women had done in the hot and dusty Iberian Peninsula. The desecration which Bonaparte's army had wreaked upon the civilians was something Deveril could never forget—but dwelling in the past was no good at this moment. The young widow was clearly afraid of him, and his mind did not have to jump far to land upon the right conclusion.

At first he could not believe it. How could he? She could have been abused by someone else. She had been without a husband for a few months; perhaps in that time of not being under anyone's protection, someone had taken advantage of her. Or perhaps there had been some unpleasant incident during her childhood.

His mind ran back over his friendship with John—the laughing, the drinking, and the gaming. To John, Major Deveril had always been his amusement-chasing friend back from the wars; to the Major, John had been the alcoholic who could never say no to a wager. He remembered John's temper that had been all too often pardoned as an irregular result of drinking.

Deveril glanced at Letty who sat so still and frozen. Had he not seen her flinch earlier? Had she not shaken a little when giving him her hand? Would he pass that off too? Realization dawned and it dawned dark.

"Curse him!" He muttered the curse, but Letty still heard it. "I should have known. I should have seen it in him...." He stuffed the handkerchief back in his pocket and walked rapidly away from her toward the window. He needed to gather his thoughts.

She watched him, unsure of what he would do now. She needed to be ready for whatever response he decided to give. He strode around the room in some kind of madness before turning again upon her.

"Madam." He bowed so low that Letty, after jumping

slightly in anxiety, thought he would be kissing her hemline in minutes. "I believe I owe you the deepest and most profound apology a man has ever made on this earth." He rose and caught her gaze. Her own eyes held a little light of humour at his affecting speech despite the pain the memories were causing.

Without ceremony or invitation, he sat down again with a resigned thump on the divan but still faced her. "Madam, I cannot know all the truths. Your husband was my friend, but I believe I was mistaken in his character, at least in regards to you." He sighed. "It is not every day you realise you have been so taken in by a friend. I should have known as soon as I saw you that you were not what he described. Lies! You would not believe the things he told me.... I am sure they cannot be true." His upper half sprang to life again as he leant in to Letty. From his countenance Letty guessed he was verging on telling her these terrible lies. Before he did, she lifted a staying hand to place on his arm but retracted it just before they touched. Although she did not complete it, the gesture was noted by him.

"Sir, please do not repeat them. I am sure that in time you shall find the falsehoods disproved and the truths validated."

He stopped trying to question her after that and instead searched for forgiveness. "I should like to put my prejudices aside and make your acquaintance without the past dictating it."

She nodded at this eloquent speech.

"I must apologise again—"

"You have no more need to apologise, for I forgive you. It is an easy thing to think ill of someone you have never met if all you hear are bad things, is it not?"

"You really need not be so gracious, madam. A sound whipping is what I need. Well, indeed it's what John needed." He was oblivious to her now, his gallantry far more important than the one to whom it was offered. Then he realised quite what he was saying and apologised yet again.

Letty did not wish him to delve any deeper. She forced herself to smile. "Let us talk of John no longer, sir. Tell me of London."

His mood changed instantly. "London? Oh yes, indeed. You are the envy of every lady in England who is not in the metropolis. London is truly wonderful. It shall be jolly good fun now Mrs. Burton is back. She always was such a droll companion."

"Indeed?" This was not the Clarissa she knew.

"Oh, yes. You are in a most enviable position."

"I swear it was not my intention to cause such thoughts of jealousy." Letty's trick of diversion had worked. Her memories would stay locked away safe.

"No, I would not have said so, but I doubt any lady would dislike being in so enviable a position?"

"I am not in an enviable position." She was sparring with him now, and his face was slowly regaining his boyish smile and laughing eyes.

"Well, I shall go on believing you to be. With Clarissa to launch you, I do not doubt you shall be a success."

Although there was peace between them, Letty could not be fully at ease, and with talk of success in Society her discomfort increased. She was fortunate, therefore, when her mother-in-law returned to them.

Clarissa re-entered the room with a bustle and a more than usual rosy tint to her face. The complaint in the kitchen had roused her temper, but still, she was all smiles for Major Deveril. After a few more minutes of pleasantries, he took his leave, making his call exactly the proper half hour Society dictated.

When he took Letty's hand to leave, she could feel all the

words he still wanted to say in the hand and eyes that held hers.

"Such a charming young man!" was all Clarissa had to say of the gentleman after his exit. Letty said nothing. Her feelings were too much in turmoil. One fact, however, remained starkly clear: John had had at least one good friend in London.

CHAPTER FIVE

Fate chooses your relations, you choose your friends.
– JACQUES DELILLE

L etty received a letter from Mr. Glenville, which had been redirected several times, on her fourth day in London. It contained the news that Highfield had been sold, along with the farm and all the old-fashioned furniture she had left behind. It was a sober note, and as the Town house was almost silent, this made it even sadder. She reflected that now she had no more than the meagre possessions she had brought with her. There was little money left to her name; she was in the world with barely any security. Thankfully, she was not left to her melancholy thoughts for many more days.

After a few weeks of solitude, ticking clocks, endless pages, and heavy silence, Clarissa decided she could bear it no more. It was now a few months since John and David had passed away, and Clarissa wished to begin renewing friendships. So at exactly half past one on a Thursday afternoon, she decided upon a promenade in Hyde Park with Major Deveril—who happened to be in the drawing room when her decision was made. Hopefully, she would meet some old acquaintances while walking.

Once Clarissa's new landaulet arrived at the gardens, the small party stepped out and made their way through the gates, starting a sedate walk along the wide pathway.

"Oh, do not worry about me!" Clarissa said to the Major, who had offered his arm. "I have been in this world long enough to take myself about, but I am sure Lettice will lean upon your arm." The old widow stepped out leaving them behind her.

Letty hesitated, eyeing the Major who looked encouragingly at her. She slowly placed her hand within the crook of his arm and began walking with him, lengthening her stride to match his.

"You do not smile very much, Mrs. Burton," the Major stated. There were lines of concern on a face that was usually carefree. The dark dress she wore blew a little in the wind, and her ribbons fluttered against her.

"I think it is the most proper thing to do when one is in mourning, Major Deveril."

"Ha!"

Letty watched the profile of his face and saw creases appear at the sides of his mouth.

"Yes, I suppose it is, but you are a little too good at it. I would rather you enjoy yourself."

"What makes you think I am not enjoying myself? And I think it is probably more proper for you not to laugh at a widow for her mourning."

"Mrs. Burton, there is no need to continue that charade with me. I can be trusted." He glanced at Clarissa who was slightly out of earshot in front, peering inquisitively over hedges for any chance acquaintance while he and Letty conversed.

"I have led soldiers into battle. I am one of the most trust-worthy men in London, I promise."

Letty laughed. "How can I not trust that?" She was becoming accustomed to his talk.

"I have fought for honour."

"And tell me, was it something you enjoyed fighting for?"

He did not answer. His face was darkened by the same shadows she had seen before at their first meeting. Further acquaintance had taught her that they were rare on his cheerful countenance, but from time to time, the shadows did come, and she was slowly learning their causes.

"Enjoy war? I believe you can enjoy being a skilled soldier. But whether one should ever enjoy war itself—I will say no, though others may dispute it if they wish."

It was clear he did not want to pursue this topic. The surface-deep comments he had made earlier were easy to say. To speak openly about his military career was obviously far more difficult, and she did not wish to push him.

"I did service for my King abroad, but I am far happier here than I ever was at war on the front line. Now—" His face lit up as he changed the subject.

Letty felt the first glimmer of admiration for this honourable man.

"One thing my years as an officer have taught me is to be no man's fool. I have seen very clearly that you are a mourning woman, but not one that mourns for the loss of her husband."

Her face was gentled by a slight smile. "You are very sure I should trust you. Tell me: what else could I possibly be mourning?" She enjoyed the Major's lightheartedness but was wary of where his conversation was headed.

"I would be a scoundrel and a cad to assume your thoughts. It is only that I understand perhaps a little of you and your past. I believe that maybe you are in mourning for your freedom, at least, that is what I think."

"What, I? Do not be ridiculous! I am as free as anyone could ever hope to be." She felt a tightening of her chest.

"Or maybe as free as a pet bird, moved from one cage to another. It does not matter how big your cage is, you are still a prisoner."

Letty was about to take exception to Deveril and use a fork in the path to separate from him and disappear when he did something quite unexpected.

"But see here, Mrs. Burton." He pulled her with a definite strength toward the side of the path and pointed out a bee. It was feasting itself on a large rose, only its furry tail in view from between the velvet petals. Major Deveril shook the stem of the rose a little and the insect flew off, bobbing here and there. "Behold, the humble worker bee, following the rules of the world into which it was born. Here it is fetching nectar, but, although it must go to and from the hive, it can choose its own way in between. So in this life Mrs. Burton, though we must follow the rules of Society, we can at least enjoy this little freedom we have, do you not think?" His green eyes locked onto her face and filled with the light of mischievous humour.

Letty could not help but let a small smile embrace her lips again. "Indeed, Major? You must educate me—how does one enjoy oneself in Town? Especially when there are only rules to follow?" His words had hit almost too close to the truth, but they intrigued her.

"Quite simply, Mrs. Burton, you must become an observer, or, a watcher of people, if you will. Learn to laugh at the many rules Society puts upon us and amuse yourself with watching others obey every fickle dictate of fashion. For instance, that hat." He pointed discreetly to a very fashionable lady's hat, made of bronzed silk and sporting a steep cylindrical bonnet with large feathers to complete the extravagance. "You could indeed praise that lady on her sense of fashion, or, if your nature is of a meaner sort, you could easily be envious of her. I choose however to think upon the similarities that the hat has to a flowerpot. You see she is more a slave to Society than we are as she has resorted to the wearing of garden-like millinery upon her head."

Letty could not but acknowledge the truth and humour of Major Deveril's observation.

"And there, farther down on the green, is Mrs. Ponsonby's daughter." He gestured slightly at a small, smartly dressed woman walking on the heels of her taller progenitor. "You could observe her as a lady very fortunate in her mother's sense of fashion and generosity. Or you could observe her as a lap dog, following her owner and obeying the instructions she is given for the treats of clothes."

Dimples had appeared on either side of her mouth and her lips were beginning to quiver. "Major, I think you are quite cruel in your perception, however true it may be."

"Ah, but is it not freeing? At least, I have obtained what I wished: a smile from you. And I shall cherish that more than all the money in my pockets."

"If I had not heard from my mother-in-law of your flirtations with Miss Gray, I should think you were entering the dangerous waters of starting a flirtation with me." Her sparring was good-natured, although the words did carry a hint of warning.

"No, indeed, I am perhaps a little bit of a scoundrel, but I prefer only to be a scoundrel to one lady at a time, otherwise it becomes most confusing. No, I have decided that you and I must become friends. You are the sort of companion to keep me sane at the parties and balls that we shall attend once you are out of blacks. Perhaps the tittle-tattling of the ton can be better enjoyed if I can at least make it ridiculous with your help. In return, I promise you my protection and guidance whilst you navigate Society."

"It seems you have given me a great offer of friendship,

Major Deveril. Might I beg time to consider your generous proposal?"

"Oh, indeed, though I must require your answer soon, for now I see you partake of the same humour as I do, I am anxious to start this friendship of ours sooner rather than later." He gave another of his boyish grins.

Clarissa had, until this point, purposely strode ahead, not only to look for acquaintances but also to give the two young people a chance to talk. She had always approved of the Major; a grasp of fashion and Town gossip was very agreeable in a man, and he was so wonderfully charming! He claimed to be besotted by a Miss Gray, but perhaps he could be persuaded to fall in love with Letty? She seemed disinterested, but who could resist a charmer in a scarlet coat? Clarissa's musings were cut short when she caught sight of what she had been looking for all along.

"My dear! My dear!" she whispered urgently. She had rejoined Letty and the Major as quickly as possible without behaving improperly and was now panting heavily. "There is a party of quite the most fashionable afternoon promenaders coming this way. We must appear most respectable and pleasing—perhaps they shall look well upon us, and we may even be introduced to them at the assemblies when we are able to go! Though, to be sure, we may never receive invitations, for I have not met any of my previous acquaintances yet."

"What a brilliant idea, madam!" replied the Major in excitement, diverting her melancholy and encouraging her to consider the approaching promenaders. He threw a quick wink to Letty. "Perhaps if we continue to walk towards them and smile affably?"

"Yes, Major, I think that is the best plan. Let us just hope the Lord is in a provident mood." They implemented their military friend's strategy, and continued to walk slowly down the path just as they had been doing before. The party passed

by them, Clarissa issued smiles to all, and Letty forced one
onto her face to please her mother-in-law.

Letty noticed that the two ladies in the party were
extremely handsome, one with guinea-gold curls and the other
with raven locks peeking from beneath each of their modish
bonnets. There were several gentlemen escorting these two
ladies. All of them seemed fairly young, and most were
members of the dandy set. But while most looked upon
Letty's party quite genially, one man did not.

Letty tried to ignore the slight, but it was obvious to her, if
not to her mother-in-law. The gentleman in question, if he
might be so called, had a plain face fixed with a frown, and
when he deigned to look upon the passing party of three, he
threw an appraising look in their direction. Seeing nothing of
value, he lifted his nose in the air, his look growing disdainful.
Perhaps he disapproved of women in mourning touring the
gardens with a handsome man in a scarlet coat. He looked
away shortly afterwards and did not look back again.

Letty caught all this as they passed, and although she was
not affected by the delicate sensibilities which some women lay
claim to, she knew a cut when she saw one. She hoped,
contrary to her mother-in-law's wishes, that they would not
see this party again in the near future.

The exciting moment was soon over, and when Clarissa
had stared after the members of the ton for a few moments in
a sort of mournful trance, the three walkers began to loop
around the path and walk back towards the landaulet.

They were just reaching one of the main paths when they
met with a mother and her eldest daughter. Not only was the
mother an old acquaintance of Clarissa's, she was also happy
to renew the friendship. They started a rapid dialogue that
none of the younger set could decipher, and after this joyous
reunion was somewhat over, Clarissa presented Letty and the
Major to the mother and daughter.

The Major, happy to let the women talk amongst themselves, stood to one side. Letty smiled at the shy girl whose Christian name, as she had just learned, was Sophie. "Have you been in Town long, Miss Egleton?"

"Oh, yes. Mama insists we come to London for the entire Season."

"And do you enjoy the Season?"

Miss Egleton's plain face frowned as if confused by the question, and then, as her brow cleared, she looked frankly back at Letty. "No, I don't think I particularly do. Not that I complain, of course—there are so many things to do in London."

"Yes, indeed there are. I am coming to learn that." Letty's eyes appraised her companion who was a little smaller than herself. "So, what is it that you do not enjoy?"

"Oh, Mrs. Burton, if you carry on asking me these questions, I am sure to say something I oughtn't."

Letty chuckled. The girl was genuinely worried about her own words.

"Oh, I know, I am rather silly, it is just that Mama is forever telling me off for saying things I should not. Just the other day, I happened to tell a gentleman that I disliked Byron intensely, and he was such an admirer of his. I had no idea, of course, but Mama said that was no excuse. I simply should have said nothing on the subject." Miss Egleton was whispering slightly so that her mother, busily chatting, would not hear. She did not really know why she was sharing so much with a perfect stranger, but the young widow had such a sweet face and Sophie could not help but trust it.

"I do not know much of Byron. Why is it you do not like him?"

"Well, he is deemed to be quite the poet, but I have heard from my brother, who is up at Oxford, that he is also quite a...

I can't remember the word he used, but I know from the tone that it was not a good one."

"I see. And the gentleman to whom you were speaking was an admirer of Byron's poetry?"

"I think so. Oh, I am no good at speaking the correct things and even worse in the company of gentlemen. You must forgive me, if we see each other again, if I say things I oughtn't."

Letty was grinning broadly now. The brown-haired Miss Egleton was really rather sweet. "You need not worry what you say to me. I am not easily offended."

"In that case we must sit with each other at any parties in which we find ourselves together. You can stop me from speaking to anyone, and I shall be your companion."

"That sounds delightful." Letty chuckled and Miss Egleton joined in.

Letty could not help but like her new acquaintance. She was honest, and that made her quite charming. After she explained about her habit of saying the wrong things, she also confided in Letty about her love of walks, architecture, and books. Letty enjoyed these things also, and determined that Sophie Egleton, with her pleasing manner, was someone she wished to see more of. She was happy to hear Clarissa accept Mrs. Egleton's offer to call upon them the following morning.

Once that had been decided, Clarissa announced that her legs were aching and expressed a wish to be home immediately. She excused herself and her daughter-in-law from the Egletons' company, and they both made their way towards the carriage with tomorrow's visit to look forward to.

As they reached the landaulet, the women saw the Major, who had slipped away while they were acquainting themselves with the Egletons, standing nearby, deep in conversation with another gentleman. Who the man was they could not say for his back was the only view afforded them.

Not wanting to seem rude by interrupting, Letty persuaded her mother-in-law—with difficulty—that they should wait in the carriage. Clarissa climbed in first, her weight making the landaulet lean precariously to one side before she sat down. Letty gathered her skirts about her and put a tentative foot on the step. She glanced in the direction of the two men to see if they had concluded their conversation—but instead of meeting the Major's cheerful green eyes, she caught sight of a pair of eyes that were much darker and that were ever so slightly familiar.

"You seem a little distracted?" The Major was allowing himself to speak frankly to Letty since Clarissa had drifted off almost immediately once the carriage had set into motion.

"Do I?"

"Well, I could ignore it and be polite, but seeing as I have been talking to you for a full five minutes and asked several questions without being awarded a response, I must put it to you that you are distracted."

"Oh, I am sorry, Major Deveril." Letty's eyes were a little anxious, worrying she had caused offence.

"No need to apologise, Mrs. B., for if you accept my offer, we shall be friends, and there is no need to apologise to a friend. I shall also be permitted to call you Mrs. B. instead of Mrs. Burton—which I think does not suit you at all."

"Ah, but I have not accepted your offer yet, and, therefore, my apology still stands. What was it you said while my mind was elsewhere?" In truth, her mind had been occupied in placing those dark eyes she had just seen. It had not taken her long.

"Nothing much of interest. I merely thanked you for waiting so patiently for me while I finished talking with Beauford. Hadn't seen the fellow in an age, you see, and I had to check up on him. Oh, I do beg your pardon—you do not know of him yet, I suppose?"

The memory of the library at Truro, which she had been trying to ignore, surfaced unpleasantly. "I have heard a little, though not enough to proclaim I know of him." She decided not to tell the Major she had already spoken with the Viscount. It would only stir up her anger and cause some kind of trouble if she were to repeat the Viscount's words to the Major.

"Yes, and I feel for you, I do. You have been so deprived of Society. He is, in fact, one of my friends and the most eligible man this side of thirty." He gave another of his reckless grins.

"Indeed? What a fine friend you have. What exactly is it that makes him so very eligible?" For the first time, Letty was a little interested in Society gossip.

"He is a viscount, one of the few not in debt, and he is reputed to be not just tolerable to look at but, in fact, rather handsome. What did you think?" Deveril laughed, but she could see he was examining her quite closely; she could not help being a little ruffled by his study. She swallowed, trying hard to conceal her emotions.

He could see something had come over her, and it had nothing to do with her conversation with the plain Miss Egleton. No, indeed, she had been quite happy when he had left her chatting. It was not until they returned to the carriage that she had reverted to her quieter self. He had started to coax open her hard outer shell, but he felt it was shutting on him once again.

Letty relived the blazing anger of the man who had dropped his books in Truro. "Oh, he is handsome, I suppose. Though he seems a little serious, do you not think?"

"Well, yes, he is now...." The Major seemed ready to expand upon something and then thought better of it. "But most of the time he is an excellent fellow to spend an evening with. Perhaps I can introduce him to you, though there is a proviso—I only introduce my friends to my friends. What say you, Mrs. B.?"

"Oh, Major Deveril! You are becoming quite intolerable!" cried Letty, her deep thoughts forgotten as she burst into a fit of laughter.

The house was silent, once more in sleep, and Letty was alone and awake. She sat upon her covers, wrapped in a large blanket which kept a little of the warmth in, and stared into the nothingness. The smell of a guttering fire reached her nose and she braced herself for the cold that would come with its death.

The young widow had not had time to digest everything that had happened since coming to London. She would have to think and ponder adequately before her mind would allow her to rest. In Cornwall, she had barely known anybody, yet here she had been introduced to several people whether directly or indirectly in a matter of weeks. She felt she was sitting on the tip of a world she did not fully comprehend, a world she had not hitherto come into contact with. She knew of London, of course, and of the Society which surrounded it, but it was one thing hearing about it and quite another beginning to experience it.

She had not yet been to a social gathering, but she already felt overwhelmed. She hoped her calm reserve would be able to handle the situation when the time came, but in these late hours of the night which passed inevitably into the small hours of the morning, she found herself sitting sleepless upon her bed, thinking and thinking.

One thought continued to dominate—she could not keep the Viscount Beauford's face from her mind. His dark, scowling eyes and his harsh words had incensed her in Truro, and still, even now, she could see him so clearly before her. His face was so very distinct, or perhaps it was more the look it bore—one of anger and impatience, as far as Letty could ascertain. It had certainly succeeded in calling up a similar anger in her, but, unlike him, she had not let it show. She wondered if there would ever be a time when she could not rein her temper in, a time when it would break loose and go bucking, galloping, and wreaking havoc everywhere.

When her thoughts were not distracted by the Viscount, she considered the offer of friendship from Major Deveril. She had been thinking over the answer she would give. She had not been reliant on anyone for a long time, and to enter into a close friendship was something she was not sure she was ready for. It felt a little like standing on the edge of a cliff and trusting in someone else to support her.

The strongest inducement to accept his offer was the possibility of being introduced to Lord Beauford. She was interested to see what the aristocrat's reaction would be, whether he would remember her or whether she could deliver him a perfect set-down without him being any the wiser. But that would be precisely the situation in which her temper could be lost. No, perhaps it was better to accept that the ton would always live by their rules and the rest of society by others. If she could at least accept that, then she could meet him with equanimity. Though even as this thought floated into her head, she doubted her ability to remain calm during the introduction.

She mused over the Major and his interesting perception of Society. The more time she spent with the Major, the more she warmed to him. He seemed a safe place. After two years which no woman should have to face at twenty years of age, there was solace in the fact that someone in the world knew her past—the past which she had always tried to hide. Even in her marriage she had hidden her hurt from her husband, not to mention everyone else. She had become skilled at it. It took time to develop an expressionless countenance no matter what one was confronted with, to keep calm tones and a mask-like face in spite of the worst circumstances. It was an art that took others, who were willing, decades to learn, but she, who had been unwilling, had learned it in two years.

Once the comments became abuse and then turned into a raised hand, she had learned there was no use in tears; they did nothing to stop a man in fury. There was no use crying out in a house that was empty except for you and the man you had vowed your life to. When villagers shunned you and tenants resented your husband, there was no one after that. There was no friend to speak to but God.

Now, however, there was Major Deveril.

He did not despise her or find her disgusting. In fact, in recent weeks she had begun to see a protective glint in his eyes when he looked at her. That same look had come into his eyes when they were driving home in the carriage today. She had been distracted, but it was the first time anybody had cared enough to notice it. He would be a good friend, she thought, though she had no concept of what their friendship would be like. She began to think on it. He made her smile, he made her laugh, and she felt she could trust him. She thought about his attributes and his actions. Minutes passed into hours and the night faded away not long after she faded into sleep.

The next morning Letty awoke in a sunlit room. Maria bustled in a few moments later with water for the basin. She said her morning greetings and beamed a smile at her beloved mistress as she helped her into her black dress.

The Egletons arrived. Letty spent an enjoyable half hour discussing novels with Miss Egleton and began looking forward to a walk they were planning for the next day.

"I hope you will settle well in Town, Mrs. Burton." The

girl had lost almost all of her shyness around Letty. "It will be wonderful to go to balls and the like with you. For then, it will not be so embarrassing not to be asked to dance. You can stop my errant talk and I can sit with you, for you cannot dance in mourning. Oh!" she gasped, a hand flying to her mouth. "I am sorry. I expect you do not wish to be reminded. Did you like dancing?" She was blushing and stumbling over her words.

"Not at all," replied Letty, wanting to soothe the girl's embarrassment. "I am forever tripping over invisible things! Though, Sophie, I'm sure you shall be asked to dance and, please, do call me Letty." The young widow felt a deep sympathy for the plain girl rising within her.

"Oh, yes, I will, and no, there is no need for flattery. I know as well as you do that I am plain and quite soon will be on the shelf. But do not pity me, for I actually enjoy the freedom of it. I am fairly independent and, without the need to impress gentlemen, I feel at ease. It is only in certain social gatherings, like balls, that I find myself in a little discomfort. That discomfort probably contributes to my foolish talk, as mama calls it." Her soft face was smiling, and Letty could not help but admire her for her confidence in singleness. Many a girl would have gone to pieces.

"Very well, I shall not pity you, only join you instead when the time comes!"

"Do you miss your husband very much?" Sophie's slight naivety and easy talking had led her into saying something which would not normally be said. Whether it was the sweet and innocent look on Miss Egleton's face, or the fact that her words had lanced something filled to bursting, Letty answered her.

"Sometimes. It is strange to go from being constantly attached to someone to being alone again."

Sophie digested this information, her brow puckering and her eyes looking serious. "Well," she said suddenly, a brightness overcoming her face, "one of the few benefits of Town is that you almost never can be alone. Even if you do not make other acquaintances because of your current state of mourning, I would be most happy to keep you company!"

Letty's face broke into a genuine smile, and she nodded, not knowing what else to do in this situation. She could not remember the last time she had had a friendship with another woman near her age.

"Though I suppose you must know," spoke the young woman, her eyes turning serious again, "I am inordinately fond of architecture, as I have told you, and you may have to listen to me speak of it on occasion."

"Indeed! I am sure that is a hardship I can endure."

"You laugh at me. Well, I have forewarned you—that you cannot deny." The plain girl grinned. "I have to say, I am coming to like you immensely, Letty."

"And I you, Sophie."

"I have recently been reading a novel." The young girl changed the conversation easily. She seemed to have relaxed now she had been in Letty's company more than once. They had both exchanged a little unspoken humour, and their acquaintance was fast becoming a friendship. "It is the one by Walter Scott. Have you read it?"

"Sophie? Sophie?" Mrs. Egleton demanded her daughter's immediate attention. "What is the name of the millinery shop we frequent?"

After a discussion about milliners and hats, in which Letty was quite lost, Sophie turned back to her.

"Where was I? Oh yes, *Waverly*. Have you read it?"

Letty had, of course, but she was happier listening to another young woman who was now her friend. "Tell me about it," she replied.

The two continued to chat along quite amiably until propriety bade the guests leave. The hostesses bid them good day, and after the door had been shut, Letty walked to the window and smiled to Sophie as the Egletons' carriage drew away. She sat back down upon the sofa and realised, with not a little joy, that she was finally feeling at home.

The Egletons' visit had also imparted the same full measure of joy to Clarissa. She swept round. "I have good news, dear Lettice, for the first time in such a long time!" Her hand held out, like some kind of trophy, an invitation to a card party at the Egletons'. "Oh, it shall be such fun! And it is quite proper for you to go, as long as you refrain from playing. I only hope you do not find it too boring, my dear!"

"Not at all. I am sure I shall find the games interesting to watch." Letty smiled at Clarissa's joyfulness and was happy to accommodate it. The promise of seeing Sophie again was persuasion enough for Letty. They could sit together and talk while everyone played about them.

"And just think of who will be there! The Major is invited, Mrs. Egleton tells me, and what other eligible men, I do not know!" Clarissa clapped her hands together in glee, causing the invitation to flap about noisily. "We are finally making our way back into Society, and I only hope the Lord continues to look kindly upon us!"

Letty smiled affably at her mother-in-law. Unlike her relative, Letty was content not knowing which gentlemen would be at the card party. She left the fantasizing, quite decidedly, to Clarissa.

CHAPTER SIX

Love sought is good, but giv'n unsought is better.
– WILLIAM SHAKESPEARE

The two ladies stepped out into the foggy London evening. They were happy that they need not take a chair to the party since Tibbs was ready and waiting with a carriage. Before she entered the carriage, Clarissa even spoke two words in his favour, and Letty could see the odd friendship between servant and mistress when he grunted in reply.

As they made their way through the night, Letty watched figures appear through the gloom and form into people. She glanced down at her lap and pressed a hand to the material of her dress. This was the first social appearance that she was making in Town, and therefore, she had donned the plainest gown she could find and dressed her hair very simply. Drawing attention from anyone tonight was not her aim, especially from male attendees. She was not vain enough to consider herself beautiful, but no risk could be taken—hence, her plain toilette. Clarissa, for obvious reasons, had opposed these choices violently.

"I shall not pretty myself," Letty protested, but Clarissa would not be thwarted. Finding she was unable to explain her actions, she tried to soothe her mother-in-law's frayed nerves instead. "But, Clarissa, do you not see? I do not want to lead a gentleman into affection of any kind if they cannot marry me for six months! That would be a thing too cruel." She was slightly shocked at her own cunning.

"Oh, you are the most conscientious girl I have ever met, my dear! I am sorry for doubting you. I am just so used to failing plans and things not working correctly." Clarissa dabbed her eyes with her handkerchief and pressed an understanding hand on Letty's forearm.

Letty listened to the older widow's gloomy sighs, thanking God she had escaped this time. At least tonight she would not draw any attention to her plainly dressed self, especially attention from any man.

However, upon entering the Egletons' apartments, her courage began to fail her. She was confronted by a room that positively glittered. There was such quantity of satin, silk, and taffeta—materials Letty had only seen in pictures. Pearls, diamonds and rubies winked at her from their hiding places in bosom brooches and cravat pins. As her gaze swept around the people and their stunning attire, she began to wonder if it had been a good idea to choose such a particularly plain gown.

Thankfully, for the first few moments, the crowds did not notice her shocked expression, an expression caused by her total lack of knowledge and complete underestimation of London Society. The other guests were too busy talking, whispering loudly, and crying out with laughter.

Letty's reprieve did not last long. The hum of voices, the music they had entered on, gradually petered out. The people, one by one, turned to look upon the newcomers. Mortified, Letty realised that nearly all the attention had passed over Clarissa as the gathered guests examined the younger widow and her inelegant dress. Every hair on the back of her neck rose, and a prickling sensation ran down her spine. She wanted to run out of the room and leave all these beady-eyed people to their party, but she knew she could not. Even if she tried, would her feet move at her command? She swallowed as several decades seemed to tick by and scolded herself for being so stupid.

Suddenly, through the crowd, a figure came striding forward, a knight coming to her rescue in the form of Major Deveril. He bowed to both ladies.

"Mrs. Burton, always a pleasure." He grinned at Clarissa, bending over her hand as one would do for the belle of Society. Clarissa smiled and tapped him admonishingly with her fan.

"Good evening, Major. You look in fine fettle, probably due to the attendance of Miss Gray at this little card party." She allowed a knowing smile to form on her old lips. "Now, perhaps you would be good enough to direct me to our hostess?" She could see faces she recognised from the past, but all of them would need a new introduction from Mrs. Egleton. It had been too long, and their curious glances left Mrs. Burton with the knowledge that she must repair the damage caused by her family's departure from Town and the misery that had overtaken them. As always, she looked forward to this task with little hope of success.

The Major directed Clarissa to Mrs. Egleton who invited her to join a whist table as her partner. Then he turned back to offer his arm to Letty. This time the younger widow did not hesitate. She was slowly learning to trust the Major.

He drew Letty further into the room and whispered in her ear. "How interesting you look, my dear Mrs. Burton. You have caused quite a stir though, and as a would-be friend, I must tell you I am not sure it is of admiration!"

Letty smiled a little shakily. "I swear the opposite to my

intention has happened. I wished to go unnoticed. Perhaps I would have been better putting a flower-pot on my head, do you not think?"

The Major shook with laughter. It was the spark that caused the rest of the room to spontaneously combust into conversation again as the guests dismissed from their minds the young widow in the frightful dress.

"Am I to hope that is a yes to my offer of friendship?" He guided her through the crowds to a sofa free of people. Releasing her arm, he allowed her to sit while he retained his standing position. He smiled charmingly down at her, awaiting her reply.

Letty sunk gratefully into the chair. "I think I shall need all the help I can obtain in Society." She looked about her pointedly. "So I say yes."

"Thank the Lord!" said the Major. "From now on, if you decide to wear a dress like this to a social engagement of any kind, please consult me beforehand so that I can—as a friend —do my best to dissuade you." His words were so good-natured that Letty took no offence. He cast an eye about the room. "I suppose now is as good a time as any for me to introduce my other friends to you."

Before Letty could protest, he had crossed the room in three long strides and, to her horror, was speaking to the dark-eyed Beauford. How could she not have observed him when she first came in? That was a mistake indeed. Apparently, even the most eligible bachelor in London deigned to accept an invitation to the little card party at the Egletons'. Perhaps these Egletons were higher in Society than she had apprehended— though Clarissa must have known it and praised God when they had met in Hyde Park a week ago. Later, Letty would find out that Mrs. Egleton's father was an Earl and so naturally, despite her rather non-advantageous marriage, dues had to be paid by all of the ton.

At this moment, however, all her attention was needed to calm herself. In a vain attempt at distraction, she began examining the contents of the room as though she were a purveyor of fine artefacts. There were several very pretty ladies present, all with beautifully made dresses and hair dressed in a way no one could correct. Satin hung thickly and luxuriously from dresses, silk swished with even the tiniest of movements, and already secret conversations were abounding behind the ingenious fans. Little did she know, she was, in fact, the topic of most, and more than one unflattering word was said on her account. One lady in particular, with a rather enormous bosom, was leaning in to her plain-faced, but wealthy, friend.

"You just wait until Corianna hears of this. I guarantee she shall snub the girl for dressing like that and then all others will follow." Her words were as solemn as an oracle.

"Well," replied her friend in disparaging tones, "the Duchess only sets the lead thanks to her husband's title and wealth, and before that, it was her father's wealth,"

The corner of Letty's eye caught sight of an upturned nose.

The plain friend carried on in her over-loud fashion, "Though I must say in this case I would snub the girl as well—such a plain-looking woman with no sensitivity to the demands of fashion." She held a set of spectacles to her face and gave Letty a look of distaste that the widow found hard to ignore.

Having heard every word of this particular tete-a-tete, Letty turned to face her critic. She could not allow herself to sit idly by whilst being insulted. The young widow kept her accuser's gaze a moment, her eyes emotionless and yet unrelenting. It was not without a little guilty satisfaction that she saw the woman become ruffled and look back to her friend.

Besides turning away from Letty's challenging stare, the lady also responded by quickly changing the conversation.

"The Duchess of Bedford is such a beautiful young thing, though I am amazed she is still leading the ton after the trouble she caused with the Viscount Beauford. It almost ended in—dare I say it?—blood!" The whisper was ominous, and brisk fanning ensued from both ladies.

"Hush, my dear,"—the lady leant in again—"one must remember that disreputable man is present. Of course, I would not say anything untoward, especially not about the many light-skirts he keeps chasing, but he has most certainly tarnished his family name."

Turning their gaze back to Letty, the two ladies noted that she was still observing them. They dropped the volume of their voices, the plain woman raised her fan to shield her gossip, and Letty lost the infinite joy of overhearing the rest of their conversation.

Shaking off her annoyance, she moved on to observing the gentlemen. All were dressed very well, most boasting well-fitted jackets and high shirt collars, the former probably Weston's creations. As much as she would have loved to study the room all evening without any necessity of interacting with the other guests, she would not be allowed that privilege.

Beauford and the Major advanced toward her through the crowd at full charge, and she found herself standing to face them.

"Lord Beauford, may I present Mrs. Burton." The Major flourished a ridiculous hand, making her smile a little before she curtseyed to the other man.

The perfectly dressed gentleman stepped forward and bowed. "It is a pleasure to make your acquaintance, Mrs. Burton." The words were said without the least enthusiasm.

"Thank you, my lord."

"Excellent!" said the Major, rubbing his hands together. "And now that we all know each other, shall I obtain some drinks?" Beauford nodded and thanked him while Letty cast an urgent look that the Major could not translate. Being committed to this new endeavour, he left her stranded and alone with this Viscount. She watched the Major retreat, trying hard to overcome her fear and, more importantly, her temper.

The Viscount and the widow stood in silence. She averted her eyes and searched the rest of the busy room for something else to concentrate on. She was more than a little dismayed to find several pairs of eyes observing her—and the gentleman Major Deveril had abandoned her to.

"I take it you remember meeting me before in the West Country?" His voice was bored. His eyes roamed around the room, more interested in everything else than her it seemed.

She turned her cold gaze upon him before answering his blunt question. He did not return the perusal.

"Vaguely, though I believe it is your manners that are more clearly imprinted on my memory."

"Indeed?" His eyes turned to her and widened a little, though his mouth stayed firmly under control. "And do my name and circumstances, now known to you, rub my impolite manners from your memory?"

His voice was tinged with sarcasm, yet she thought she heard a little curiosity also.

He had cut through propriety with a sharp tongue, though it was clear neither of them cared for propriety in the first place. And seeing as their conversation was only heard by them, it really did not matter. As long as they both kept smiling, the rest of the room would never be the wiser. Letty could already see this was his tack and she must follow.

She looked over his face—his black hair, the clear lines, the strong brow, and darkened eyes. She did not have time for arrogance no matter how handsome the face that wore it. She was used to backing down and conceding, but this fight she refused to lose. She threw off any attempts to hide her displeasure.

"No, it only brands the memory deeper. For knowing now that you are a gentleman of high rank, I am all the more disgusted with your behaviour." Why had he not apologised and instead gone on in this fashion?

"Does that mean that I should be quite at ease with your lack of propriety shown now because you are obviously of low breeding?"

Even for Letty, who knew her position and was quite happy in it, this remark cut deeply and drew from her a small gasp. She shot a quick look at his countenance and saw there a smile at her expense. Drawing herself together, she made ready for her escape.

"Well, as it seems that we are both predisposed to dislike one another's manners, there is no need for us to suffer any longer in each other's company. I believe my friend, Miss Egleton, is asking for me. Good evening, my lord." She inclined her head and took herself gracefully across the room to where Sophie had been beckoning to her.

"Whatever did you say to frighten Mrs. Burton off?" asked Deveril as he arrived back with three glasses of ratafia in his hands.

Beauford tossed one of them off. "It seems she does not approve of my manners, Deveril." He avoided his friend's gaze, looking down to study the glass in his hand instead.

"They don't seem to frighten off the rest of the ladies in London," mused Deveril, sipping at his drink and watching his friend over the rim of the glass. "Definitely not that delightful opera dancer you were seeing a few weeks back. What was her name again?"

Beauford did not answer. The firm line of his mouth and the twitching of his cravat showed a decidedly irritated Viscount. Deveril was tempted to push.

"It is a hard thing when one realises one is no longer the object of every woman's admiration, is it not?" He was barely containing his mirth now; it seemed too easy to tease his friend.

"Harrumph!" was all he received as an answer.

"Yes, a very hard thing. It seems, my dear man, I am more in demand than you are."

"Go and spend your time with that harpy then, but I warn you she has a sharp tongue. You will not succeed in any love-making with her."

"We shall see." As soon as he had turned away from his friend, Deveril's face broke into a big, childish grin. How splendid that Beauford, a man who knew his rank and was used to people doing whatever he wanted, was rattled!

Nettled, the Viscount watched the retreating back of his friend. He was annoyed beyond measure—although one would not have known it by looking at his well-schooled expression. But when he considered how rewarding it would be to watch the intercourse between Deveril and the widow, his spirits improved. She would snub him within a few moments. The Major was forever overstepping his boundaries; the prudish widow would send him back like a smacked pup.

Unfortunately, however, events did not transpire as the Viscount had foreseen. Although Beauford could not hear the conversation on the other side of the crowded room, his view from afar showed only cordiality betwixt the Major and the widow. With one last disgruntled noise, Beauford turned to talk to Sir Antony Margate, a boring man obsessed with horse-flesh, who droned on for a full three-quarters of an hour about one of his mares.

Meanwhile, the Major was still smiling. "I must congratulate you Mrs. B. I have never met someone who has irritated the Viscount so beautifully. You must inform me tomorrow exactly what you said, for now I cannot hear well enough to extract all the possible glee from it." Deveril passed her the glass of ratafia that he had promised her. "Though you appear meek and mild as the Virgin Mary, you are in fact more like an Amazon, Mrs. B.! Yes, indeed, you are not at all what you first appear." He ran his eyes over her plain dress and simple hair and grinned roguishly.

"I will return the compliment, Major, and say the same to you—for when we first were introduced, I certainly pegged you as a member of the dandy set."

"Dandy, indeed!"

She laughed at his mock anger.

"I see now why the Viscount was so irritated with you, though he said it was about manners."

"Yes, it was, but I do not wish to speak of it. That collar is far more interesting." She nodded towards a foppish looking youth who was fawning over one of the pretty young ladies.

"Yes, that is true," said Deveril, allowing himself to be sidetracked. "What do you think of it?" The collar points reached as high as the youth's cheekbones and looked quite ridiculous.

"I think he looks rather more like a blinkered hackney than a man."

"Very perceptive, Mrs. B. My hat goes off to you." He bowed mockingly, and they both erupted into laughter.

The rest of the evening was filled with more ridiculous banter. It was, however, kept slightly more discreet after Clarissa warned Letty that if she did not divide her attentions among other gentlemen she would cause quite a scandal. Clarissa was frustrated at their lack of delicacy, especially as she was trying to form quality connections.

The two potential scandal-causers did as they were bid. Deveril left Letty's side, and she was quite happy to remain with Sophie. The younger girl picked up where they had last left off. She continued her narrative that described almost every person present, and soon the widow was quite the connoisseur of the ton.

As for the rest of the Viscount's evening, it was spent quietly. He stayed on the edge of a small gathering without paying the slightest attention to their conversation. He could not help but spend his time watching the plain Mrs. Burton journey through the evening. She was undeniably a most peculiar woman.

"So, what do you think of the young Mrs. Burton?" asked the Major who had gone to dine at White's with Beauford the next evening.

"Who? Oh, the widow. Insufferable!"

"Come now," said Deveril to the blunt reply. "You barely know the girl. What on earth can you have against her?"

The Viscount stretched his legs out in front of him and pushed the plate of beef away. He picked up his full glass and sipped it slowly, making Deveril wait for what he knew would be a cutting reply. At long last, he replaced the glass on the now slightly soiled tablecloth.

"There is nothing worse than an arrogant woman who is disposed to think herself above her betters. It is the same as a prize colt thinking himself better than the one who is master over him. Ridiculous!" He ended somewhat more loudly than he had begun.

"Oh, you call her arrogant? I do not think you know her well enough. Perhaps you are more vexed that she did not fall at your feet like others, but challenged your manners instead!" Deveril enjoyed teasing the Viscount, and besides, arrogant was not the way to think of Mrs. Letty Burton. No, whatever else she was, she was certainly not arrogant.

"Oh, curse it all! You know very well how I feel about that

particular breed of female. All pretension and sharpness. Missish—that is the way to describe that behaviour, a trait that the middle-classes are particularly fond of displaying. However, the one thing that did the widow credit was her dignity. You know she actually said it made my manners all the more despicable to her when she found out I had a title and fortune? I could scarce believe my ears, for it is my title and fortune that allow me to act so abominably to everybody and still expect to be treated well." This reference seemed even more pointed now since recent events only proved the truth he so bitterly recited.

"Beauford, you are scandalous. I profess myself a scoundrel, but you are an entirely different breed. I am half inclined to think Mrs. B. has a point."

"Ah, Mrs. B., is it now? I suppose you'll be asking soon for my blessing upon your approaching nuptials with the widow?" Beauford raised a quizzical brow, his dark eyes gleaming a little in the candlelight.

"No, don't be absurd!" Deveril took on the voice of an injured pup. "She would not have me even if I wanted her. I do not think her in the market for a man, y'know. No, I say to myself the pretty Miss Gray is who I shall have to be content with."

"Nonsense. Even if you have not taken a fancy to her yet, I think you will soon succumb to her feminine wiles. It is an old trick to pretend indifference in order to spark interest in the opposite sex, is it not? Why, that is exactly what all the young rakes do nowadays, and then they treat their conquests with contempt only to keep them wanting more. And then there are all the small foibles of love—the trinkets and presents, the sonnets and letters. I must say, I am quite at a loose end when it comes to the opposite sex. There are so many rules to follow, how can one possibly keep up?"

The glibness of these statements masked something much

sharper underneath. Deveril knew the callous words were armour against the pain caused by a broken heart. Now, however, was not the time to speak about too recent events. He must play along with his friend if he wished to remain in that position.

"So you are keen yourself to keep out of love's way?" Even a joking question like this was too close to the mark.

"Indeed, the confusion of love is to be avoided at all costs." The tall man stood and strolled about the room very slowly, examining small objects and peering out the smudged windowpanes—anything but face his friend. What would he have to say? His previous actions already spoke for themselves, and besides, explaining himself out loud was something he never wished to do. When the Viscount had come back to Town, the one thing that singled out Deveril as a good friend was the fact that he had never, not once, referred to what had happened.

"It sounds like *you* are the one pretending indifference." A mischievous smile played about the Major's lips.

The Viscount, coming back to the present, shot a sharp look at Deveril. Quite suddenly, he abandoned his dignity and fell to chuckling at the Major's wickedly satisfied countenance.

"Touché, Major Deveril!"

"Thank you, Viscount." Deveril saluted his friend. "And now a game of piquet, I believe, simply to prove how easy it is to win against you." He gestured to the door as he stood, and they both retired to the card room.

"I have been told it is not arrogance you exude, madam, so what am I to think?" Viscount Beauford bowed courteously.

"No one can have the power to tell you what to think, my lord." Letty spoke the title with a careless tone. "It is your decision to think of me what you will and none of my affair." She affected a look of indifference.

"Indeed, though would you not like a say in my opinion of you?"

"Hardly. For whatever I say, I believe you will think as you please, and therefore, there is nothing further to discuss on the matter."

Letty had maintained her calm charade as the Viscount singled her out in the large upper rooms of the Grays' apartments. She and Clarissa were attending a small soiree with perhaps a little dancing, in which Letty and Sophie Egleton would not partake. Clarissa had immediately joined their hostess for a friendly chat on the sofa in the corner, where the ample Mrs. Gray was sampling sweetmeats and stroking a languorous lap dog. The Major had been flattering the young Miss Gray, a pretty girl with, it seemed, not an ounce of common sense, and Letty and Sophie were happy to stand and chat for a while.

Her friend had only just been called away when Letty saw the Viscount bearing down upon her. She dreaded the conversation he would make after the set down she had given him at their last meeting. She had managed to converse with fairly coherent sentences until now, but the authoritative bearing of the man was something which, though she disliked admitting it, put her on tenterhooks.

"Oh, come now, Mrs. Burton. Let us at least converse despite our unfortunate beginnings. I have it on good authority, from Major Deveril, that you are not looking for a husband. That, coupled with your non-arrogance, means we can at least make the most of each other's company when attending the same parties, for, I believe, you are not the usual specimen of the opposite sex."

"I do not know what the Major has been telling you." She paused, holding in a retort, then she thought better of it. "I thank you for your praise, however improper you may sound, but I would rather spend my time in that dog's company than yours." She gestured to the fat lap dog on Mrs. Gray's sofa that was observing them with its squished face. Widow and bachelor were mesmerized for a moment watching the owner and dog, both of whom were feeding themselves on treats. If they had been able to read each other's thoughts they would have found their minds were on similar tracks—both thinking how alike the owner and the pet were.

Letty smiled a little, then looked away. The Viscount saw it and repeated his offer for conversation, but to no avail. She would not accept. She would not be the entertainment for some libertine when his bored tendencies felt so inclined. "No, thank you, you may save your conversation."

"Really?" asked the Viscount, determined not to let his quarry get away. He leant onto his other foot to block her escape and smiled teasingly down at her. "But please tell me, what exact merits does the dog have that you favour him over myself?"

She gritted her teeth. She could not very well leave his company now without causing an unpleasant scene. Very well, if the Viscount would not let her go, perhaps she should become at least affable and converse with him for a moment. Though she had much rather bombard him with set downs, she knew such behaviour was not good for her mother-in-law's reputation—especially if he decided to snub them. Curse propriety and all its earthly shackles! She held back the biting remark she had on the tip of her tongue and smiled politely.

"That's better. Have you decided to stay, young widow?" He spoke as if to a pet dog or horse, and Letty's blood boiled within her. When her temper finally got the better of her, propriety's shackles were broken beyond repair.

"The dog has better conversation than you, as he has none! Better manners, as he does not tend to bite one's head off in anger! And the creature is in fact of jovial disposition and always ready to play, not subject to unpredictable flashes of rude temper!" Her cheeks flushed.

"Hmm, a fair prognosis. I salute you in your perception." He carried on completely unshaken by her outburst; in fact, he almost seemed pleased she had just insulted him. The realization of the ridiculous finally dawned upon Letty, and she could not help but giggle behind her fan.

"Ah," he said in low accents. "It seems you are not just the stern woman you at first appear. Fascinating! Tell me, Mrs. Burton, why have you come to Town if you are not in search of a husband? It perplexes me greatly that at one time I see you in Truro and at another here in London."

"Oh, I am sorry that I have caused you such distress and perplexity. Perhaps some smelling salts to calm your nerves?" She was too much amused to stop now. "My mother-in-law is always in charge of some." The corners of her wide mouth twitched, unable to contain her humour.

"I think I am safe from an attack of the vapors, but perhaps your explanation will cure me completely?" The flicker of a smile appeared upon his own straight lips but was gone as soon as it came.

"It is very simple, my lord. My husband died shortly after my mother-in-law's own husband's demise, and she wished to return to Town with me as her companion. I obliged. For although you may be a stranger to it, loneliness is something quite abominable." Her tone had changed; it was matter-of-fact and somewhat harder.

"Well, then, I am glad for her having your company and happy that it should afford me some decent conversation." He settled for straightforward pleasantries rather than pulling at the cracks in the mask she wore.

"You are too kind."

"Not at all. It was a wonder when the Burtons left

London Society and exiled themselves in the country. Apparently, some of the family married very low and this caused some disgrace."

Letty began to feel cold; her palms were moist and clammy. She clasped her hand tighter around her fan and tried to block the picture of her father's parsonage from her mind. This Viscount obviously thought her a woman of breeding or fortune, and although she felt ashamed of the deception, she was far too embarrassed to disabuse him of the notion.

"Sir, I believe I have been selfish in keeping you from the company of the rest of this adoring room. I must release you to enjoy yourself, and if you will excuse me, I shall go and rejoin my friend." She managed to speak with clarity, which surprised her a little. From the smile and bow she received, she guessed he suspected nothing of her panicked thoughts.

"I shall not enjoy the crowds without you, but I shall let you return to your friend." He managed a half-smile as he bowed, a welcome relief from his implacable countenance. Watching the back of her small figure retreating, he raised one eyebrow slightly. This woman was indeed interesting.

CHAPTER SEVEN

Now faith is the substance of things hoped for, the evidence of things not seen.
    THE GOOD OLD BOOK

The next morning brought with it the promise of a drive out to a nearby cathedral. Clarissa was staying at home as she had a little shopping to do in Town and, though she would not admit it, she had quite the headache after last night. She could not think how she had managed to drink so many glasses of punch.

The party that set out was made up of the Major, Letty, Sophie Egleton, and Viscount Beauford, who was the Major's choice of companion. They managed to venture out at ten o'clock in eager anticipation of the day ahead. When Letty stepped out onto the cobbled street, she could feel the heat of the sun on her cheeks and the promise of blue skies for the entire day. She could barely contain herself as she entered the carriage with Sophie and the Major, and it was an effort to resign herself to the journey's length.

The young widow could not keep from staring out of the

carriage window on their journey, just waiting for the moment the outside world would turn green. Occasionally, she caught glimpses of the Viscount who had chosen to ride and whose presence she so desperately wanted to ignore. She still felt slightly baffled when he was near, not knowing whether to like him for his dry wit or loathe him for his seeming arrogance.

As she watched him ride beside the carriage, Letty decided that if he were to boast in anything, it would be his horsemanship. She watched the beautiful bay gelding he rode, its muscles strong yet sensitive and yielding to its master's commands. The movement of the large animal was nothing short of graceful, but it was the rider's immovable seat and effortless control that captivated her. She watched the silent conversation between horse and master—the nudging of the legs, the gentle squeezing of the fingertips, and the movement of his weight as he asked for more or less. The gelding rose and fell in steady time, frequently lengthening his stride when a straight stretch presented itself. When a turn in the road appeared, the Viscount would combine a squeeze of the reins with reassurance from the leg. The horse would gather itself, ears twitching, listening for its master's next command while it took the bend in a balanced stride.

The Viscount never once looked towards the carriage. He had, in point of fact, omitted his good morning salute when the ladies had joined the gentlemen outside the house, refused to ride in the carriage, and had barely spoken to his friend the Major. Even Clarissa—who had come outside to see them off, had been introduced by Deveril, and had proclaimed her acquaintance with the Viscount's late mother—was rewarded with no more than monosyllabic answers. He had resisted any civility before their departure, and now, from the dark look upon his face, he seemed sullen or perhaps even angry.

The Major, however, was quite the opposite in spirits and seemed to not even have noticed his friend's mood. He chatted for most of the journey with Sophie, who relaxed once he smiled a little. The journey was not too long, and Letty did not put two words together the entire time as she watched the increasing growth of countryside outside the window. Thankfully, the other two were quite content to talk to one another, and her conversation was not missed. The grinding of the carriage wheels on gravel signified that they had reached their destination. Letty could not wait to be the second to step down from the carriage. She was up immediately and almost leapt out before the carriage came to a full stop.

"Have a care, Mrs. Burton," called the Major. "I do not wish to deliver you back to your guardian with a broken limb!" He might as well have spoken to the wind.

"She seems rather excited." Beauford's words had no intonation. He dismounted and threw the reins of his horse to his groom. Deveril shrugged. He had not expected his friend to have a jovial disposition today. How could a man feel happiness after receiving such a letter from the woman he thought he loved, a letter which both tantalized and repelled, a letter so scandalous the Viscount had handed it to Deveril in disbelief?

The Major had read it, of course. His boyish self would have encouraged the flirtation, but his moral self and the knowledge of the Viscount's unhappiness led him to give the advice he did. He had told the Viscount to leave it, to refrain from answering Corianna, Duchess of Bedford, until he had cooled his temper and calmed his thoughts. And what better way to cool one's temper than with a drive through the idyllic countryside? The Major had asked for the Viscount's company on the outing today, and he had accepted despite his inner turmoil.

Letty was already beyond earshot when the Viscount let out his cool words. She was bounding happily ahead into the countryside, her arms flung out carelessly to the sides and her lungs inhaling the biggest breaths possible.

"There is nothing like a breath of country air, do you not think?" Letty called back to the three stragglers, her cheeks already glowing from the fresh air and exercise.

"No, nothing!" cried Sophie. "It does so invigorate one, and makes one feel as though one can conquer anything!" She was so at one with Letty's thoughts that for once she overcame the shyness to which she so easily succumbed.

"If fresh air had *that* ability, I do not think we would have the need for wars or soldiers," said the Major, bringing them both back down from their metaphorical clouds with a bump.

The Viscount remained silent, his walking stick whipping harshly at the grass as he strode briskly forwards. It was clear his thoughts were elsewhere. He felt a heavy burning in his heart, a burning that was so hard to decipher. Was it pain or temptation? The burn of betrayal or the sweet heat of lust? In spite of his morose state, the widow's next words did catch him a little.

"Major, you must not be so sensible, not when you're in the country. For there are no rules out here to obey or even to laugh at!" Letty giggled, spinning about in the freedom and mocking his motto.

The wet grass was making her feet damp. The wind that blew against her sent her into shivers. Her hair flew into disarray. And yet, for all that, she had not felt so alive, so well in all the time she had been in Town. Her three companions could clearly see it, the light in her brown eyes, the wildness to her hair, and the exuberance of her spirit.

"I think her quite beautiful, do you not, Major?" whispered Sophie, not even looking at the Major, so transfixed was she by the sight of her friend.

"Indeed, quite a goddess in her natural habitat, or, perhaps this is her heaven, her paradise?"

"Yes, yes, that must be it. Perhaps this is where she belongs, away from Town?" Sophie felt a warming inside at seeing Mrs.

Burton so happy, a woman who was rapidly becoming her closest friend.

"But if she were away from Town, then she would miss parties. True, she cannot enjoy them as one should, but for the next one she shall be quite at the point of being able to dance!" The Major was triumphant and failed to notice a sad light pass over Sophie's face as the woman realised she would no longer have a companion to sit with while others danced.

"What party is this you speak of?"

"Have you not heard? Not merely a party, but a ball! Thrown by the Viscount himself." The Major gestured to Beauford who had paced on ahead, almost staying level with the exuberant Letty. "I believe he has asked his dowager aunt to host. It is quite unlike him to throw a ball. I cannot think how he has agreed to it, but I think it a brilliant notion!"

"Oh yes, it shall be most agreeable." Sophie was barely paying attention by this point. "Now, Major, I believe we must catch up with Mrs. Burton and the Viscount unless we wish to lose them both for the rest of the day!" And with that, she hastened after the rebellious goddess and the surly gentleman.

When they came upon the cathedral, the party slowed and quite happily formed into two pairs. Unfortunately for Letty, she was doomed to bear the sullen mood of the Viscount. Half of her wondered at his mood, but the other half was determined not to let it ruin the day. Above them, as they walked, she saw gothic architecture clearly portrayed in the gargoyles and carved decorations of the thick stone arches. The atmosphere of the building from this outside vantage point was lightened by the bright coloured stone and yet kept in mourning by the dilapidated masonry. She looked from gargoyle to Viscount and, for the first time, felt a touch of pity for the gentleman.

"What do you think of the building, my lord?"

"Desolate." He had perfected the heavily bored voice, and

she waited for more conversation in vain. He was not looking at her but examining the indentation his walking stick was making in the damp grass.

"You do not favour ecclesiastical architecture then?"

"If I did, Deveril would not have had to coerce me into accompanying you."

"I see." She nodded in swift understanding and clasped her hands, walking on.

The tone caught the Viscount's attention. He looked up from the vegetation he was trampling underfoot and examined the woman. She was looking quite calmly at the stonework at the foot of an arch a short way off.

"And what do you see, O widow?" His words tried her calm.

"A building." She wandered on. He walked behind her slowly, now examining *her* rather than the battered vegetation.

"Yes, a building it is, made grand by its architecture."

"Not just that, surely?" She halted and turned her large brown eyes upon him. "Does the fact it has housed worshippers for the past five hundred and fifty years hold no weight?"

"For that long? I had not read the history. I am surprised you have—you must have had a very thorough governess."

"No, my lord." She tensed for a moment at the allusion to her childhood and her own admittance. Then quite suddenly she smiled with confidence. "But the age of the cathedral is quite clear to any fool."

"Yes, of course." His face broke into what almost constituted a smile; the firm mouth took on a crooked angle and his eyes lighted with amusement.

She had diverted his attention from her personal life once again, but something in those dark eyes disquieted her. She decided to go along with whatever game he was playing.

"You're laughing at me? Perhaps you think me a bluestocking, and yet, I think you miss the point of such a building." She turned and walked away again, leaving him to follow.

"It is only a church." He was once again level with her.

"No, it isn't." This time the smile was to lace *her* lips.

His brows furrowed and he stopped their gradual walk to look upon her properly. She seemed to speak the truth, or at least what she believed to be true.

"It is a church." His voice was quite firm, the sort of tone that suggested it had been obeyed hundreds of times before.

"The people make up the church, my lord, not the bricks and mortar." Her father had said that often, and it sprang unbidden to her lips. "Do you not find that even more interesting than the building itself—the thought of all the people throughout the centuries who sat here, prayed here, suffered here, hoped here?"

"I can well imagine how they would have suffered kneeling on such hard stone. And as for their hopes, I doubt that many of them were ever fulfilled." His voice was as bitter as a mouthful of seawater. "Hope makes beggars of us all. And that—to use your words—is quite clear to any fool."

"But, my lord!" Her eyes locked firmly on his. "There is always hope." She said it because she could not help herself. She said it because it was true.

Her voice challenged him to counter her, but he did not. For the first time since he had re-entered society he felt a ray of light shining on those parts of him that he had thought would remain dark and closed forever. She said it with such certainty, with such quiet assurance that he could not believe otherwise. He watched the line of her mouth change its gradient as she smiled. No, he could not argue with this woman.

For the rest of the day, the small party admired the architecture of the cathedral, commented on the amount of people visiting at a cool time of year, and finally abandoned the holy building when the sunlight began to fade behind thin clouds.

They set Miss Egleton down at her home and arrived back at Clarissa's lodgings at a quarter past four. The Viscount nodded to the Major and bade Letty good night after she had climbed down from the carriage.

"Good night, my lord." She curtseyed in return. He still sat atop his bay gelding and she thought she saw the shadow of a smile upon his lips before he turned away. It was most probably sarcastic or at least a smile at her expense. She watched the animal and its rider disappear beyond the lamplight, not any the wiser to the rider's thoughts. Indeed, she could not know that the Viscount had thought upon the word *hope* long and hard on his ride home. Neither could she know how her words had shocked and challenged him to his very core, leaving him with one resolve: to know her better.

The Major began taking his leave and refused an offer of the carriage to take him home. "No, I am quite all right, I assure you. I feel in the mood for a walk this evening, and the weather is fair."

"Very well, Major. We shall see you on the morrow," yawned Letty, barely able to keep her eyes open.

"Really? Oh yes, the theatre! It shall be entertaining, methinks, and perhaps my Miss Gray will be there." He walked away, his cane scraping against the cobbles of the street.

"My dear," said Clarissa once they had retreated back into the hall. "You are quite exhausted. Why not go to bed and I shall send up a small supper? I expect you shall want only a little to eat."

Letty was too tired to resist and allowed her mother-in-law to send her to bed like a child.

"The fresh air has brought out such a glow in your cheeks," called out Clarissa as Maria ushered Letty upstairs to undress her and put her to bed. "You look much revived, my dear!"

When Letty's head finally found the soft pillows and she

felt the warmth of the covers about her, she fell heavily into sleep and dreamt of the countryside, a wild and rugged landscape, a familiar paradise.

The next day brought with it heavy rain. Letty could hear the droplets thrumming on the windowpanes before she even climbed out of bed. The sound was rhythmic, pleasing, and natural. She allowed the melody to guide her in and out of consciousness until the sun finally made its debut between the thick fabric of the curtains. As she washed and dressed with the help of Maria, she thought about yesterday, the feel of the cold country air pinching at her skin and the lack of formality that she had missed so much. Even Beauford had not destroyed her calm, which he usually seemed so able to do.

"What dress will madam be wanting me to put out for her tonight, if you please?" Timid Maria bobbed a ridiculous amount of curtseys as though she had committed some atrocity. She was still settling into her new position, and though sometimes she seemed quite comfortable, she still held her mistress in god-like awe.

"Oh!" said Letty, drawn from her daydreams back into the sun-filled room. "I had not even thought about that." She dropped the thick length of her brown hair that she had been un-plaiting. As she pondered what would be the right thing to wear out of all of the dresses Clarissa had bought her, she saw the room darken a little. The window showed grey clouds thickening in the heavens. The rain would be falling all day, she thought—she must find some occupation.

"Ma'am?" The maid allowed herself to smile as Letty responded.

"To be quite honest, I have no idea, Maria. What do you think is appropriate for the theatre?"

The maid was shocked to be asked a direct question that demanded her opinion. It took quite a few brisk brushings of her apron before she came to terms with the unprecedented situation and decided on an answer.

"Well, ma'am, I think perhaps this one?" Maria opened the tall wardrobe and drew out a Grecian evening dress of lavender gossamer satin. "I do not believe you have had a chance to wear this yet." She laid the dress upon the bed and ran a hand gently over the soft fabric. "And Mrs. Burton was so excited when she bought it for you—said it was just the thing for you."

The gown was beautiful and something Letty could not object to. It was simple in its design, accenting the female figure well with draping material and delicate pleating. No one would call it immodest, though the neckline did come almost down to the bosom.

"I am not quite sure. Do you not think something more concealing?" Letty was acutely aware she had not worn anything that came below her neck since John's death.

"Oh no, ma'am, this will look so pretty. I daresay gentlemen will think so too?" The maid let a cheeky grin transform her impish features. This charming appearance, however, did not save her from Letty's outburst.

"Maria! You are most improper!" She cast a pair of sharp eyes at the maid who now stood cowering beside the dress laid out on the bed.

"I'm sorry ma'am. I did not mean anything by it, honest, honest!"

Letty was suddenly filled with compassion for the girl who had been looking after her for a full two months. Why had she lost her temper? It was not the impertinence. No, Letty knew that did not bother her. It was the implication that a man might be interested in her that had upset her. She felt the stab and prickling of guilt. Red stained her cheeks as she looked away to regain her composure. Eventually, turning back, she let her face break into a gentle smile, and she gave a little chuckle. "You are so naughty, Maria. What would Mrs. Burton say to hear a maid speak such things?"

"Oh, ma'am!" gasped the maid. "I wouldn't say it to her, but I like you, ma'am. You're kind and I thought it would make you laugh!"

"And so it did. I do not mind, as long as the mistress does not hear. But no more silliness about gentlemen. I did not come to London to look for a husband, and I stick by that resolution."

"As you please, ma'am, but will you wear the dress? It will look so pretty on you, and you have been wearing black for ever so long."

"Very well." Letty knew her half year's mourning that Society required had been fully paid. "I shall wear the dress! However, I shall have the liberty of dressing my own hair, if you please."

"Yes, ma'am." The maid smiled, and a few moments later, blissfully scurried from the room, so glad that her mistress would look as pretty as a picture for the theatre tonight.

The thought that she would have to face the Viscount Beauford again this evening did not occur to Letty all day. She picked at embroidery, plucked at an out-of-tune spinet, and finally sat down to read an entire novel. These diversions were necessary since her mother-in-law had refused to allow her to make herself useful around the house.

"It is servants' work, my dear, not yours!"

"Yes, but I feel so useless. I can be of some assistance instead of lying about in this fashion."

"Do not be silly, my dear. It is the rain. It makes all of us unhappy!" Clarissa's shrill voice penetrated everything while she touched a handkerchief to her face. "It always made Percy unhappy," she added in maudlin tones.

When the post came, there were several letters for Clarissa. She paused while looking over them, a shadow coming over her countenance. Soon after opening them, she refolded them carefully and tucked them into her skirts. Letty tried not to notice, but her curiosity was piqued. She thought of saying something and then decided against it. After all, was private correspondence any of her business, even if it made her mother-in-law so unnaturally quiet? No, Letty would leave it. She withdrew her eyes from Clarissa, finding the thick pages of her book and beginning to decipher the printed letters once again.

Clarissa must have noticed her look, however, for she now took pains to hide her secrecy with a display of frankness. She took the final letter from the tray, opened it, and displayed it to Letty in an obvious way.

"Look, a letter from my cousins, the Spencers. One does not have a part in choosing one's relations, but I have been considerably blessed in this matter, for the Spencers are quite lovely. In this letter they even write to invite us to stay once the Season is over. What a kind gesture."

"Indeed," agreed Letty. "And where is their residence?"

"Devon, my dear, Devon—a house with a stunning prospect, and I understand Lady Spencer has made many changes to it since the birth of her two children."

"We should go, if you wish it."

"Oh, yes," replied Clarissa, satisfied Letty's attention had been diverted from the other two letters hidden in her skirts.

She was right in this respect. Letty was thinking, quite happily, of their return to the West Country. It would be wonderful to be in that part of the world again—but what was that she felt? A twinge of sadness at parting from her current place. Would she really miss Town? No, not the city itself, she decided, but perhaps some of the residents.

At about midday, the sky grew progressively darker. The

ominous heavens were layered with great plumes of iron grey, and the clouds seemed ready to burst open at any moment. Letty sat beside the window, watching the comings and goings in the street, her finished novel lying beside her. A little boy scurried about with what looked like his brother, both of them causing mischief. They almost upset two women who were walking this way. Letty giggled at their vivaciousness, though, perhaps Clarissa would have thought it a vice. Her eyes moved away from the children and drifted down to her hands resting gently on her stomach. How she had wanted what John would not give her! How she had yearned so desperately for life! Looking up again in a fit of restlessness, she caught sight of a carriage drawing up beneath the window. Who could that be at this time?

The tinkle of the bell could be heard below. Clarissa stirred in her chair; the box of chocolates resting on her breast shifted slightly, in danger of plummeting to the floor. Letty rose and walked down to the hall before a servant could come up and disturb her mother-in-law further.

"Who is it, Tibbs?"

"A Miss Egleton," replied the disgruntled footman-come-butler. "Claims she must see you right away." Despite his tone, his face was as impassive as a servant's ought to be.

"Yes, of course. I will bring her into the sitting room myself." Letty was unsure what Sophie would want to discuss at so unusual an hour. The butler retreated below stairs, allowing Letty to walk the last flight down and see a slightly damp and upset looking Sophie standing before her.

"My dear, what is it?" asked Letty, most anxious of the answer. Sophie's eyes were wide, and she looked as though she had been crying. Her dress was rumpled, and her hair fell about her face haphazardly.

"I am come to tell you that we are to leave Town, today!"

she said in a quiet voice, not the vivacious one Letty had come to know.

"Why so suddenly?" For once Letty's control was lost and despair flooded her voice.

"My aunt has been taken very ill, and we are to travel directly to her residence in Somerset. We think the worst is come for her."

"Oh, my dear, I am so sorry." Letty placed her arm around Sophie's shoulder and guided her into the small sitting room on the ground floor of the house.

"Oh, it is not for her that I fear—she is forever on the brink of death!" Sophie's voice was exasperated and her eyes alight with anger. She muttered a little under her breath before sitting down and regaining her melancholy looks.

Letty smiled involuntarily at Sophie's frustration towards her invalid aunt. The woman obviously enjoyed her smelling salts and hysterics, and Letty knew what a trial it must be to pander to one whose only ailment was her boredom with life.

"No, Letty, it is you I am sad to leave. I have never been so happy as I have been since you came to Town. I will be so lonely when I leave you—*that* is what I am afraid of! And of leaving you to the mercy of Society, going to all those parties alone." She took hold of Letty's hand forcefully.

"Oh, do not worry for my sake!" said Letty, with a resilience she was far from feeling.

"You do not understand. Oh! I have heard talk, my mother has heard talk...."

"Talk of what, Sophie?" Letty felt herself stiffen and almost did not want to hear the answer to her question.

"Just nasty, nasty things about you being spread over Town, that you are a fortune hunter and now that your first husband is dead—and still warm in his grave—you are after another one, a viscount." Sophie knew the harshness of her words. Her eyes were already brimming over with tears of apology as she spoke what must hurt her friend. *She* knew Letty was determined not to marry. Anyone who had spoken to her knew that as well, and those who had said differently were simply heartless.

"I see." Letty retracted her hands and clasped them firmly in her lap. "And who is it that has decided to spread these rumours? Perhaps a jealous mother or schoolroom miss?" Her voice rose with anger. "This is ridiculous!" she cried, before receiving an answer. "All I have done is argue with the Viscount. Who could possibly think we are conducting a flirtation?"

Sophie hesitated. "Anyone who listens to the gossipers. They can create a mountain out of a molehill in a few days. You have been seen in the company of the Viscount on regular occasions—it does not matter that you were arguing, for who could have known what passed between you? I would not have known myself if you had not told me how much you loathed him. And I do not know who is the instigator of these wicked lies, but Letty, that is why I do not wish to leave you. They are baying for blood! That is what Mama says, and they will just wait until you slip!" She was sobbing out the words now, horrified of what the future would bring.

The widow was quiet a moment before speaking. "Pray, Sophie, do not despair. If I were to care what everyone was saying about me, I swear I would be a wreck! No, do not fret about me. Just think, we can write to each other, why, every day if you want. Twice a day!"

Sophie laughed at this. "I think Mama would be most upset if I used that much paper! But you promise to write to me? You will tell me how you are, what has been happening? And you promise to tell me the truth?"

"Yes, of course, have I ever not? We shall have some tea and say goodbye with smiles not tears." Letty rubbed the droplets from Sophie's cheeks and rang the bell. She was trying her best to ignore the horrid feelings Sophie's news had brought, the pain and the yearning for escape she felt.

They did just as Letty had said. They drank tea, they chatted about life's difficulties, and they parted with smiles and embraces. After Sophie had finally taken her leave half an hour later, Letty sank back onto the window seat near her slumbering mother-in-law. Her brow puckered a little as she felt emptiness within herself and, suddenly, a weariness.

She watched Sophie's carriage take her away and then stared into the street until she knew not when. She could not help but let a little despair seep through her carefully constructed walls. Then, as she looked down at the direction that was clasped so tightly in her right hand, she felt a little hope and sat down to write her first letter to Sophie. Perhaps if she sent it soon, it would arrive before her friend did and be a welcome surprise. Besides, doing this would keep her from her own thoughts, and if she were kept from thinking, it would mean she would not need to confront the fact that she was without her new friend in uncharted waters. After dusting and blotting the paper, Letty strode about the room before deciding to disobey her mother-in-law and venture down to the kitchen to be "put to use" as she had so aptly said.

"Lettice Grace Burton!" yelled Clarissa, huffing and puffing down the stairs into the kitchen. The rotund woman rounded the last corner and was shocked at the state of her daughter-in-law.

"Before you shout further, Clarissa, just look at your curtains!" Letty stood triumphantly with a pinny over the top of one of her old day dresses, perspiration on her brow, and smudges of dust on her cheeks. What she was holding, however, was of far more interest to her mother-in-law than her daughter-in-law's appearance had been thirty seconds ago.

"Oh, how beautiful! How wonderful! And to think I have been wondering whether or not to buy new ones, but no! These have come out so well from the wash. Just admire the colour, so rich—it is simply a miracle!" Clapping her hands, the recovered Clarissa hop skipped her weight forwards and felt the heavy fabric between her fingers.

"We thought you would be happy," Letty giggled, smearing another line of dirt across her cheek as she attempted to scrape her hair out of her face. The use to which she had been put had washed away the feelings of loss and confusion. With her mind and hands busy, she had not been given the time to think over her predicament.

"Yes, indeed I am!" cried Clarissa, and then, taking in her daughter-in-law's appearance once again, she added a hasty reprimand. "But I would much prefer it if you stayed above stairs, no matter the curtains. I am sure Maria will draw you a bath, for you cannot dress for the theatre looking so dishevelled, my dear."

Although Letty objected to not being allowed to work, she was happy Clarissa had ordered a bath. She felt hot and sticky from ironing the curtains, and a bath was yet another distraction from the unpleasant news Sophie had shared.

"Very well, if I must!" she sang in maudlin tones before mounting the stairs dejectedly. Then, casting a wicked glance backwards, she skipped the rest of the way to the top, which provoked Clarissa immeasurably and amused the servants no end.

CHAPTER EIGHT

I am no bird; and no net ensnares me; I am a free human
being with an independent will.
   – Charlotte Bronte

After the longest time she had ever spent washing and dressing, Letty walked down the stairs of the London house. Her fingers slid over the polished wood of the banister as she descended the stairs. Her graceful steps and upright carriage showed her figure off to full advantage. Her gown fitted well, the satin drawing together under her bust and then falling away to outline the curve of her hips and the movements of her legs. The mass of hair she laid claim to was piled high on her head with several floral bands containing it while small tendrils fell about her face. Even Clarissa had to admit she did look attractive, far more so than she could have hoped. At this rate she might even marry despite her lack of fortune.

To Letty, however, that thought was pushed away into a corner. She was happy with her appearance, pleased with the symmetry of her hair, and she enjoyed the slight glow the warmth of the fire had given to her cheeks. At the same time, she was somewhat apprehensive of the comments people might make on her appearance—previously, she had worn plain gowns of black while in public, and this change could only help to further the gossip about her. This fear was made all the worse by the flattery of her mother-in-law and the possibility of the Viscount Beauford's presence tonight. Then again, maybe she should see it as a sort of release; after all, if those people already thought badly of her, she had nothing to lose. Indeed, her reputation, as she would like it, was already gone.

She knew she would at least be able to speak to the Major without feelings of self-consciousness. But how she wished Sophie could be here with her too, someone to sit and talk with while Society danced along on its merry way completely oblivious of them.

They took chairs to the theatre, and she was left alone with her thoughts for a little while longer. The small windows afforded a miniature view of the outside world. Most of the city, however, was already shrouded with darkness with only a few small lights flickering here and there. She clasped her hands in her lap, but a jolt of the chair sent them flying out to take hold of the sides of her enclosure.

They reached the theatre in time for a brief round of chit-chat before finding their seats. Letty kept her eyes on the floor as they entered and left them there almost all of the time they stood talking.

Clarissa was having a jolly time, chatting to all the acquaintances she could find as her dutiful daughter-in-law stood by. Letty spoke when someone addressed her, but only necessary civilities. She knew that Clarissa's friends would demand little more than silence from her.

"You look ravishing."

She was wrong. One of Clarissa's friends would of course want to talk. Letty saw a scarlet coat from the corner of her eye and reacted in a brisk fashion to the Major. "What rubbish!"

Unperturbed, he pointed to a red haired girl in a pink gauze gown. "If I was talking rubbish, I would have said that woman in that dress looks beautiful."

"Major, that is cruel. Who is to say you look beautiful in your coats?"

"Well, it simply needn't be said." He sniffed and smoothed a lapel.

"You are insufferable, Major."

"That is interesting—I know for a fact that somebody used the exact same word when describing you."

"Yes, I think that sounds just about correct considering my popularity in, well, just about any circle!" Letty smiled and fluttered a fan at Deveril.

"That reminds me—how have you found Beauford?" His eyes twinkled.

"Oh, I see, am I to believe it was him? I am not surprised that I am not popular with him, for I insulted him on no less than three occasions, and yesterday I was not even sure if he was listening while conversing with me. If he is here tonight, I am sure I shall insult him for a fourth time."

"I believe he will be here tonight. Perhaps I should go in search of him just so I can witness this intriguing and most definitely amusing insult?"

"No, indeed." She touched a hand to his arm. She did not wish to talk to the Viscount; he delved too deeply in matters she would rather keep hidden. "Please do not."

"Very well, but I find it odd you should quake before him."

"Quake before whom?" A cool voice had joined their conversation. They both turned to see the Viscount Beauford who had walked purposefully over. "I could not imagine Mrs. Burton quaking before anyone. She is a veritable Amazon."

"Indeed, I thought the same, but apparently the dowagers' beady eyes are more than a match for her." The Major slipped her a wink, and a brief flash of thanks passed from Letty's eyes to his.

"I doubt that." The Viscount's voice was cool and his eyes a cold examination.

"One must always know one's place, my lord," replied Letty without looking at him. "I merely adhere to Society's expectations of being respectful to one's elders."

"You, adhering to Society's expectations? How very amusing." The corners of his mouth curved into a dark smile. He took her hand, bowing over it. She froze, shocked by the sudden contact with his strong fingers. Then he surprised her further by brushing a kiss against her glove. The action set her heart racing, but it was not from attraction. She pulled her hand away a little too quickly, and her surprised face was confronted with another dark smile as he rose again.

The Major, understanding far more of this non-verbal intercourse than the Viscount, thought a change of topic vital for Letty's equanimity.

"Mrs. B., would you please continue your adherence to Society's expectations by accompanying me to the box *before* the play begins?" He made his own extravagant bow and reached for her hand. She held it out only too willingly, desperate to escape. However, it was not Deveril's hand, which closed around hers, but the Viscount's.

"No, I think you have been far too greedy with Mrs. Burton's company, my dear man. Madam, would you be so kind as to join *my* party for the remainder of the evening?"

Letty's heartbeat quickened. She was a rabbit watching the snare close around her.

"I am sorry, my lord, but I am afraid I am already engaged to my party."

"Nonsense. Deveril, do you really object?"

"Well, it is scandalous that you should abduct her from me and Mrs. Clarissa Burton."

"What is this I hear?" The elderly widow had come to collect her party.

"Madam, the Viscount...."

Beauford stepped around and bowed taking her hand with his free one. "Madam, so pleased to see you once again—though I am embarrassed that it is only to request the company of your lovely daughter-in-law for my party this evening."

"Oh, my!" The Viscount's request fit in perfectly with her plans for Letty to make an advantageous match. But, recognizing that the situation was unusual, Clarissa began to play the protective mother-in-law for effect. "Well, I suppose I may spare her, though I love her company, and the evening shall be dull without it. But I will only release her in the knowledge that she shall be well looked after. I suppose I may trust you, for I have known your mother a very long time and watched you grow up from a small boy. And I am sure our mutual friend, Major Deveril, will vouch for you?" If her heartbeat and thoughts were audible to the rest of the room in that moment, the theatre-goers would have heard great cries and thuds of joy. It would have been a very different sound than her usual melancholy thoughts.

"I can, madam, but are we sure we wish to lose her company tonight?" Deveril tried to save her.

"I am sure we can—now come, Major! I am yearning to sit down." Now on Deveril's arm, Clarissa looked around to the other two one last time. "Look after my daughter-in-law, if you please, my lord."

"I shall guard her with my life," the Viscount replied in his irritatingly confident voice.

Letty was swept away to the Viscount's box with only one glance of panic thrown back at the Major, who returned it with an anxious frown. But with Clarissa clamouring for attention and assistance to her box, his worries were left to take care of themselves. Letty would be safe in the Viscount's care. At least, Deveril *hoped* so.

The Viscount did not speak as they began to walk through the theatre. Letty was almost happy at this. It was as if he had forgotten her presence. He seemed to come back to attention after a few minutes and shortened his stride until he was matching Letty's own. Still he said nothing.

He drew back a pair of red velvet curtains and led Letty into a small box at the very top of the theatre in the centre. The view of the people milling below trying to find their seats and of the large stage straight ahead was grand. Letty stared in childlike wonder at the scene for a moment before good sense knocked on her door and she resumed her mask born of apprehension.

"I suppose you have heard of my aunt, Lady Lincombe?"

Letty saw before her a rather stern-looking woman, a female counterpart to the Viscount, though twenty-five years his senior. She had the same black-brown hair, the same strong brow, and those dark eyes. Yes, they were certainly like his the way they examined her.

"Lady Lincombe, it is a pleasure." As Letty bowed, she caught those eyes judging her—then saw them lighten a little as the older lady smiled.

"Pleasure," said Lady Lincombe simply, her small mouth refusing to grace the widow with any further words.

"She likes you," whispered the Viscount, leaning toward Letty.

"Indeed?" Letty was incredulous.

"You do not believe me, but I know she does. Trust me." He guided her past the aunt, and she exchanged the briefest of greetings with the aunt's companion, a simpering creature of no fortune but an impressive grasp of the Season's gossip. Letty was surprised to notice herself relaxing a little to Beauford's guiding touch, no longer shying away from it as she had at first.

She was not afforded much more conversation with the aunt, and for this she was grateful. She was not versed in conversation with a well-schooled Lady of Society, and this particular lady seemed as though she did not speak unless she was the creator of the conversation. With those dark eyes so very like the Viscount's, Letty could not help thinking that perhaps they would see her for what she was—a penniless parson's daughter out of place in London Society.

Beauford guided her away from his relative and over into the corner of the box.

"You shall be quite safe from the civilities of my aunt here, I think."

Letty had trouble reading him. His face was rigid and his manners polite but stiff. Once they were seated and the curtain had gone up, she felt so uncomfortable that she turned away from him and began to look about the audience in a vain attempt to find her mother-in-law.

Beauford was not watching the play either. At first, he made an absentminded survey of the audience with his quizzing glass. Seeing nothing of interest, he moved his perusal closer to home. He turned, facing almost exactly towards Letty, examining her profile, her dress, her hair, and most of all, her distress.

"Is it not your habit to sit still during a play?" Letty almost jumped out of her skin as the Viscount's voice whispered in her ear and his cravat came close enough to tickle her chin.

"I am sorry—I was looking for my mother-in-law." The smell of cloves lingered in her nostrils. She reprimanded herself for letting her voice waver but could not refrain from edging farther away from him.

"Am I that dull? Surely, you gave Deveril more of a chance

than this. I have only had your attention for these ten minutes together."

"No, of course not. Not at all."

"If you wish to sit nearer a woman for support, I can move and you may sit nearer my aunt—though I did not think you uncomfortable in men's company."

Letty did not respond.

"What do you think of the play so far?" Beauford's tone was disinterested but his dark eyes refused to leave her countenance.

"To own the truth, I have not really followed it. Can you tell me what has happened?"

"Certainly, I have watched it many times. Do you observe the man with the dark hair?"

"Yes."

"He is in love with a woman, but they cannot be together."

"Why?"

"Because of a curse that binds the man and prevents him from happiness with anyone."

Letty nodded, and fixed all of her attention on the stage. Perhaps this would save her from further conversation with the Viscount. She watched the man stride about the stage in misery.

After fifteen minutes had passed, the Viscount leaned in again and asked her again how she was enjoying the play now that she understood it.

"It is interesting."

"But not *very*, judging by the expression of boredom on your face." He paused for a moment. "This may be impertinent, but may I ask, does watching this type of play upset you?"

"No, why should it?" Her brows drew together, and she

turned to look at him for the first time this evening, surprise written on her face.

"With the death of your husband, I assumed any allusion to romance and love would upset you, though you seem to be in high spirits the rest of the time."

"Well...I...." Her head jolted back in surprise at the assertion and at her own impropriety. She had never really thought about it, never considered playing the heartbroken widow. Perhaps that made her cold; perhaps it made her reproachable in the Viscount's eyes. Her gaze dropped to her lap; she was lost in her thoughts. But when her eyes crept back up to his face again, he did not seem reproachful, but intrigued. For once, those dark, disinterested eyes were slightly wider, a little gleam in them as they studied her. There seemed to be something in them of comprehension—but how could he possibly understand? Only the Major fully understood, and she had not even intended him to know. Yet still, Beauford's eyes saw right into her.

"It seems a long time ago now." The dark farmhouse was so far removed from this full, glowing theatre. Yet still, that was not the reason for her lack of sorrow and she knew it.

"Do you miss your home country?"

The gentleman's addresses were not precisely proper, but Letty still answered him. She was so lost in the past that she spoke without even thinking.

"Parts of it." The image of paradise arose water-coloured and misty in her mind's eye and yet so clear in her heart. Suddenly, she was no longer in a theatre dancing to Society's song; she was away in the heath land with the briny sea air stinging her nostrils and the coarse terrain beneath her boots.

"Your friends, I suppose. Tell me, how can it be that you have no acquaintances in Town?"

Letty awoke from her dream and was suddenly aware to

whom she was speaking and how much she should divulge. "Why do you suppose that?"

"Simply by your never mentioning them, and that whenever I see you, you have been only in the company of my friend Deveril and that Miss Egleton, both of whom I understand you only met upon coming to Town."

"I see." She said no more.

"So, I put it to you again, how is it that you can have no acquaintances in Town?"

"I cannot say," she replied, shrugging her narrow shoulders a little as though it were nothing.

"Do you miss your acquaintances from the West Country?"

"You take a keen interest in my private life, my lord."

"And you take a keen interest in dodging my questions, madam."

"It is my life, my lord."

"Well, of course," he said, slightly ruffled at the woman's abrupt change. "I simply wondered what you did to entertain yourself when you were married!" Curse it! Why was she so evasive? Any other woman would be dying to tell him anything and everything.

Letty bit her lip, remaining silent despite his frustration. She could not disclose anything further to this man without being completely improper and foolish. He was a known rake as Theo had told her. She could not trust him. Already she had said too much. She tried frantically to rebuild the walls of her privacy by maintaining utter silence.

"You do not seem to me to be a woman who would be satisfied with embroidering cushions and joining in with village gossip. Therefore, it is a mystery what you would do when married, for it would obviously be something going quite against the dictates of Society."

She knew she could not remain silent forever unless she wished to evoke this man's anger.

"No, indeed, I abhor embroidery, if you must know. I have always been quite envious of men's liberty. For you may go where you will and when you will, marry if and when you choose, and indulge in far more activities than a female." She was doing an excellent job avoiding having to answer.

"Ah, so you think women have a far harder lot in life than men? You are being quite outlandish, Mrs. Burton."

"I suppose I should titter like a young schoolgirl and recant what I have just said, but I am afraid it would be false to say that I should ever be content in marriage, if my only pastimes were listening to gossip and embroidering—as you put it."

She certainly was not a schoolgirl, he thought, as he glanced over her again, and certainly unlike the females he had encountered before, especially...but he did not want to think on that right now.

"Just as I thought." His voice was infuriatingly self-assured. "What exactly would you prefer to do? Speak to stewards, arrange business, and be loaded down with hundreds of business correspondences a week?"

"You seem most unhappy in your situation too then?" She was interested. "Though I am surprised you resent it so. For though you may be weighed down with business, it is a small price to pay for the freedom you receive as one of your sex."

"It is intriguing to hear your opinion. But even if I were to agree to it in my heart, I would never admit so much—for then you would have triumphed over me in being right."

"Yes, that would be most devastating. I cannot even begin to imagine the irreparable damage it would do to your pride." She smiled daringly, but kept her eyes keenly watching the play.

"You seem to be the most comfortable in my company when you are insulting me."

"Yes, what a shame the Major is not here." She spoke without thinking.

His lip curled into a sneer. "If I did not know better, I would think that you and he were in love with one another."

"Yes, it might appear that way to outsiders." She schooled her voice to be calm. "I can only imagine the conversations currently running throughout the theatre about how you have taken a nobody widow to join your party this evening. Just think of the scandal we are creating. I think I should disappear as I am afraid I shall never quite be able to blend into the tapestry that is Society."

"Well put, Mrs. Burton—though I myself quite enjoy creating a scandal and have no intention of disappearing. There are far too many beady-eyed dowagers to disconcert." He glanced sideways at his aunt.

Letty's mouth fell into a genuine but most involuntary smile.

He was watching her smile, his own lips wishing to mirror hers.

"I have heard of some scandals you have caused. Most amusing. Pray tell me, are you the black sheep of the family?" She could not stop herself now, too caught up in the banter they had created. She was at home in this; she was able to control it.

"Some have said so. Do you believe everything you hear of me?" His voice took on an edge.

"Not everything, only everything I believe you capable of."

"Oh dear, I fear your opinion of me must be very low if that is the case."

"You say that as if it bothers you, though you have already proclaimed your unwillingness to quit the scandals you so enjoy making, despite my opinion or anyone else's."

"I am a stubborn man, as anyone will tell you. Some scandals I would take back if I could, others I would cause again, and again, and again." His dark eyes became impossibly darker and he caught her stare as she turned from the stage to him. For a brief moment their eyes were locked in an inseparable gaze, every second of which made Letty realise there was more to this man than she had at first assumed.

"Tell me,"—their eyes parted and rested on the actors once again—"are you so set on never marrying again?"

"I think the answer to that has already been well established." Her voice was cold and abrupt, her control over the conversation lost.

"You would not marry a second time, even if Cupid's arrow pierced your heart once again?" His voice dripped with sarcasm, and his smile was sardonic. He was the man she had first met, intent upon incensing her.

"If love does exist, that might be possible. But even if I thought it did, I would never allow myself to be a target for Cupid's arrow."

"But why not, Mrs. Burton, when there is such joy to be had?"

If she had been listening without anger she would have heard his bitterness.

"My lord, can we please change the conversation?" She could feel perspiration on the back of her neck, and the wall that held her feelings in check was swiftly crumbling.

"I simply cannot accept your position on this."

"Please try, my lord!"

Gathering her skirts in her hands, she ignored the perplexed looks of the aunt and her companion and exited the box rapidly. The Viscount's brow rose quizzically as she disappeared in a flourish of red velvet.

When the curtain had obscured the sight of the widow, Lady Lincombe leaned across to her nephew.

"Does she have no thought to propriety?"

"No, aunt, I cannot lie to you. I do not think she does."

"Then I think she suits you very well, William."

The Viscount was slightly startled at this and stared the older woman in the eye to know whether she was serious. He saw the gleam that was there. His aunt, after the recent and nasty scandal, had a desire to see her sister's son settled. Having the same blood in her veins, she knew it would not be an easy task. She had doubted Corianna, now the Duchess of Bedford, and her ability to understand and equal her nephew, but this young widow, she seemed far more taking.

The Viscount said no more during the course of the play. The widow's conversation and his aunt's provoking comments had left him with much to think on. But however much he tried to puzzle out matters, his mind was still as foggy as the coast of Cornwall. Nothing was clear. The way was obscured.

CHAPTER NINE

Life is thickly sown with thorns, and I know no other remedy than to pass quickly through them. The longer we dwell on our misfortunes, the greater is their power to harm us.

– VOLTAIRE

The weather had changed during the night, leaving behind any hint of rain and growing cold even to the point of frost. The sky and the streets were all variations of a pale grey, and apart from a few people here and there, London was deserted at this early hour.

The Viscount, whose steady steps echoed from walls that rose up about him, kept his eyes on the road ahead. It would be easy to think a man of his calibre, walking the streets at this hour, simply had not slept since the night previous and was making his way home from his favourite club. It was much harder to guess the truth—that the Viscount was up at this hour on business, or rather, that he had already attended to it.

He had been to his bank where he had withdrawn a rather obscene amount of money—money which he would give his aunt full rein over. After all, if he was to throw the first ball in his name, it simply had to be done properly. Those were his aunt's exact words. It had been her idea as well as Deveril's encouragement that had brought this dratted event about. Something about pulling his name out of the mud and displaying a proper return to Society. He had to admit, most of his friends tiptoed about him at the moment. Perhaps the ball would be the thing to bring them all round. Though, when his aunt had insisted on inviting Corianna, Duchess of Bedford, Beauford had almost killed his relative before Deveril got a good hold of him. The old woman had not even looked abashed when he lost his temper. She had tapped a bony finger on the desk as though she were waiting for a naughty child's tantrum to end.

"Are you quite finished? William, you know very well that the only way to get over this scandal that—may I remind you? —you did in fact create, is to invite the Duke and Duchess as if nothing had ever happened. If you can control your infernal temper at the ball, then perhaps you will not have destroyed the family name forever. Now be a good boy and allow me to begin preparations, yes?"

He had of course agreed. That aunt of his always found her way around him. It was not that he was giving in, exactly —only that she was right and that he knew how much she enjoyed bossing servants about. The sooner she could start planning the ball, the sooner she would leave him alone. He did love the old bat for her stubborn will, but sometimes it could become a trifle much.

So here he was, inside his pocket a roll of soft as thick as his arm and his legs making quick work of the cobbled street. He rounded a corner to see the market sellers setting up shop. Their calls would be filling the air by the time he was back at home writing letters of business. Though he knew he had a good deal to attend to today, he simply could not shake the events of last night from his thoughts. Apart from the ball, the one other thing that consumed his mind was Mrs. Burton.

He had spent the second half of last night's play in tight-lipped silence, assuring himself over and over again that it was not he who was at fault but she. He had not seen her for the rest of the evening, despite looking for a loud mother-in-law and a scoundrel of a Major. True, he had been pushing and probing the widow, but it had proved so interesting and distracting to do so. The more time he spent with that young woman, the less he thought upon any recent matters. He was merely asking questions; it was not his fault that she had reacted so badly. Now he was sure she was not who she appeared to be. Not that he could discern what she was at all, curse her! He felt frustration but also shame. He had upset her last night. No, he could not admit to that, could he? And yet, despite his attempt at denial, the heavy feelings increased.

He was near the park now, the trees blurring the grey buildings into non-existence. Two heavy horses pulled a dray, the steam rising off their flanks and bringing the salty smell of sweat to Beauford's nostrils. He glanced over to the vehicle that intruded upon his silence—why was that Burton woman constantly making him feel guilty?

His steady step faltered. What was that shape in the trees? He could see a woman. Her head flickered in and out of view from behind the sycamores. He had unconsciously stopped in his tracks, the cane poised in one hand, ready to change direction. The flash of a dark cloak shot out from between the branches.

"Speak of the devil!" His cane struck down on the road, and his feet propelled him in front of the dray almost causing the horses to shy.

"Oi, watch it!" shouted one of the angry drivers, all thoughts directed toward the precious ice they pulled.

Beauford ignored them. He was already on the other side

of the road walking parallel with the wanderer. There was no way into the park this far down; all he could do was follow her this side of the trees and railings.

She was walking fast. He struggled to keep up but managed to always keep the flash of black in sight. He could see brown hair falling recklessly out of its bonds. He was not close enough to see her face. The trees were suddenly denser; her shape was fading behind the living screen.

His wooden heels clicked rapidly on the pavement, and he almost cursed with relief when the gate to the park presented itself. His footsteps dulled when he stepped onto the earth, but his heart beat faster still. Where had she gone? Had she really been here or had he been carried away by his thoughts? Perhaps she was an apparition. Perhaps he was going insane.

No! There she was, just emerging from between some shrubs, her boots feeling their way across the cold, frosted grass. Her cloak swished and flared. Her cheeks were flushed red with the cold, and the tip of her nose was rosy. Her head was down as though she thought intently while she watched the grass pass beneath her. She was so oblivious that when she came upon the Viscount she was startled and stepped back gasping loudly.

"Oh, sorry, sir! Viscount Beauford! My lord...I did not think to see...to see anyone here." Letty's eyes flashed about her as she began to realise the predicament into which her recklessness had placed her. "I beg your pardon." She curtseyed and tried to pass, raw panic loosing itself inside her.

"Now, now, madam. Please do not distress yourself." His hand came out to stop her, but seeing it, she halted before they touched. "Are you walking alone?"

Fear flooded into her eyes. What did he want? She did not want to answer. "Yes." Soon enough she would know if that admission had been a mistake. She could see John in her mind's eye and could feel the coldness of old fear growing inside her once again.

"You realise that it is not the thing to do here in London? Especially at this hour. You cannot trust who is about."

Relief flooded through her. She almost laughed out loud. She could trust him, and with that knowledge every fiber in her body relaxed.

"Here." He offered his arm. "Allow me to escort you home."

"That will not be necessary, thank you." She tried to get past again, not knowing what to think anymore. "Let me pass." What was his game? Why had he moved, as if to block her passage, and then drawn back again?

"Please?" His voice was concerned and his eyes searched hers, looking for the fear that had, moments ago, been so apparent in them.

"Very well." She hesitated before putting a cold hand in the crook of his arm.

As they exited the park, his only thoughts were to allay her fear, whatever the reason for it.

"Do you think my manners have improved? Observe that I used the word *please*." Their pace had fallen into an easy rhythm, and she could feel rather than see his smile.

"Indeed, you are progressing very well, my lord."

"So tell me, what on earth are you doing out alone this morning? It is most improper, you know."

"So is walking alone with you," she countered, ignoring the question.

"Yes, but better walking with me than getting set upon by some vagabond."

The danger she had put herself in struck her like a hard slap. "Oh, I am so foolish!" She paused in her stride before walking on again.

"Yes."

She wanted to give him a set down for such bluntness and for his unmannerly agreement with her own insult, but he carried on too quickly.

"It is easy to walk alone in the country, I understand. Here, however, Society and safety forbid it. Though I realise you are probably not so anxious over the former." The corner of his mouth curved up, and he flashed a pair of dark, amused eyes down at her.

"No, of course, I just thought...that is...I was hoping...."

"Hoping that you would not meet anybody of consequence? I am afraid in that mission you have failed most miserably."

"You are very confident that you are of consequence." She grinned quickly before turning serious. "There are so many rules here it is hard to remember to keep them all. In the country, I could roam where I wished, and I am not used to Town ways."

"Well, that husband of yours should have brought you to Town more often."

Immediately, thoughts of the nightmares that had kept her awake most of the night flooded back. Walking had always calmed her, but it seemed walking with this Viscount would only be a reminder of the past.

Beauford felt her hand tense as he spoke. Now she was so quiet, her thoughts clearly elsewhere. He needed to distract her once again even if he did not know why. More than that, he *wanted* to distract her from whatever caused her upset.

"Will you be at the concert tonight? I hear most people of consequence are going, which will of course include myself."

She managed a faint smile. "Yes, I believe I am engaged to attend."

"Good. Then there shall be at least one sane person there."

"Yes," she said, a gleam in her eyes. "But only one—you

blend in better than you know with the ones you would term insane."

He chuckled.

They had arrived at her mother-in-law's door. She paused to thank him but before she could turn away, he took her hand.

"Madam, if I am insane, then I do not know what you are to be considered, walking around London so early and alone. Promise me not to do so again?"

Letty waited for the satirical gleam in his eyes to appear, but it did not come. He was, in fact, staring quite seriously at her. His hand did not loosen its grasp. He was waiting for her answer.

"Yes, of course, my lord."

It was as though the words undid a spell. Her hand was her own again, and before he turned on his heel, his face broke into a most genuine smile. Who was this man that defied his own reputation? At least this morning, he had not been a hell-bent libertine. No, he had been a gentleman.

Letty was so shocked at the look of happiness on the Viscount's face that after sneaking back into the house and upstairs to her room, she did not even notice Maria's scolding.

"Ma'am! Really, you do not even seem to be paying attention, and you must, you must!" Maria pushed her little hand against Letty's cold cheek and tutted. "Honestly, if Mrs. Clarissa was to find out, you would be in such trouble and you know it, ma'am."

This brought Letty out of her daydreams. "Oh, Maria, please don't mention it! Promise me you won't say a word—I will not go off without telling you again!"

The maid, wearing a face of smug self-righteousness, nodded slightly. "Well, yes, that goes without sayin', ma'am. Now come on, let's put you to rights."

She had the cloak's strings undone in a trice. Truly, Letty

could not remember when she had come to depend upon Maria so much!

The Viscount's stance was relaxed. His shirt collar was removed, his feet bared, and his cravat discarded on the floor. The Major's attitude was quite different. Perhaps it was his natural propensity to be cautious and ready. Perhaps it was the years he had spent fighting the frogs on the continent, marching through deserts, and being set upon by half-starved, half-crazed soldiers. Whatever the reason, the Major was far more alert. He stood in the same amount of clothes as the Viscount, but he was not leaning sleepily on one leg or only half listening to Gentleman Jackson who was giving them each pointers after their last round.

The champion boxer stepped back, signaling for them to start again. The Major's arms were up, his feet moving swiftly across the floor as he began to circle his opponent. His eyes were not lazy like the Viscount's. They darted over his opponent, examining every subtle movement. After a minute, the Viscount began to move as well. He was slower, taking his time to watch the Major rather than plan his next strike. He brought his hands up a little and grinned.

Noting the smug smile upon his opponent's lips, the Major took a shot. He threw a right fist aimed for Beauford's face. The Viscount rapidly deflected it. He was quick—that was where his strength lay in boxing. No matter how many times Deveril reminded himself of Beauford's speed, he always managed to underestimate it.

But where Beauford had the speed, Deveril had the strength. Several years in His Majesty's service had seen him in more than one fight, sometimes not against the enemy. This experience had only honed the fighting skills which, ever since he was a child, had always come easily to the Major. Deveril was so skilled with the blade that, if it were dipped in ink and a canvas laid before him, it would be an easy task for him to paint an intricate picture with the sword tip. He was an excellent shot too, able to estimate accurately where a moving target would be when the bullet found him.

The Major tried a few testing blows with little force behind them. Then, just after delivering a half-hearted right-hander, he delivered a facer with his left. The distraction was good enough, and his fist hit home.

If he were not in Gentlemen Jackson's club at this moment, but in a rather less proper bout without rules constraining them, he would have Beauford to the floor in a second. Though, as he looked at his recovering friend now, he realised he could probably do anything to the man and he would not even know it.

"I say, old boy, I know I always beat you when we're in here, but you usually have the wit to block!"

Gentleman Jackson, who was occupied with another student, called over some instruction which Deveril and Beauford promptly ignored.

A trickle of blood came down from the corner of Beauford's mouth. "Good shot that was, mmm, well done, should have blocked...."

The Major stared at him, unsure whether to laugh or to do something else entirely. "What the devil is the matter with you?"

"Hmm? What? Nothing, nothing. Why?" Beauford's eyes cleared a little, and he looked upon his friend with lucidity.

"No reason at all, though I may as well box with myself. Not up on the social graces today, are we?" The Major had been looking forward to a good sparring session today—all thanks to the tormenting Miss Gray who had not spoken to him or thanked him for the flowers he had sent her. He had not even seen her since the Grays' party and was pining for the dear, sweet thing.

"Sorry. My mind is all gone to pieces over that infernal ball you're making me throw." He made as if to stop talking and then spoke suddenly. "Deveril?"

"Still here."

"What was I like when I came back?"

Deveril did not have to ask what he was referring to. The only place where the Viscount had been in the past few months was Cornwall, and all of London knew why he had gone there. There was nothing like disappearing in order to deal with a scandal.

"From the West Country?" Deveril needed more time in which to form his answer.

"Yes." Beauford stared at him expectantly, waiting for an answer that he knew would be the truth.

"Bit of a hard question really. You were lots of things—cheerful certainly was not one of them." Deveril laughed nervously, realizing he was probably saying the wrong thing. "You were like ice, and it took you a good deal of time to thaw." Even as he said it, Deveril was not sure if his friend had completely thawed out yet. He could be perfectly amiable one minute and completely shut off the next.

Beauford did not move for a moment, and then, jerking his head as if in acceptance, he began to spar again.

Eager to lighten the mood, as well as to assuage his own curiosity, Deveril changed the subject as he lifted his fists. "How was your evening with Mrs. Burton yesterday at the theatre?" There had been a part of Deveril that had been worrying during the play. After all, maybe it had been an awful call of judgment to leave Letty on the arm a known rake.

"Pleasant, I thank you." Beauford ducked a sudden swing from Deveril. "She is a most interesting woman, don't you think? There is something strange about her—and her rela-

tionship with her late husband—that I cannot quite fathom."
He lunged forward, catching Deveril's arms as he defended
himself.

The Major muttered agreement, knowing this was a
subject which led into deep waters—waters which he was
convinced Letty would not want the Viscount swimming in.
He should not speak of what he knew about the widow, and
he would not be fool enough to share it with the Viscount. He
already had a slight apprehension concerning the aristocrat,
for it was hard to read what one of Society's worst libertines
was thinking of Mrs. Burton. Maybe it had been a mistake to
introduce him to Mrs. Burton altogether.

"Very good! Very good!" cried Jackson, suddenly coming
over to them once again. His arms were raised, and he clapped
them both on the back as he began to usher them out of the
ring.

Deveril and Beauford looked at each other slightly
bemused. They had only been halfway through their lesson.
Surely, Jackson realised that? But the man continued to act as
though they had finished.

"You will go round to Angelo's now for your fencing?"

Still unsure of what was happening, the gentlemen went
to the side of the room.

"We're not finished, Jackson," said the Major. "Hadn't
you realised we were part way through a bout?"

"Really? Well, I believe Angelo's waiting for you." Jackson
averted his eyes from theirs. He was not a convincing liar, and
within seconds the reason for his ruse had been brought into
the light.

"Jackson! Jackson! I'm ready now. I've been working on
my stance—light feet, I remember. I've been improving."

The heavy, authoritative voice grated on every part of
Beauford's being. His eyes shot around the room to where the
voice originated. Sure enough, the Duke whom he had called

out months ago was here—the Duke who had married the woman Beauford loved.

For a moment, when the two rivals' eyes met across the room, Deveril was sure that he was going to have to restrain the Viscount. He saw the anger, no, the fury in Beauford's eyes. It brewed up and boiled over. He was not sure if his friend was aware that his fists were clenched and his whole body was shaking.

Before Deveril had to intervene, however, Beauford managed to draw his eyes away from the Duke. His blood cooled, though only a little, and he knew that he needed to be out of this place, now.

He began to dress again and Deveril followed suit without a word. They replaced their hessians, pulled on their perfectly fitted jackets, set hats on their heads and gloves on their hands, and left Gentleman Jackson's as fast as dignity would permit. Neither had been quite aware of how many eyes had been watching them in the club, or rather, watching Beauford and wondering what he would do.

Once they were out on the street, it felt as though air had been let back into the world. Beauford dragged in a few gulps to calm himself. He was thankful when Deveril said nothing.

All the emotions he thought he had dealt with had come boiling up to the surface so quickly—all the emotions caused by the Duke and Duchess of Bedford, both of whom his aunt insisted on inviting to this cursed ball!

Some days he believed he had almost forgiven the two. Then, a chance meeting like this happened, and all his work at keeping calm and continuing his life as normal evaporated.

Deveril had been a saint as they walked away from the club and down the street, not uttering a word, just leading the way and leaving the Viscount to his thoughts. Now, however, the aristocrat managed to draw himself out of them, and as he looked about himself, he saw that this was near the spot he had been walking this morning. He could see the park and the trees behind which he had found a woman, or the phantom of a woman. He could remember the distinctively protective feelings he had felt towards Mrs. Burton—feelings which were just as strong as the anger he had felt a few moments ago.

She had looked troubled. Despite her denial and her protestations of simply wanting to walk, Beauford was convinced that there was more to it than that. Whatever it had been last night at the theatre that had made her leave the box so suddenly, that was what had impelled her to go out walking early in the morning, on the streets of London alone.

What had he said? He could barely remember now. All he could remember was how intriguing it had been to watch her —how with every word he could see her mind working hard, deciding what to reveal and what to conceal.

"I know she's on your mind." Deveril spoke quietly.

Startled, Beauford swung round, his eyes wide and his mouth opening a little in protest or shock. "You do?"

"Yes. It's not easy, old man, and I do not blame you for any of your actions. I would have done the same if I were in your position. I think you did jolly well to leave Jackson's so amicably."

"Oh." That word did not satisfy Deveril, but it did sum up the feelings of the Viscount. After all, he had not been thinking about his old flame who was now a Duchess. He had been thinking about quite another lady of quite a different mold—a lady who was a widow and an enigma. And the fact that she could occupy his thoughts so completely was in itself a mystery to him.

CHAPTER TEN

Love is a canvas furnished by nature and embroidered by imagination.

    – Voltaire

The concert room was nearly full and Letty was seated beside the Major and her mother-in-law, both of whom were trying to convince her to agree to attend the Viscount Beauford's private ball. The invitation, sent by Lady Lincombe, had arrived soon after Letty had returned home from her walk that morning.

"Oh, come, my dear woman! It will be the crush of the Season and you are denying it? You must come. What can you possibly have against the poor chap?"

"Nothing." At least nothing she could admit to herself, let alone to them. "I simply think it would be a bore, for I cannot dance, and...."

"Oh, but you can, my dear!" chimed in Clarissa. "For you are already in lavender, and you have served enough time in mourning."

"See? If your mother-in-law is saying that you should attend, you must!" The Major was pleading.

"And the Viscount, he will be there. Of course he will, it is his own ball!" Clarissa was now scolding herself. "Do you not want to go just for the chance of dancing with him?"

Letty had hoped that the Viscount's numerous conversations with her had gone unnoticed by Clarissa, but it seemed that hope had been vain. Indeed, if half of Town knew of and despised her for those conversations, then of course Clarissa must know.

The Major, who was looking at Letty, saw her stiffen at Clarissa's comment. "But, of course, you have every right to say no to dancing, my dear. We both just want you there, especially as Miss Gray will be there, and I wish very much for you to speak to her—pop in a few words about how marvelously brave I am, battling the frogs and all that."

"Of course, you are!" Letty nudged him with her fan but did not give an answer. He had protected her well, and Letty felt that she did wish to repay him in some way.

"So, is that a yes?"

She did not have time to reply. The man of whose ball they spoke was approaching.

"Good evening." He bowed most courteously.

"Ah, just the chap! We were just trying to convince Mrs. Burton to attend your ball."

"You were decided against it?"

"I...um...." Letty felt heat rise to her cheeks. What was wrong with her? She was like a schoolgirl again.

"You *must* grace it with your presence. Promise me you will come?"

Now she could not say no and, to her surprise, she did not want to. "I would be delighted to attend."

He gave a satisfied smile and then sat down beside her. It seemed he was intent on placing her in gossip's way again.

Clarissa turned pointedly away, and started talking loudly to the Major.

"Am I to think that my previous behaviour warrants you declining the invitation to my ball?—which, by the way, you accepted most beautifully just now, in spite of your clear discomfort."

How could he read her so well?

"I could have sworn you knew all of Society's rules by heart, despite what you said to me earlier today. You obey them so well when the occasion demands." He raised an eyebrow at her.

Letty ignored his allusion to this morning's walk, but he leaned in closer so that she could not escape him.

"When we first met in the West Country, I am afraid you caught me at a rather dark time."

"So I understand. And is this an apology or an excuse, my lord?"

"A little of both." A small grin appeared on his handsome face. "I shall not go into details...."

"Good, for I have no desire to know them."

"Really? But all of Society enjoys knowing my details—and not just mine. For instance, I have learned that you are both plain, and—what was it? An upstart, I believe. Though I think the latter may be because of my irritating presence at your side too regularly. And as for the former—I am not at all sure that you are plain."

"Indeed." She ignored his final comment. "I have heard such grumblings of the public myself. In fact, I feel the irritation of your presence now. So perhaps you could leave the upstart's side, for, I believe, there is someone beckoning you." She gestured to a person over his shoulder.

"Oh, my poor pet, did I touch a nerve?" he asked sarcastically, then turned to look at who she was referring to.

The secret smile that had broken his face during most of

the conversation disappeared entirely when he caught sight of the fair Duchess of Bedford. She was here, waving her fan for him, and expecting him to come at her beck and call. Letty saw a muscle in his jaw twitch before he rose and left her without a word.

"What?" Clarissa said, leaning in with a coy smile. "Has the Viscount left us so soon? Never fear—I am certain he will return. The music is about to begin. I believe you shall like this piece; it is of love, and there is nothing like a little music for moving your heart towards that feeling."

Letty smiled sweetly back at her before opening her fan and hiding her face and, more importantly, her mouth from the gossipers.

"Clarissa?"

"Yes, dear?" The woman was already whispering as though she were discussing government secrets.

"Who is that beautiful woman the Viscount is talking to?" Letty indicated the couple in the corner who were smiling gaily at everyone else while they exchanged a few, rather short words.

"Oh, she is indeed very beautiful. She is Miss Corianna— well, the Duchess of Bedford now, but she still has all the men dangling after her." Clarissa saw something in Letty's eyes and then patted her daughter-in-law's hand gently. "There, there dear. It is of no consequence."

Letty snatched her hand away and forced herself to relax. She chose not to look at the Viscount anymore, nor the woman with the guinea-gold hair, curving lips, and tempting figure. Instead, she watched as the small gathering of musicians made ready and the opera singer took her place in the centre of the room.

People found their places slowly, and as the last person sat down, the music began. The first notes drifted through the room soft and slow. Letty's large eyes were transfixed by the girl who stood in the centre of the players. She had not begun singing yet, and as she stood there, all alone, a look of fear fleeted across her face. She was small in stature. The gown she wore clung to her body as though she were a statue of some Roman goddess. Her dark hair was brought up in all its curling glory and placed on the top of her head with great tresses escaping the satin headband that secured it. On the floor a circle was marked around the singer, separating her from her fellow musicians. She seemed alone on that stage facing the audience whose critical eyes were already surveying her young face.

Her cue was coming. The music reached a crescendo and then, as it dropped down so low it was barely audible, the young woman stepped forward, her shoulders drew back, and her eyes searched for something in the heavens. Her voice came as pure and unadulterated as the wind on the western cliffs, deep and clear. And as she threaded between notes, the pitch and strength increased until it seemed the very building was trembling. The whole room was overcome by the beauty of her voice, enthralled by the innocence of what she sang.

Letty was so engaged she did not realise that the Viscount had come back to sit beside her again. It was unnecessary for him to do so, for he was not of her party. But nevertheless, he returned and seated himself confidently as if the chair had been saved expressly for him.

As Letty listened to the song, a large tear fell down her cheek that she was not even aware of until it pattered onto the back of her hand. She looked down and stroked the salty water with her thumb, and—out of the corner of her eye—caught sight of the man sitting beside her again.

Instead of looking him in the eye, she focused all her attention on the singer. She felt shame burning in her cheeks at showing so much emotion publicly. He would think her a fool if his sarcastic conversations were anything to judge by. She almost leapt from the chair when she felt the soft cotton of his handkerchief pressed against her hand.

She glanced up at him, the embarrassment growing, but he was not looking at her. His dark gaze was fixed intently upon the singer. She took the offered gift, the fabric slipping through her fingers, and her hand encountered his for the briefest of moments. It was warm. Why did that surprise her so?

When the beautiful piece of music drew to a close, she felt him change his sitting position so that he was facing her, willing her to look at him. But as she turned she caught sight of someone else over his shoulder—someone who had earlier caused her an inordinate amount of distress. She met his eyes, and neither of them spoke a word that would break the spell that the music had cast.

His eyes were not smiling or sarcastic now. They were tracing the evidence of her tears, the miniature droplets on her dark eyelashes.

She still did not speak but instead nodded towards the beautiful woman over his shoulder who had so captivated him before the song and was once again standing not far behind him.

"You wish me to leave?" he said, his voice savouring of bitterness.

"No, my lord, only it seems you are wanted by another, and you are, after all, not of my party. If you carry on in such ways, we shall set the Town talking."

The look he cast upon her showed he clearly did not care; and she did not either, not in truth.

"You enjoyed the music?" He changed the subject easily but not his tone.

"Very much. She has a beautiful voice." Letty watched the singer who was now talking to her musicians. "And you, my lord?"

He laughed, and her suspicion that he laughed at her was proved by his next words.

"You are always so eager to keep others happy, but in answer, yes, she has a beautiful voice. Is it not interesting that she is slight, quite small in fact, and seemingly inferior—and yet, she has such an ability to wield power over people? Quite incredible." He was not looking at the singer anymore.

"It seems your friend is still beckoning to you."

"Indeed, it is most infuriating. But I have obtained a promise from you to attend my ball?"

"Yes, my lord." She offered him back his handkerchief.

"Consider it a token of apology for my previous manners." He tilted his head in a mock bow, then rising swiftly, left her. And though she had the Major and Clarissa to converse with, Letty felt—for a moment—alone, with feelings she was at a loss to decipher.

CHAPTER ELEVEN

Illusion is the first of all pleasures.

– Voltaire

Clarissa's cutlery fell from her grip, clattering on the plate in the breakfast room and making Letty jump. The younger widow looked up to see Clarissa holding a letter in one of her podgy hands and wearing an expression of worry quite alien to her.

"Clarissa, what is it?" Letty hurried straight over to her side, her own face worried and her voice all concern. "Clarissa?" She was not answering, and Letty could see a pile of already opened letters that had been refolded and nearly hidden in her mother-in-law's skirts. "You can tell me, Clarissa. Can I help with anything?"

The older woman looked up, her face so tired in the stark morning light. She rested a small hand briefly over Letty's, letting a wan smile fall over her countenance.

"Oh, my dear, no, no. Nothing for you to worry about. It shall all be sorted out soon. Mr. Pottle is already working on it.

Now, do not worry. You must be excited—it is the ball tonight!"

Letty thought of inquiring further, but, seeing Clarissa withdraw her hand and turn away, she knew this was not something to press her about. Still, as she left the breakfast room to go and read, she could not help but let a few worries seep in.

It had been so long since she had had to worry about anything apart from her manners, but she remembered the heavy feelings well. She could only hope that Mr. Pottle, Clarissa's solicitor, would be able to resolve whatever was troubling her.

She picked a book from the shelf and sat down by her favourite window, staring out of it for a moment, lost in the busyness below. When she opened the cover of the volume and finally turned to it, worries fled away; she was in another world now, with another past and another future.

The hours flew by while she read and before she knew it, Maria was readying her for the ball. The carriage was waiting, the driver was ready, and soon they were flying through London to the most fashionable party of the Season.

Once they had reached their destination, Letty was handed down from the carriage and left alone a moment to admire while Clarissa exited the enclosed vehicle. The great stone building rose up before her, its many floors merging with the night sky and its width extending farther than she could see on this dark night. Torches lit up the way to the entrance. Up and down the street, people were arriving and converging on the door of the stately house.

"Come now, my dear! I'm looking forward to sampling a glass of the Viscount's punch!" Clarissa, who had recovered from this morning's worries, was in high spirits and skipped, as much as her ampleness would allow, to the door. Letty suspected that her mother-in-law would not confine herself to a single glass of her favourite beverage. Clarissa handed the gilt invitation over to the doorman.

Letty would not allow herself to look inside just yet. She was waiting until she could obtain the best view. She felt her stomach fluttering and jumping around inside her; she could not tether it down for anyone. Her cheeks were flushed, and, despite the cold evening, she was already perspiring. She did not want to credit it to nerves, even if that were the case.

As they stepped over the threshold, Clarissa was talking a thousand words a minute. "And we shall have to find out where the Major is, for he is bound to be here. He and Beauford are the best of friends. The Major shall look after us and introduce us to people—oh, my dear! This is going to be the best ball of the Season, and here we are brushing shoulders with the ton. We must look at the dresses and enjoy this while we can!" The last words of her rousing speech took on a saddened tone.

Letty, however, missed the strange inflection and nearly the whole of Clarissa's rapid conversation. When she stepped over the threshold and allowed the hood of her evening cloak to drop back, she halted. She stood in awe. The building was the most beautiful she had ever seen. The hallway alone was as big as Clarissa's London house.

The walls on either side of them were covered with baroque paintings of angels and men. Her gaze wandered higher to the gilt coving that rimmed the ceiling. She followed the murals across the ceiling in all their deep colours until her eyes rested on the chandelier that took all the focus. The crystals flashed light everywhere like fireflies darting in a million directions.

Letty could not believe this was all the Viscount Beauford's. This was his house. He lived here. The grandeur of the hall was offset by the modern mahogany tables which were placed in equal spacing against opposite walls, with their slim legs and polished tops on display for all to admire. There was no harking back to the gothic fashions of past decades nor a new feel of chinoiserie; this place stood in a time of its own.

A servant brought Letty out of her trance for a moment when he offered to take her cloak. She handed it over as quickly as she could just so she could look about her again. However, she found that even when she was turned away from the ball, she could still hear it all. She closed her eyes. The buzz of conversation echoed above. A hundred heels clicked on the marble hall. Satin, silk, taffeta, and lace swished about the room.

"Lettice, dear, what are you doing? You cannot enjoy a ball with your eyes closed! Now come on, let us go and obtain some drinks." Letty was dragged through the throng in the hallway with Clarissa's bobbing ostrich plume leading the way.

On the way to the refreshments, it was their good fortune to bump into the Major.

"Ah! Good evening, ladies." He bowed most beautifully.

"Good evening, Major. How lovely it is to see you here!"

"And you also, madam! May I say you two ladies are looking ravishing this evening?"

"You may only say so if no one overhears!"

"Ah, but it seems the younger Mrs. Burton is rather distracted at present."

"Hmm?" Letty was not paying attention to either of them. Instead, she was trying to take in everyone else.

"Oh look," said her mother-in-law, "there is the Duchess of Bedford!"

Letty came back to attention. Both she and Deveril followed the line of Clarissa's gaze up to the head of the staircase.

Clarissa carried on as more people appeared. "This ball has

attracted all of the ton. Look there! The Duke and Duchess of Rutland are on the stairs and behind them Lord Courtenay."

Letty ignored the reference to others, her eyes fastened on the Duchess of Bedford. Corianna was looking attractive in a crimson gown, the silks swathed around her shapely frame and gathered tightly beneath her bust. Her head of golden curls glowed in the candlelight, the elaborate twists of hair adding to her beauty. Beside her, an older man in pristine eveningwear surveyed the crowds from his high vantage point. If Letty had not known whose house this was, she could almost have believed it to be this Duke's, so confident was his air while he stood above them.

"That is her husband?" Letty was surprised, but her question was spoken quietly.

"Indeed," replied the Major. There was something pregnant in the way he spoke that word and in the way he looked at the grey-haired man who was easily twenty years Corianna's senior. A new sight greeted his eyes and his voice changed. "Ah, Miss Gray. Oh, Mrs. B., you must greet the lovely Miss Gray!"

The ominous moment was gone, and the young widow agreed to talk to the charming Miss Gray. She could only have been lately out of the schoolroom, and that truth was obvious tonight by the way her large blue eyes looked just as awed as Letty's had a moment ago. The girl stood a little way off in the crowds, surrounded by what Letty guessed was her family and a few rather zealous young dandies.

"Yes, of course!" Letty smiled towards the young miss who, in spite of the young men immediately in front of her, could not keep her eyes from the Major across the room.

Clarissa was busy chatting to an old friend who had so far snubbed her—but did not have the courage to do it to her face —and Letty was only too happy for the Major to bring Miss Gray over to speak to her.

The Major disappeared for only a moment to retrieve Miss Gray, and yet that was time enough. The Viscount had Letty in his sights. His easy stride brought him to her side a little too soon for his liking. He had enjoyed examining her from a distance as he had done since she arrived. Her brown hair was braided and piled atop her head as though she were some Grecian goddess. Her large brown eyes were looking about her, trying to drink everything in. Though so many were gathered around her, she still stood out alone, something remarkable and unnamable setting her apart from everybody else. He stared at her midnight blue ball dress; it was a deeper blue than he would have expected a girl of her age to wear, yet it became her well. The nighttime fabric brought out the deep brown of her eyes, the lustre of her hair, and the creamy complexion of her smooth skin.

"Good evening."

He was here. He had found her already, and inside she was cursing him for finding the one opportunity to corner her on her own. She had not been able to decipher her feelings since last seeing him, and now that he was here in front of her all she could hear was the thudding of her heart.

He bent over the hand she held out dumbly. His scent wafted up to her, the warm smell of cloves and oranges. His hair was the ebony of a raven's feather and his dark eyes inescapable. What did he want with her?

"Are you enjoying my ball?" He seemed stiffer than usual and without his usual languid air.

She nodded.

"I believe my aunt was asking after you."

"Truly?"

"Yes. Perhaps after you dance with me I could take you to her."

"Oh, and am I to dance with you?" She was regaining her composure enough to manage some banter.

"Yes." He did not wait for her to answer but instead led her away through the crowds.

It was like a dream; it all happened in a haze. Before she knew it, the music was rising up about them. She was already sailing across the dance floor before she realised just what dance it was.

They moved together in the waltz, spinning and slowing, then speeding and turning. His arms were strong about her, guiding her to follow him, ensuring that she would not fall. The other dancers blurred together in a flood of colour. She could not see the people that watched—what must they all be thinking? She did not know, and in this moment, it seemed like it did not matter. His scent was so strong now, enveloping her, making her heady. She could feel the warmth of his hands on her body.

She was concentrating hard on her steps, but she soon realised she did not have to. He moved so easily about the dance floor, leading them this way and that with little effort. He had been looking about him, and now his gaze was upon her. She could feel it burning into her, perceiving everything as though she were a book and he the reader.

"What's wrong?" She took more studying than others, but he was beginning to understand her subtle moods. He could tell, or rather could see that her thoughts were scattered all about her.

"The Duchess of Bedford is here tonight." She averted her eyes, willing them to be indiscernible.

His grip tightened about her, and he turned her faster.

"Will you dance with her also?" She could not stop herself from asking. Her eyes flicked to his face and then quickly away again.

His voice was heavy with feeling. "Why?"

"Will you?" She felt as though he was about to stop, to break step in the dance. But through an act of will, he carried on, pressing forward in a sweeping motion. He still did not answer, but she could see the lines of his jaw muscles clenching and unclenching.

"And you, will you dance with another?" Now it was his turn to question.

"No."

They made another circuit of the floor, the faces staring at them now coming into focus.

"Are you still so intent on not marrying?"

She did not have the opportunity to answer; she would not have known what to say even if she had the time. The dance had finished, the music fading into non-existence and the dancers slowing to a halt. The Viscount held her longer than he needed to. She could feel heat building in her cheeks again. Finally, she moved a little to escape him and his grip relaxed. He released her but still watched her intently—as did the rest of the outraged room.

"Will I ever be able to understand you?" He bowed.

"Or I you?"

She curtseyed so low that he could see the line of her neck leading down to the curve of her bosom.

"I believe I am to take you to my aunt now."

When she looked up into his face, it no longer seemed angular and harsh; it had softened as he looked down at her, his mouth hinting at a smile.

"Indeed—though, might I be excused first? I shall return in a moment."

He nodded and led her off the dance floor to many a matron's disbelief. The whispering grew. Who was this girl, this chit dancing with the most eligible bachelor in London? She seemed to have no connections. As far as the gossipmongers knew, she had no fortune worth speaking of.

The Viscount stood tall, watching the small figure of his dance partner disappear through the gossiping crowds to the ladies' room. He was not blind to the looks she received. Even now he felt anger growing at all those disparaging eyes. She would not be blind to them either, that he knew. Yet still he watched her keep her poise until she was out of sight, her shoulders drawn back and strong, her head carried with quiet calm, a figure to be admired.

"Oh, William, how sweet! You dancing with the little widow. I remember when you used to dance with me like that." The soft tones hissed at him from a close proximity. He did not want to turn; he could already feel the old anger and bitterness—emotions which the thought of Letty had momentarily banished—returning once more. His eyelids slid slowly shut and then opened as he turned to face the Duchess.

"Yes, and thankfully I shall be spared from that. It is the Duke's work now." Ready to ignore her response, he pulled a snuffbox from his pocket.

"Oh, you must not be so difficult about it. You know I would let you hold me like that again if you wished." Her words were spoken in low, sensual tones.

"What an inviting offer. I think, however, I shall decline it. The thought of holding a serpent close holds no appeal, I confess." He still would not look her in the eye. Inhaling the snuff, he replaced the box in his pocket.

"You did not used to object so. Is it that little widow? Have you been entertaining yourself with her then?"

Was that snide comment the spawn of jealousy? His shoulders pulled back as he straightened up to his full towering height. "Corianna, please try not to be under any misapprehension—you were invited here at my aunt's request not mine, and even her request stems from propriety not pleasure. How is it that my attempt to shoot your husband because of your behaviour does not prevent you from coming to me with the same offer again?"

"Because I know very well your petty anger comes from

love for me, and if you are not answering about that woman, then I am right." She managed a gloriously serene face.

"Corianna, dear," the Viscount's voice softened. "You were titillating, believe me. I found you quite the most delightful flirt in all London and most artful in love-making...."

The back of his neck prickled as if he were being watched. His head whipped round. His feeling had been right. He could see Letty's dark blue dress dissolving back into the crowd. She had been coming back, but now she was disappearing again—what had she overheard?

"Yes?" Corianna put a hand to his face to turn him back to her, awaiting further flattery.

"But now you are nothing more than Society's whore dressed as a Duchess."

The fair Duchess' jaw dropped, but she was left to close her open mouth by herself as the Viscount walked away without adding to his statement. He had someone to find, something to explain before it was too late.

Major Deveril had been enjoying Beauford's ball very much, mostly on account of the fair creature who was all smiles and sympathy toward him tonight. He had returned to Letty with Miss Gray on his arm only to find she had disappeared from the place he had left her. Ah, well—he had no objection to entertaining his fair partner all by himself. Nothing could dampen the delight of this evening!

But as Deveril flirted outrageously with his Miss Gray, Clarissa had come upon him and drawn him aside. The things she told him turned his joy-filled face to sorrow. He was aghast to hear of the financial burdens cast upon the mother and daughter-in-law he cared so much about. Now it seemed the situation had worsened; they were farther into dun territory than even Clarissa had realised, and a letter had arrived this morning threatening legal prosecution.

Clarissa was not sure what to do, but the Major was. They had to leave at once. This situation needed to be rectified, and tomorrow would be too late if they did not want the whole of Society to hear of it.

"It's all right, marm, I'll find Mrs. B." He rested a steadying hand on her shoulder.

"Oh, thank you, thank you! But she does not know."

"I see. We shall have to leave and explain the whole to her when we are in safer quarters."

"You have always been so good to my family, bless you, Major!" Clarissa had crumpled into a chair while the Major went in search of her daughter-in-law. He had searched among the sitting debutantes, the standing matrons, the talking crowds, everywhere.

The elusive Letty was, however, in the last place he would have ever expected. Like the rest of the crowd, Deveril watched in disbelief as Letty and the Viscount waltzed about the floor, abandoned to the world.

What was Beauford doing waltzing with Letty? Surely he would not make up to her as he had done in the past with so many opera girls? No, even Beauford knew to leave a lady of quality alone. Or did he? Curse him—if he hurt Letty! Deveril would not allow it. He had vowed he would not let anyone harm this girl, not after the pain she had already suffered.

In a horrid way, it seemed Clarissa's troubles could not have come at a more opportune time. The sooner Letty could be spirited away from Beauford, the safer she would be. There was no telling what his designs on her could be; he was as unstable as water after the torments he had suffered over the Duchess of Bedford.

The Major had only seen the end of the dance, and, before

he could reach the other side of the dance floor, the widow was already disappearing into the crowds. Beauford stood there, waiting for her and ignoring his other invited guests. Typical of him to cause a scandal at his own ball! Then, as the Major watched, the Duchess Corianna approached. This scandal was about to get a thousand times worse!

Deveril was still fighting his way through the crowds while Beauford and Corianna spoke. From the look on Beauford's face, Corianna was playing with fire. That furious glint in his eye did not bode well for anyone.

Wait, why had he spun round? Was that Mrs. B.? The Major saw the widow falter, turn abruptly, and head towards the door. He wrestled his way past the rest of the crowd until he had her before him.

"Oh, Major!" Letty was shocked to see him. Her voice trembled. "Major, I am afraid I do not feel quite well. Could we...?" Her eyes were already brimming with tears. She could feel a lump rising in her throat and had the distinct knowledge that her reserve was cracking. She needed to leave—now.

"Go home? Yes, that was why I was coming to collect you. I'll explain it all in the carriage, my dear." He put a reassuring arm about her and guided her out of the ballroom—away from the vicious vision of the gossips, away from the poisonous rumours that Corianna had already begun to spread.

She did not look back. She could not bear it. She knew only that the Major was taking her away—away from this ball, away from Society, and away from the Viscount Beauford.

CHAPTER TWELVE

*Absence diminishes mediocre passions and increases great
ones, as the wind extinguishes candles and fans fires.*
  – FRANCOIS DE LA ROCHEFOUCAULD

The grey walls of London's buildings bled away and,
slowly, green began to grow back into the windows of
Clarissa's carriage. Neither of the women inside conversed,
apart from a few perfunctory laments from Clarissa on the
loss of London Society. Letty answered vaguely to these
words, though both the women's thoughts were on other
things.

Clarissa was allowing herself, for once, to feel guilt for her
own selfishness and her refusal to take action sooner. Her face
was pale and drawn as she looked from the windows remembering Deveril's words. He had been so good to them—they
could never repay him. And, in truth, Clarissa did not know if
they would even see him again.

He had explained the situation to Letty last night in the
carriage bringing them home from the Viscount's ball. He had
done so with far more clarity than the old widow could ever

have managed. All that was demanded of Clarissa was to watch Letty's reaction to this news.

Although the young widow had kept her composure, the flicker of emotions that passed over her face had shown she was not insensible to this disaster. Letty had nodded a few times, clasped and unclasped her hands, and then finally replied. "Yes, of course, Major, you are quite right. Leaving London is the best course of action."

What else could they do? They were in tremendous debt, and if they did not want worse trouble, they needed to curtail their expenses immediately. When the carriage arrived home, Clarissa had fallen onto the nearest sofa, moaning with bitterness about their wretched circumstances and expressing her fear and foreboding of the Debtors' Prison. The Major, meanwhile, made the necessary arrangements for the ladies' departure and returned in the morning at an unearthly hour to see them off.

Now here they were in this carriage, travelling west with almost no money, with a series of unpaid debts in Town, and with the prospect of more promissory notes surfacing that would destroy them completely. Despite Clarissa's loose purse strings, they were not in debt solely from their own expenditures. Rather, a series of debts, caused by both of their husbands, had been left for the widows to pay. The Burton men's food, tailors, gambling, drinking—all had been left on Clarissa and Letty's shoulders. Of this, Letty had known nothing—if she had, she would never have agreed to go to Town. And, considering the current state of affairs, perhaps that would have been better.

The previous morning, when Clarissa had opened a letter from Mr. Pottle her solicitor declaring her in a hopeless situation and disclosing her creditors' threats, she realised she could no longer conceal her lack of finances from Letty. The solicitor had been going through her accounts for weeks, trying to discover some way to right them. However, it seemed that since her husband's death, she had not been the thriftiest creature and had only added to her husband's outstanding debts in Town. Now, they must take extreme action and hope that by surrendering the Town house, the servants, the carriage, and all the comforts of life, they would enable Mr. Pottle to sort out the finances. If he could not, at least they would not be in Town when the scandal broke.

This journey had become a time for guilt, and Clarissa, though very adept at transferring blame and bemoaning God's curses upon her, had decided in this moment to feel the full weight of her faults, if only for a short while.

Letty's thoughts were also distracted. She wrestled with many facts, not the least of which was the financial crisis that she and her mother-in-law had found themselves in. Even after he was dead, John was still causing pain in her life.

She was also distracted by the disruption she had caused in Town. So far, she had managed to alienate almost every eligible woman's friendship, apart from Sophie's, due to her lack of fashion and her exceptional manners. She had also become the object of the most eligible bachelor's interest without desiring it.

Whenever they found themselves in the same place, he had marked her out and spent a considerable amount of time conversing with her. It had simply made the mothers of eligible, non-mourning debutantes fume. Letty reflected that if they had heard the content of the conversations—conversations that she had certainly not enjoyed—they would probably have been somewhat mollified. They had only seen, not heard, however, and so she had caused more than one aspiring parent and preening chit to loathe her. Perhaps it had been just in time that Letty was removed from Town.

Her whole time in London, Letty had felt constantly on guard, as though one slip would send her over the edge of a cliff, into a canyon so deep that she would never reach the bottom. She could not trust another soul with the details of her life, with the things that had happened to her, with what she had felt. Yet last night at the ball, all these cares had disappeared while they danced. For a few moments, the gossip and stares, the ill-concealed malice, and the fear of trusting anyone were non-existent.

What had he meant when he asked, "Are you still determined not to marry?"

She did not know, and now it did not seem to matter. She was not of his world. That much had been clear to her last night when she had overheard him talking to Corianna.

She bit her lip. Why had it taken her so long to realise who the Duchess really was? Over the last few weeks she had had her suspicions, and when she overheard that conversation, those suspicions had all been confirmed. Corianna was the woman whom Beauford had fought over, the one whom Theo had told her about so many months ago, and the one whom Beauford still loved. It had taken her only a few seconds to realise their involvement and not many more for her to turn away in disgust.

How could she have been so stupid? Oh, she did not care anymore! It was painful to remember last night, and now there were far more important things to worry about than a proven rake of a Viscount. It was harder, however, than she had at first assumed it would be to blot out last night's happenings from her mind. She was usually so good at it, but this time her heart felt heavy and there was a sickening feeling in her stomach.

Fresh tears trickled down her pale face, tears that she carefully hid from her mother-in-law. Everything in her life was crashing down about her, and worst of all her heart—the heart which she had tried so valiantly to protect—was in pain. It was the one part of herself that she had never wanted exposed again. Now it was slashed open, a gouge running down its centre, and no matter how she tried to bind it with silence, distraction, or indifference, it still lay exposed, stinging, and bleeding. She would have to carry it like this, perhaps forever, and she did not know whether she could bear it.

As she stared out of the window, she breathed in deeply. From watching the beggars, as they had escaped the clutches of London, and seeing now the farmers who were tending the growth of the earth, she gained some perspective. What did the events of her life matter in the face of the grander schemes of this world? She was only another human being amongst the thousands—thousands of lives that would be proven dust in the face of eternity. It did not matter that she had been dealt an unfair hand; she must still see it through.

Perhaps it had been God's will that she was there to look after Clarissa in this chaos. Letty could not imagine what would have happened to the old woman without her there. That gave her a little purpose to live for, and yet, the bleak world outside kept her new optimism within its limits. The carriage jostled as it ran over a bump. The journey would not allow her to rest and so her thoughts carried on their lonely procession through her mind.

During their journey, they arrived at various posting houses where ostlers ran out to attend them. It was a sad reminder of Clarissa's gruff groom-come-butler whom they had sent to Mr. Pottle who would find him a new engagement. Tibbs would be missed by his mistress when she had stopped thinking of herself. Maria, Letty's trustworthy maid and now a friend, was travelling with them for now, but it would not be long before Letty would have to make a decision regarding the girl's future.

The posting houses treated them well enough until other carriages, ones without chipped paintwork and creaking doors, drew up needing attendance. The ostlers would immediately leave the Burtons' hired carriage to attend whichever member of the ton was emerging from the newer equipage.

When Letty and Clarissa finally did get waited on and their horses fed and watered, Letty was in charge of paying. She had been given Clarissa's reticule with an audible sigh.

"You had better take this, my dear. My darling husband used to take care of all payments, and as you can see, I am clearly not capable of dealing with monetary matters. The Lord has cursed me in them!" The old woman's podgy hand wiped tears from her cheeks.

Biting her tongue, Letty bowed her head and used the mind God had given her to begin to take care of *all* the practicalities. In truth, she did not trust Clarissa with money anymore; it would be her own responsibility from now on.

To be back in the freedom of the countryside was at least some comfort. It was not the ferocious beauty of the edge of Britain, but to even have entered the border of the West Country was lavender water to a burning brow.

It had been much too long since Letty's last solitary walk. The wind billowed about her dress, rouging her cheeks with an angry red independence. Her hands became a chapped pink, the skin dried by resentful winds, and her hair was one great lock of tangled beauty. Trees were struggling to bud while winter seemed to be making a last-charge attempt to halt the advance of its nemesis spring. It was easy, as the wild coastline came into sight, for her to forget everything.

She would not dwell in a cave of self-pity. Clarissa was living proof that that particular method of dealing with disaster did nothing. Tears were no currency for a debt-collector, and how could you sign away family silver to a tradesman when your hand quaked from sobbing? No, frugality and careful budgeting, coupled with an illusion of being well-to-do was the play that must be enacted by mother and daughter-in-law—though Letty knew that there was no doubt they would sink further in social circles.

Act one of this play had been settling with the creditors in Town, or at least keeping them at bay a little longer. It had been hard to avoid public exposure, something Letty cared little for anymore, but she knew how much it affected Clarissa. They were able to escape Town the day after Beauford's ball due to Mr. Pottle's assiduous attempts to stave off the creditors in London. The solicitor had been a mask for his clients, enabling them to avoid the embarrassment of meeting debt collectors face to face.

Act two involved Clarissa accepting the Spencers' invitation for a visit and requesting permission to arrive at her cousins' earliest convenience. It was the only way she and Letty could remain housed now that the Town house was given up and the country manor had been rented out.

It was a terrible blow to Clarissa's pride to rent out the manor house, to have somebody else sitting in her dead husband's winged chair by the ornate marble fireplace, to have her butler-come-footman Tibbs, now engaged to the new tenants, waiting on and being reproached by somebody else. She knew the men in her family must be rolling in their graves. If only they were here now to sort everything out. She had frequently said this to Letty who had born it better than a saint, never once exclaiming that it was *their* extravagances, coupled with Clarissa's own, that were bringing about the Burton widows' destruction. To almost every pronouncement of Clarissa's, Letty merely replied, "We will survive."

Act three, which was yet to come, would be the most painful for her mother-in-law, but it was vital due to their circumstances. The young widow had been taught by her father, the parson scholar, and was quite capable of fulfilling a governess' role. She had resolved to compose a letter to Lady Spencer, prior to their arrival, inquiring after a governess position for the family's two children. They could not hope to live on as guests at the Spencers' home forever, and Letty hoped that Clarissa's connection with the family would strengthen her application. If she were chosen, it would give her and Clarissa far more hope for the future and even the chance of a new home.

They had spent the last two weeks at an inn in Devon, only just being able to pay board and desperate to hear from the Spencers. Many a candle had extinguished itself late at night while Letty slept on budgets she had drawn up, the ink splotching her thin cheeks and staining her overworked hands.

Finally, they had received a letter from the Spencers informing them that they had been travelling for the last fortnight but were now at home to receive them. They had gone from the inn to the house immediately, and tomorrow was the day of Letty's appointment with Lady Spencer concerning the governess position. If Letty was successful, she had hopes of being able to support Clarissa through this position and install her in a small cottage not far from the house. Success was paramount, and fervent prayers for it were frequent visitors to Letty's lips.

But now as she walked, and while the sea boiled on the jagged black rocks below, it was time to forget her worries for a short while. The cool wind breezed through the muslin day dress which hung loosely on her thinning frame. She tried to submerge her thoughts in the craggy landscape that surrounded her and the glimpse of freedom she saw in the gulls that swooped and played on the wind, but her mind refused to submit.

It was not only she who suffered. Clarissa herself had lost a great deal of rosiness from her cheeks, and her hair had greyed considerably. She had gone back to blacks when the seriousness of their situations had dawned upon her, and the former ceaseless chatter was replaced with intermittent speech.

This time Letty knew she grieved for her money and for the lost status, not just for the husband who had provided her with both. She did not judge her. Letty knew Clarissa had never known a life of thrift or a lack of money. To be thrown into this at an age beyond learning was difficult. She would come around eventually, and Letty would help her to come to terms with it.

"Now cease!" shouted Letty, her voice taken away by the wind as quickly as it had come. "Cease thinking of all this!" She wrapped her hands in her thick hair, which had loosed itself disgracefully from her pins. Vainly, she hoped that the action would stop the worries that consumed her mind. What would she give to be a gull and fly away over the oceans with no thought of money, status, or Society!

She had been stripped of all joys. And oddly enough, she even looked upon her time in London with nostalgia. "For at least there I could laugh!" Although it surprised her, she realised how very much she missed the Major and his humour. It was clear now she would not see him again. They had been removed from Society as they knew it, dumped into the briny depths like jetsom from a wave-tossed boat.

Most of all, as she picked her way through the tufts of grass and the sandy soil of the coastland path, she realised how she missed Sophie. She must write to her soon, as soon as she had the money to accept her reply. In her, at least, she could have confidence. With her she could discuss a little of her heartache.

10 March 1816

Dearest Sophie,

How I miss you and your conversation. How I miss the times we spent together in humour and confidence. It feels lonely here without you. I have become orphaned of my only friend. Now let me stop bringing you down into the doldrums! I shall talk of happier things—though where to start? For if I do not tell you the whole, you shall not think them happy things at all.

I trust utterly your wisdom and confidence in this issue. You will have already seen from the address that we have removed from London. To own the truth (and you shall be the only creature apart from myself, my mother-in-law, and dear Major Deveril to know), we have been destroyed by debts owed to creditors.

Do not be alarmed by the desperate language I use, for it was at first a disaster, but it has been righted. I must admit I have prayed more in these last weeks than possibly in my whole life. And it must be God who has seen us through to where we are now, for how else it could have happened I do not know.

I have taken up the position of governess to two adorable children who are the children of Sir and Lady Spencer. They are far relatives of Clarissa's as she was married to Sir Philip's first cousin. The children are slightly boisterous, but I find myself liking them despite—or is it because of?—their antics.

I am able to support Clarissa in her own establishment through this employment. Though Clarissa's abode is remarkably smaller than her own house which we now let out (for there is no other way to repay the mortgage to the bank), it suits her well enough.

I confess I do find employment better suits me than being a lady of Society. I can hear your laughter at these words from here in Devon! I know you shall think me a "silly Letty", but you know how I loathe being useless. Though, I confess, it is a trifle challenging at times.

Last week, for instance, Master Frederick took it into his head that the tree house built outside for him was rather dull, and decided he would much rather scale his father's bookshelves in the library. Thankfully, he was brought down before breaking anything and only sustained a sprained ankle when he jumped from the last shelf. Ten-year-old boys are so amusing. And little Cecile is a beautiful cherub of eight, though she acts more like her brother than a cherub! Two children are enough, I fancy, to keep me occupied, though I will find time to read a letter if you should wish to reply.

Now, as to the bearer of this letter—I am trusting in our strong bond that you shall not want to take back your friendship with me! It is indeed my maid Maria whom I have sent to you. You see, I could not just leave her unemployed in London. Sending her to you was the least I could do for her after all she has done for me. I have provided her with a little money I had stored, and she is to give it to you if you wish to re-advertise her rather than keep her. But for now, let me speak two words in her favour, dear Sophie; she is both kind and ever so hard working. If you were to keep her for your own care, she would not disappoint. And indeed, this is what I desire in my heart. Can you tell me what you decide, friend?

I long to hear of you and all you are doing. Is your invalid aunt still being attacked by vicious vapors? Or have they subsided to being merely irritating vapors? How do you go on?

I have returned to my maiden name for the time being—it is far less question-filled—so you will need to direct your letters to Miss Lettice May. I hope you do not mind.

Your faithful friend,
Lettice May (Burton)

30 March 1816

Dearest Letty,

I am so very sorry for the delay in my reply, but you see, I have removed from my aunt's house back to my family's home in Somerset. It is a mere fifteen miles apart, and yet see how long it has taken for your letter to reach me?

Before I say anything of the present, I will tell you that Maria arrived safely at our home, but had no money left to her thanks to her extended travels (and I think they were rather confusing for her). But have no fear! I shall, of course, take her in, for I know how much she means to you. And if my hopes are founded, I will only be borrowing her until she can one day be returned to you!

In reply to your kind, though suspiciously humourous, inquiries after my aunt, she has recovered surprisingly well from her knock at death's door—quite miraculously, in fact. The story, I am persuaded, you will love to hear.

It was on a morning like any other, and she awoke with the traditional spasms of her left side and usual faintness plaguing her. A letter arrived. She was quite wild with vexed nerves and ignored it, saying that she was near death and could not be concerned with reading it. In fact, Poppy the maid, was scolded most horribly for bringing it in. I had to console the poor girl for a full ten minutes before returning to the room and seeing that my aunt, despite her outcries, was now reading the letter anyway.

She was sitting up in bed quite composed and suddenly became very excited. She called Poppy back to make her presentable, for she was to go at once to the dressmaker's so she might order a gown for herself to be made in the latest London style. She then informed us all that the most eligible bachelor had arrived in Somerset and that she had been invited to a small private ball—which he was apparently going to attend.

Oh, Letty! I giggled excessively after this episode and so wished you could have been with me to laugh as well. It was, in fact, the Viscount Beauford! He is in the country visiting friends, and I think Major Deveril was with him too, though I only saw the Viscount. We received an invitation as well to the private ball; I saw the Viscount and we spoke for a few minutes on the weather. He asked after me and my family most kindly, and then after you. He told me to tell you he wondered if you had run away from him with a fat lapdog for company. I confess, I had no idea what he meant, but he seemed to smile so I think he did like you quite well, you know, though I remember you loathed him.

Oh, I am so sorry—my mother has just called me to go into the village. I shall have to post this letter on my way so that it will not be delayed even further. Forgive the little information in it, but I do hope you shall reply soon for I love hearing from you. You do make me laugh so. How are the children? Still boisterous?

Your friend,
Sophie Egleton

5 April 1816

Dear Sophie,

I am afraid I only have a moment to write as the children have both succumbed to chickenpox. I feel for the darlings. They are so sore, but I am sure it shall be over soon. I keep to their rooms and read them story upon story until all I have left are the ones they make me imagine and tell them.

I am utterly and completely in your debt on Maria's account. You are the kindest creature. Has she already proved her worth? I fear your hope to return her to me shall be unfounded, but that is no matter. All I can say is thank you!

How amusing that the Viscount and Major Deveril seem to

have followed you to Somerset. Are you finding much amusement at home?

Yours,
Letty

14 April 1816

Dear Letty,

Oh, how dreadful for the poor dears! I do feel for them. It
was only last year that my youngest nieces had chickenpox. They
were ill for a long while, but I hope it shall not be that long
before your charges recover.

It is, in fact, a pleasure to be at home at the moment. I find
it strange, but it seems almost pleasant to meet with previous
acquaintances, and I was even asked to dance twice at the last
village assembly!

Once was by a young man with shockingly red hair. I think
it rather becomes him, though the sun, which has now decided to
shine, has brought out more than a hundred freckles across his
cheeks. He is, however, so very kind and caring. At the assembly
he obtained a drink for me and insisted on escorting me back to
the carriage when the evening drew near to an end.

I do not know the other man who asked me to dance very
well, but he is a younger son and, I have to admit, it seemed as
though I was dancing with my younger brother. He barely made
my height and had little conversation; it was most awkward.
Though I suppose you would have laughed at the sight, I found it
quite embarrassing. I was so thankful to Mr. Simpkin, for that
is the red-haired gentleman's name, for it was after the dance
with the other man that he brought me a drink and saved me
from awkward conversation with my partner.

I cannot imagine what Mr. Simpkin gains from talking to

me, for he has spoken to me quite frequently since the assembly, at dinners and picnics and such. In fact, a great proportion of the time I think he is laughing at me for my fussiness. I find him most amiable though, and besides, if you laugh at my silliness then I suppose a man would too, and I believe he does it kindly.

Maria is a gem! Truly, she is an efficient girl if ever there was one. As soon as she received her wages, most of them went straight off to that family of hers. I understand now why you were so concerned about her. She has been marvelous at making my hair ready each night for dinner and at taking it down for the night. She does the most fantastic plaits.

Tell me more about this place where you live. What is the family like? Are they kind to you?

I am to go for afternoon tea at Mrs. Norman's house today. She is a funny, elderly lady, and some of the things her wrinkled old mouth utters are almost scandalous. You would like her, I think. I would love to acquaint you with her if you can ever obtain some holiday and come and see me. She is just like you when you are in your funning mood, constantly watching the people of the village and deriving amusement from them. I think if she were an animal, then she would be a hawk, for she is so sharp in her perception of what is going on in the village. She predicted a wedding a year before it came about!

I hope you are well, dear Letty. Please do look after yourself. I know you are probably being brave, but even the brave need to look after themselves and be well rested!

Your faithful friend,
Sophie

19 April 1816

Dear Sophie,

The children are well, thank goodness! Poor Cecile was quite ill at one point. I think she must have caught a cold whilst fighting the chickenpox, but she has finally recovered. I was so worried I cried when she could not stop coughing one night. I know it seems silly, but to see a child in so much pain is very dreadful.

I am, I confess, a little tired now. But do not worry about me. I shall keep well and keep going—I must for Clarissa's sake.

She does well in her little cottage. She has even learnt to garden and has an impressive vegetable patch which she shares with me when I go to visit in the afternoons. Her cottage is in easy walking distance which means I can see her most days. She is able to just about keep herself happily on my small income with a cook coming in the evening to make dinner for her. I am sorry if it is unseemly to talk of monetary matters, though I will say that you did ask about my position at the moment. I am so happily situated that, if all goes well, I think we shall be just able to survive the debts besetting us.

As for the house, it is quite a beautiful place and very well maintained by Sir Philip and Lady Spencer. Do you remember that day we first met? Well, I distinctly remember you declaring your love of architecture, so I thought I would include some sketches I have done of the house. I thought it would interest you, and I am sure you will be able to tell me more about the house just from glancing at these than I would be able to tell you from living here!

The family is lovely, and I am very fortunate to have them as employers. Sir Philip is quite a serious man and very good when it comes to business matters, which is why, I think, his estate thrives. When he is with his children, however, he lets his guard down and becomes as loveable as a playful old dog.

Her Ladyship is attentive to my every need. She knows a little about my circumstances, and since they let the cottage in which Clarissa resides, she has overseen some renovations to it.

She is a quiet woman, clearly quite beautiful in her time, and even though she is older now, she remains quite striking.

They are much in love; it makes one happy just looking at them together in the evenings. They allow me some freedom when the children have gone to bed, though I often go to sit in my room as I feel as though I intrude when I sit betwixt them in the drawing room!

I have been teaching the children sums, and Cecile has proved to be quite the mathematician. She leapt onto my lap with her answers after she finished some questions exceedingly quickly, and gave me a huge, wet kiss when I was able to mark them all right! She is such a darling.

I think if I carry on as a governess, I may end up like the old lady, Mrs. Norman, of whom you wrote. I do wish to meet her after your amusing description. She sounds like quite a funny character.

As for you, I think from what you have described, this Mr. Simpkin will ensure you end up a married woman soon. And just think of all those copper haired children you could have! I do not mind what anyone says—I think freckles are most endearing. Have you danced with him again?

I must close here as the children have managed to finish all the questions I set them to keep them occupied while I wrote to you. I send all my love to you, dear Sophie, and I hope to hear from you soon. Do add in something about Mrs. Norman, for she must have said something else scandalous by the time you receive this letter!

Your ever-faithful friend,

Letty

P.S. I am glad Maria has proved her worth. I knew she would not fail you.

. . .

Letty allowed the quill to rest back in the standish and set about dusting and blotting the paper. She admired her hand which was covered in patches of ink; she really was the clumsiest writer. She would have spent the next few minutes scrubbing the ink off, but a small, insistent hand was pulling at her sleeve.

"Please, Miss May. Please, I want to go out and play in the tree house."

Letty looked into the large brown eyes and could not resist allowing the young lad out. After all, he had completed his questions so diligently.

Cecile had finished as well, and Letty ordered a small table and chair to be set upon the lawn so that she might mark the work while the two children played.

April had brought with it few showers and bountiful sunshine. Newly sprung leaves blew on the spring breeze, their citrus colours bringing bright life to a not-long-ago dreary landscape. The grass sprang up lightly under her pumps, and she could feel the hem of her skirt slightly damp with faint traces of evaporating dew. She did not mind, however, as she took her seat at the table and began again to methodically cover her hands in ink whilst marking. It was beautiful here. It had been so upon her arrival when winter's grip was still seen on the landscape, but it was more full of life now. Most of all, as birds wheeled and played above, it was tranquil.

Other women who had spent half a Season in London would have been tearing locks of hair out of their bored heads by now. It seemed, however, that life had finally stilled for Letty, and though it was a struggle to balance everything, she was on those solitary walks content, if not occasionally blissful. The tranquility had calmed her wild emotions and given her time to bandage her damaged heart even though it had not healed.

Her days were filled with much of the same, but the

monotony, as it could be termed, was also a kind of comfort. Though she spent the majority of her time with the children or in her room, while she corresponded with Sophie, she was not lonely. How she hoped Mr. Simpkin had honourable intentions! She would love to see Sophie finally become appreciated and not undermined by the gaudier charms of other schoolroom misses.

She smiled as she thought of a red haired gentleman poking fun at her dear Sophie. How she longed to see it, to analyse him down to the last copper hair on his head. She was sure, from Sophie's description, that he was just the sort of man of whom she would approve. And she saw him as just the sort of man who would suit Sophie. Perhaps that was a little too much to perceive from just a letter, but it made her the happiest to believe it.

The talk of old London friends in Sophie's letters had, for one moment, made Letty miss the conversation and friendships she had managed to gain. The Major came to mind with his easy humour, he who had made her laugh excessively and who had been their shining knight in a time of dire need. Perhaps, with time, she might see him again, though it would definitely not be in a London Season—that she knew full well.

The Viscount was a different matter. Although she had found his company interesting, sometimes infuriating, he had been stirring feelings in Letty she did not wish to recognise. Some of those feelings she had not wanted to feel again. She felt tricked by her own mind and heart. How could she think this way again so freely after two long years of unhappiness before?

She had succumbed to the charms of a rake, and now she must suffer for it. No amount of happiness and conversation could make up for the words she had heard him utter at his own ball. He had indeed led her on a merry jig and had then been caught making love to his longtime flirt. She cursed herself for believing him sincere, for giving up more information about herself than she had ever wished to. Now she was paying the price for allowing herself to feel again.

After all these weeks away from London, she could still feel her heart aching. It throbbed gently beneath the surface of her calm. Despite the pain, or perhaps because of it, she felt the walls of privacy and silence were again strengthening themselves about her mind. Yes, Letty was happy. The Viscount's delving conversation was far from her, along with his deceiving presence.

CHAPTER THIRTEEN

Courage is the first of human qualities because it is the
quality which guarantees the others.

– ARISTOTLE

May passed away in much the same fashion as April
with only minor changes to Letty's routine. The
lawn became the hive of almost all of the children's activities.
Lessons became freer and much more fun; Letty even
managed to read to them and teach them in the sunshine,
though they were under strict oath not to mention it to their
mother. She found herself growing in affection for Frederick
and Cecile as well as their parents who watched over her most
kindly.

Clarissa did well in her little cottage, though she did not
laugh as she used to. Letty was persuaded that over time the
woman was starting to enjoy herself. The young widow had
managed to engage a local girl as a cook, putting Clarissa's
vegetables to use and keeping her in good health.

After successfully cultivating the vegetable patch, Clarissa
discovered that new friendships might be cultivated here as

well. The tittle-tattle of the village was easily obtained from an old spinster named Miss Vince who lived nearby. The two women spent many a happy afternoon gasping and nodding sagely at the highly exaggerated goings-on in a small and quiet village. This kindly individual, Miss Vince, was also an exceedingly good listener, and with her Clarissa shared most of her heartache over her loss of status and fortune.

"Ah, but my dear," replied the spinster, "if you had not been reduced in circumstance, why then we would never have met! And to whom would I tell all the gossip? For you know you are the only other intellectual mind these five miles together! Now do not indulge in self-pity, for that I cannot abide. Instead, I will tell you what the chambermaid was caught doing up at Grange Manor, you know, the house that belongs to the estate's owner...." The small, grey eyes twinkled wickedly.

And so, even as Miss Vince regularly communicated the latest scandals, she also made herself useful by rebuking Clarissa's blue devils. To her credit, the widow took all such reprimands in stride until she eventually managed to spend less than four hours in self-pity a day. Sometimes, she even thought of others.

With ivy growing up the walls in the June sunshine, the cottage looked quite idyllic, and, thanks to Lady Spencer, the interior was very pleasant. Of course, a cottage would never compare to a house in Town or a country manor—the ceilings were far too low for that—however, the rooms were of an ample size and the light paint gave them an airy feel. Spring flowers were put in the vases almost daily, brought to Clarissa by Letty as she wandered through the bluebell wood on her way to visit. The furniture was comfortable, and, although not stylish, it was pleasing in design and complemented the simple rooms, making the cottage an altogether charming establishment.

It was from one of these visits that Letty returned to find a visitor at Grange House. Various squeals from the direction of the study made her suspect the children might be hiding in there, and Benson, the housekeeper, confirmed her supposition by directing her to that particular room. She began to think, with dread, of the French exercises the children must do. It was neither child's favourite subject and took Letty much patience to teach.

However, all thoughts of the French language were quickly dispelled from her mind when she entered the room and saw a figure she did not recognise. She rapidly ascertained why Frederick had been squealing just as loudly as his sister when she saw the various parcels and presents which lay on the floor, surrounded by shreds of wrapping paper.

"Ah, here is our governess, Miss May," said Lady Spencer, speaking in her sing-song voice and smiling towards Letty. "You are just in time to take the children away for their French lesson."

Letty gritted her teeth as she was reminded of the French. The problem, she feared, was not with the children's distaste for the subject but rather with her own knowledge of the language. She could speak it but could not claim to be a proficient linguist. Since she had only had her father to teach her, there were several particulars of grammar of which she herself was not certain. Nevertheless, she smiled quietly at Lady Spencer and came forward into the room, ready to be the invisible servant.

"Miss May, this is our nephew, Charles Bonville. He is come to visit us while he is convalescing after a rather bad fall he suffered while hunting." It was just like Lady Spencer to carefully remember every detail, and just like her to graciously include Letty. No longer permitted to lurk unseen, Letty came forward to face the gentleman who, up until now, had had his back to her.

He turned around with a little difficulty, a walking stick shadowing his every move. "Pleasure." He performed a stiff bow but only vaguely made eye contact.

As he chose not to look on Letty, she used this opportunity to look at him. His hair was cropped short to his head and combed into very neat order. His forehead was slightly small but was more than made up for by his strong chin and firm eyes. His coat was not of the best cut, but it became his solid body well enough. His hessians, however, in contrast with the mediocre garments upon his person, were polished so well that Letty swore she could see up his nose as he bowed over his toe. All in all, he was rather hard to evaluate with his plain, frowning face and strikingly fashionable footwear.

Where had Letty seen this frowning face before? She was sure she had encountered this gentleman sometime in the past, and the feeling which came with the recognition was not one of joy. This was the man who had cut her and her mother-in-law when they had first promenaded in the park after arriving in London. She still remembered the look of disdain he had worn, and it was not dissimilar to the look he wore now.

"Sir." She curtseyed politely. He rose from his demi-bow and, almost straight away, turned awkwardly from her to discuss shooting on the Grange estate with Sir Philip. Understanding that the introduction was over, she put her hands on the children's shoulders and ushered them out of the room. Of course, they must collect their presents first, and Letty, following them up the stairs, picked up whatever dolls or soldiers fell from their small arms. She might remember Mr. Bonville, but Mr. Bonville certainly did not remember her!

"Uncle Charlie is very cross all the time, but he does bring fine presents!" Frederick nodded with approval as he placed his scarlet-coated toy soldiers on the windowsill of the playroom.

Cecile, to whom the comment was mainly directed, was

far too busy with her tongue nearly touching her nose as she dressed and undressed the fragile china doll she now held.

"Children, come now, it is time to learn your French." The sight of their teacher bearing books was enough to send the children scurrying for cover. And so the afternoon slowly deteriorated until dinner, in which Frederick refused to eat anything until he was tempted by some venison, and Cecile sat red-faced after a bout of tears over not being allowed to bring her doll to the table.

It was not often that the children were invited to dinner with a guest present, but, seeing as Mr. Bonville was family, an exception had been made. Letty was slightly embarrassed that they had decided to be on their worst behaviour for the occasion. She tried to taste her soup and ignore the large blue eyes misted with tears that looked up at her from her right side.

"But she will be lonely and hungry upstairs all alone." Cecile's words were spoken with such worry and affliction Letty could almost believe she was countenancing a real person's starvation!

"She shall get along just fine. I am sure she is using the time to make friends with all your other toys. Now come, eat your dinner." She placed a napkin on the unsatisfied child's lap and started to cut up her meat for her.

"And you are from which part of the country, Miss...er... May? Yes, that's right," said Bonville after his aunt whispered the name to him.

"Cornwall, sir," replied Letty, unsure whether she liked this nephew. She eyed him measuredly after seeing that Cecile was finally eating some of her dinner.

"Indeed. And whom did you govern there?" He was staring at her, his eyes cold and uninviting.

"No one, sir. I was married to a gentleman."

"Yes, and I am sure you do not wish to speak of it." Lady Spencer's calm voice filtered over what could have been an awkward moment. "But tell me, Sir Philip, was shooting good today?"

"Mmm, mmm. Prime, prime, m'dear." Spencer dug into another pheasant.

"I am sorry, *Miss* May. I did not ascertain that you were married from your name." Mr. Bonville seemed almost angry, as though she had tricked him purposefully. "I hope I have not caused you any undue pain through my questioning?"

Despite the fact that the Spencers knew of her husband, Letty did not wish to tell anyone who did not need to know. She had lived in peace for several months, and now, due to a moment of blind truthfulness, she had the misfortune to make her employers' nephew curious.

"Not at all, Mr. Bonville." She spoke in calm accents and inclined her head, continuing to eat under what she chose to ignore—his close scrutiny.

She was excused after dinner, leaving to put the children to bed, but she knew she would, before long, be expected to return to the adults. She braced herself, breathing in deeply before she re-entered the room. She was sure, or rather hoped, that her customary hour for retiring would still be accepted despite its earliness and the present company.

"Ah, Miss May. Are the children well settled?"

"Yes, quite well, Lady Spencer. I eventually persuaded them to put down their presents and rest."

"Oh, good." Lady Spencer turned to Mr. Bonville. "You are so kind to them Charles."

The sombre man was meditating on a volume in his hand.

"They always so look forward to your coming." Lady Spencer smiled dreamily, carrying on oblivious of his clear disinterest.

"It is an easy task to please children," he muttered. "My secretary was happy to look out some gifts for them."

Letty picked up a book she was halfway finished with from a side table and retreated to sit in a far chair.

"And how goes your leg? Any better?" asked Lady Spencer.

"Well, standing and shooting on it didn't do it much good." Seeing her Ladyship's worried expression, Bonville added in conciliatory tones, "Though I am sure being here has helped it mend somewhat."

"Good, I am so glad."

There was a moment of silence where everyone found some occupation, even if it was simply gazing about the room and wondering if that was a spider on the room's high cornice.

"Miss May, how do you like Devon?"

Letty reluctantly lifted her gaze from the book she was reading and allowed it to fall on Mr. Bonville's frowning countenance. Was she the only person he had newly met in some weeks? Was that why he insisted on interrogating her in this unorthodox and abrupt manner?

"Very much so."

"More than Cornwall?" He seemed to be quizzing her.

"Would I be impolite to say no?" She let her frank eyes widen a little, and perhaps a glimmer of humour light them, though she would not show her amusement completely. For who was this, Mr. Bonville? A man of humour or disdain? She could not tell, at least, not yet.

"I suppose not. But I hope you do not dislike the country hereabouts. I have always found it fine hunting country."

"Oh, really? How long before you may hunt on horseback again?" It was easy to turn the conversation from herself to him.

"Not until next Season. Had a lovely mare on the go too. She was starting off nicely, very bold in the field, and now she'll be out until next year." He sounded like a schoolboy robbed of his toy.

"What a shame." She bowed her head to her book again. Then, after about a quarter of an hour, she bade her customary goodnight.

Though Bonville raised an eyebrow at her early departure, her pupils' parents nodded and saw her off with smiles.

"She is a relative?" said Bonville, once the door had clicked shut.

"Yes, Charles. Her mother-in-law was...oh, who was she again, dear?"

"Hmph?" Sir Philip stirred in his chair. "She married a cousin of mine. Wasn't the sort of marriage one talks about y'know. The lady was all right." He was starting to perk up. "She's become a tenant in one of my cottages now, you see. It was the girls who married their sons that were, well, a bit of a step down from station, don't you know? But, Miss May seems a fine filly—bit quiet, but she is in much better spirits than when she first came."

"Indeed?" Bonville was still not wholly satisfied.

"Oh, yes, become quite herself. I dare say that Town did not suit her."

"Oh, my dear!" chimed in his wife. "You say that about everybody because you dislike Town so."

"She was in London?" exclaimed Bonville.

"Yes, but they came away mid-Season," explained Lady Spencer. "I think she said the mourning was too much for both her and her mother-in-law. They both lost their husbands around the same time, you see, and she wanted some occupation. I think"—she spoke quietly, leaning in as though there was need for secrecy—"her mother-in-law needed such a change. I believe she has even rented her own house out so she may not see anywhere that reminds her of her husband."

"Unusual," Bonville said flatly. "And this, Miss May, despite her low breeding, is she good company? Lord knows,

I'll be needing plenty of that while I am healing, even if she is below me in station."

"She keeps to herself mostly and goes to see her mother-in-law almost every day. She seems a quiet soul." Lady Spencer felt like she was defending the woman.

Charles stopped his questioning then, remembering that slight mischievousness in Miss May's face when he had spoken to her. Perhaps she was not as quiet as she at first appeared, and that thought made him suspicious.

But though this particular assumption was correct, the assumption that succeeded it was not. Any lack of conversation on her part he immediately took for shyness in the presence of a handsome man like himself. He could not have been more mistaken. His looks were of small interest to any lady and least of all to Letty.

CHAPTER FOURTEEN

Better a witty fool than a foolish wit.

– WILLIAM SHAKESPEARE

She was not attractive—that was a fact Mr. Bonville would freely own as he studied her at breakfast. Her hair was only a dull brown and her complexion too pale. Together it created a harsh contrast betwixt skin and hair which could not be pleasing. Her eyes were large, but they too had only a dull brown colouration. She did not seem to be perfectly versed in all the subjects she taught, though she was adequate. And it was these reasons, coupled with her seemingly quiet nature, that made Charles wonder why on earth Lady Spencer had hired her.

Letty might have been an expert at keeping to herself, but she was nobody's fool. In those moments of invisibility, which came often, she managed to watch this Charles Bonville. It was clear, in his straight, symmetrical face and perpetually ruffled brow, that he did not approve of her. She could think of no reason for this, and in moments of weakness, when her body was already tired, she found herself angry with him.

It was these feelings that made her so surprised when he searched her out after breakfast one morning. She was even more astonished when he asked her to walk with him in the garden. All she could do was stand transfixed, gaping at the man. His serious eyes kept her gaze, his mouth refused to smile, and his brow drew together as if working some large sum.

"Of course, Mr. Bonville. Children, how would you like to play in the garden for half an hour?" Finally, she had done something sensible and answered! Though why she had given Mr. Bonville a favourable reply was unfathomable even to herself. What did she mean by walking with a man who so clearly disliked her? And what did he mean by asking her?

Squeals of delight brought her back to the present. The initial excitement was followed by chaos. Math papers fluttered to the ground as the children sprang from their seats and ran to the classroom door. They wrestled with each other over the door handle, and Letty could see they would soon be fighting in earnest.

"Children!" She placed her hands on her hips. "Please refrain from being quite so hasty! The garden will wait for your coming even if you walk."

Charles was surprised by the firmness of her reprimand compared to the usual quiet of her demeanour.

He offered her his arm, and she slid her small hand into it, stepping out slowly with him. His bad leg ensured it would take twice as long to walk anywhere, and Letty was now dreading the inquisition he was about to launch. She could not believe this walk was innocent of any ulterior motives.

She was granted a few moments silence when they first stepped out, for which she was grateful. In the quiet she was able to appreciate everything around her. Now that June was upon them, it was warm and fresh outside. Rain had fallen in the night, giving that newborn-look to the wildlife and landscape. Different scents hung everywhere. Roses grew on a trellis by the path and let their thick fragrance descend smoothly onto the couple below. The rich smell of newly watered earth rose up, mingling with the sweet roses to make a heady concoction. Letty breathed it in again and again, trying to hold on to the invigorating freshness.

Pebbles clicked and scraped against the flagstones. A squirrel scampered across their path and straight up into the boughs of a safe, green oak. Letty made a sound of surprise and then smiled, her eyes lighting slightly at the small creature's flight.

"How is your mother-in-law?"

Letty stiffened, the child-like wonder vanishing. Bonville's question was an abrupt reminder that she was not on one of her solitary walks where no one demanded anything of her, where she could be away from commands and all the hundreds of tasks she had yet to undertake. No, she was accompanied by a man of whom she was still unsure and whom she needed to answer.

She digested what he had asked; clearly, Lady Spencer had told him more than she had anticipated. Why did he want to know how Clarissa was? He did not really care. The only thing he seemed to care for was that bold mare of his.

"She is well, I thank you." She managed to reply in a level voice. She slipped a sideways glance at his face and saw a look of concentration. As they carried on walking, he made a low, grumbling sound. Another glance at him was confirmation: he was frustrated with his current condition. He was trying to walk faster, but it was clear he could not. For a brief moment, Letty felt pity for him and gave in to concern.

"How is your leg now?"

"Dashed painful actually."

She was a servant. What did it matter that he swore in her

presence? He could not know that she had heard worse from her dead husband's lips.

"Perhaps we should turn back."

"Ha! And sit inside all day in aimless chitchat? I think not. No, being out in God's creation will do me much more good." He steadied himself on her arm. She was able to balance his weight without too much trouble. "That's why I take pleasure in fox-hunting—no better way to enjoy God's creation than on the back of a horse chasing down a fox."

She nodded out of necessity, and they walked slowly on in silence. Letty, simply content in looking about her, breathed in the fresh air once again and felt the warmth of early summer sun rouging her cheeks.

"So, how do you like the children? Cecile's going to be a teaser when she's older, don't you think? So precocious."

Bonville's effort at conversation drew a chuckle from Letty. She glanced down onto the lawn where the two in question were playing. Frederick had just stolen Cecile's hair ribbon and was tearing away with it.

"Yes. She is a dear thing—very willful, but then surely it would be worse if she were to be a shy wallflower."

"You think so?"

"Yes, I believe I do. For a woman's part in life can be hard. If you have not a little courage, then you become the world's plaything."

Bonville's thin lips pursed. "You have a unique view, I see, though you make your case very persuasively. Pray tell, what of boys, or rather, what of men? What do they need to survive?"

She mused over the change in his expression before continuing. "I cannot venture an opinion on the opposite sex. I would be speaking out of place and with little accuracy." She inclined her head slightly, as if in submission. Her thoughts were running over her memories of men, one in particular coming to mind and reminding her that she could not decipher that sex at all.

"Yes, I suppose you have no experience. I would say courage is pretty essential, though perhaps more a firmness of mind and character; a resolution in all thoughts, deeds, and actions. But most of all honour. I believe it is the one attribute which holds precedence above the others. What do you say to that?"

"Yes, I would agree. Although I think these are ideals, for I have not yet met a man I could honestly say was in possession of a purely honourable character. All men are changeable, and all are susceptible to faults."

"I do not think you have had the chance to move in the first circles or the realm of politics, for there are men in these areas whose characters are sound. I know this as I have both contributed to and moved in these circles. It seems you have very little faith in humans, and particularly in men."

"No...indeed, I...." She realised the trap she had thrown herself into. She was usually so careful to hide her thoughts, and the bitterness which so often laced them. She reprimanded herself for remembering the men who had so distorted her opinions on the opposite sex, those individuals who had imprinted on her mind the idea that all men were lacking honour.

Surely, Major Deveril had been honourable? He was, indeed, very kind and had been ever since their first meeting. But it was so hard to be sure. So many times her instincts had been unfounded and her judgments had proved wrong.

She had slipped up in conversation with Bonville as she had with Beauford, giving too much away to someone she did not know—to someone she could not trust. This time the Viscount was not here, yet still he seemed to be leading her into troubled waters. His treatment of her tinged all of her emotions and feelings, like dye that had seeped slowly throughout a piece of fabric. If only Mr. Bonville would not quiz her so in the hope of tripping her up! Then she might stand a chance of remaining calm.

Her words continued to falter. She would not correct his assumption of her lack of Society, for that would bring up questions she did not wish to answer. The revived gossip of villagers was something to be avoided at all costs. Clarissa had dealt with enough. But seeing the look of growing irritation on his face, she knew there was only one way to mollify him. She took the only route possible, though it was a route she heartily despised.

"Oh, Mr. Bonville, you are trying to tease me! How you can twist my words! You are too cruel to a poor governess who does not know any better." Letty forced her eyes to twinkle at him and her face to maintain its innocent look.

His gaze shifted irritably. "If you don't know any better, then it is through your fault alone. You seem unable to recognise an honourable man when he is right in front of your face."

They walked on again, at the crushingly slow pace set by his injured leg. She would give anything to get back to the house, to the security that lay in her ability to escape and become invisible, something she valued very highly since leaving Town. She was on dangerous ground, and this man was trying his hardest to push that ground out from under her.

"Come, we do not want to spend the rest of this walk in awkwardness. Let us make peace."

Charles halted precipitately, causing her to pull a little on his arm. He ignored her obvious confusion and instead bowed stiffly towards her in acceptance of her proposal. He spent the rest of the walk in silence, and Letty was more than relieved when she was able to quit him and take the children in for their next French lesson.

"Insulting me as though she were my superior! She is not even my equal. No honourable men in any of her acquaintance, indeed!"

"Oh, Charles! I am quite certain she did not mean you." Lady Spencer tried to soothe her nephew's hurt pride. "You were a present exception, I am sure. She is the sweetest thing; she would not have meant to insult you. She must not have counted you into the equation, for she barely knows you."

"I thought it worth speaking to her in hopes she could provide some sort of entertainment in this place. It seems she is entertaining, though in a most abominable way!" He turned about and came striding, as quickly as his injury would allow, back down the centre of the room.

Sir Philip, sitting somnolently by the fire, gave a little grunt and slid lower in his chair. It was so easy for his wife's nephew to get his back up about some imagined indignity. He yawned. Thankfully, Lady Spencer was adept at quelling him.

"I know it frustrates you so to be cooped up here, but I am afraid it is what the doctor ordered. You will not have to see her apart from at meals, and she is always quite happy to eat in silence or talk to the children. She will not bother you. You shall barely notice her."

"Good. I do not wish to be insulted or to bear the ramblings of a bitter widow!"

"Oh, now, Charles! Try not to be unkind, for she is a good girl really."

He snorted in a most unflattering way and then resumed his awkward pacing of the drawing room. "That I find hard to believe. I wished to be polite, though she is obviously below my station—I even asked her questions! She has simply rein-forced my opinion that the middle class should be segregated from our own. An odd order of people, so far removed from our activities and social niceties—it is a wonder we even acknowledge that section of society. She is an exceedingly strange woman, and there is no more to be said!"

Letty knew eavesdropping was a terrible thing, but, after hearing raised voices and then catching her name spilling through the drawing room doors, she could not help but pause. Cocking her small head to one side and resting her hand on the large wooden door, she had no difficulty making out the conversation between her ladyship and Mr. Bonville.

At first, she felt cold shame growing inside her rapidly, but that was quickly heated out of existence by a burning anger. A strange woman, was she? Perhaps, but that was a fact she had never before felt shame over, and neither did she intend to be ashamed of it in the future. She would allow him to see that her middle class person could mix with the upper classes without any display of inferiority or any lapse in manners.

It took steadfast resolve to force a smile, push the door open, and step calmly over the threshold. She entered the room with more grace than she thought herself capable of. She did not lay her eyes on Mr. Bonville when she greeted him, for surely, hers were far too lowborn for him to gaze into? She turned elegantly and bestowed some kind words on a rather ruffled Lady Spencer.

Though Letty would not mention it, it was clear to both conscious occupants of the room that she must have heard a little of the conversation, if not the whole. Sir Philip, however, was snoring fitfully by the fire that crackled in the hearth. He would be happy in his dreams for a good while longer.

Letty moved over to the table and picked up her current volume. She placed herself opposite Sir Philip, knowing this would ensure no conversation was directed toward her. She was far enough away to warrant not speaking to. For, though her outward appearance seemed to be calm, her inside feelings were still boiling away close to the surface. It would take some time for her to regain control over them.

Mr. Bonville, after watching Letty's entrance and subsequent retreat to the fireside, could not keep his cheeks from flushing a violent red. Whether he was more embarrassed or furious at Letty's impromptu appearance, he could not tell. Rattling his cane on the floor, he sat abruptly and picked up any book in which he could hide his face. When he did manage to summon the courage to peek over its covers, he saw the picture of tranquility in Letty's quiet figure reading contentedly by the fire.

And so an evening of silence was all that followed this rather tempestuous start. Letty stayed longer than usual, to Mr. Bonville and Lady Spencer's dread, and to her own hidden satisfaction. When she finally rose to retire, she said a pleasant good night to them both.

This time she looked Mr. Bonville full in the eyes as she spoke. Something passed between them. She received the pleasure of seeing a rather put out gentleman. He, on the other hand, received something far more—a look of fierce defiance and unbridled independence from a woman he had severely misjudged.

CHAPTER FIFTEEN

For pleasures past I do not grieve, nor perils gathering near;
My greatest grief is that I leave nothing that claims a tear.
– LORD BYRON

Thanks to Letty's practical turn of mind, she realised that after last night's episode it would be of benefit to everyone if she became invisible on the following day. She was used to obscurity and so she bore it well. She had enjoyed putting Mr. Bonville in his place last night; however, she realised in hindsight it was perhaps an action that was not quite prudent.

She had spent most of the night awake, and in those thoughtful hours, she decided it would be best to take the children out on a long walk tomorrow. It was an excellent pretext for escaping the house and its ruffled occupants and avoiding the aftermath of the previous evening. The children had natural history and anatomy lessons from time to time, and she was happy today to teach them away from the house in the depth of the parkland.

She could almost have laughed at the ridiculousness of Mr.

Bonville's conversation concerning her, if only there was someone to laugh with. But there was no one—no Major, no sweet Sophie, and no one else of a satirical mind. And being all alone, she felt the sting of the words more than she should have; she could not help mulling over the phrases again and again in her mind.

Perhaps what Mr. Bonville had said was the reason that she had not been accepted into London Society. She would never be of their calibre. She would never be acceptable. No, she would always be tainted with the dirt that came from her origins, the muddy waters of her relations and the lowliness of her station.

It was not only the place in which she had been born but also the depravity of her past which would not let her go. How could a woman who had been beaten, abused, and broken be accepted by others? No one had to know the facts about her history in order to realise she was sullied. Now, more than ever, she could feel the pain and unworthiness on her skin, and the need to cover herself with a mask to hide what lay beneath.

Now, separated from those dark days by so many months, she could see it all more clearly. She saw the past which could not be changed, and the path which lay ahead with no real redemption. She could not alter Society's false perceptions of her, and she could not fix what was broken within her.

Could she feel peace about this conclusion? Almost.

What other options were left to her? None.

That was why she carried on, for no one would carry on for her. No one else would earn the wages she needed in order to provide for her mother-in-law. No one else would bind up her wounded heart which continued to bleed. No one else would wipe away the tears she could not shed. And this was something Mr. Bonville would never know, something which Letty kept between herself and God.

She slept little, and as soon as the sharp arrows of daylight flew up and pierced the night sky, she rose. She dressed quickly, took little care about her unruly hair, and went to wake the children. It was early, but once the little ones were awake, they began bouncing about the room, full of excitement to have lessons outdoors. The woods, which to Letty were a welcome sanctuary, were to Cecile and Frederick a magical world.

"We will be out until lunchtime," Letty said to the maid, trying in vain to put Cecile in a short, stiff little jacket. The child's arms would not cease flailing about as she tried to hit her teasing brother.

The curly-haired parlour maid bobbed her head. "Yes, Miss May."

"Right," said Letty, standing up and smoothing the creases from her skirts. "Come along, children. Lots to see and not nearly enough time to see it in."

They went marching into the corridor. Thankfully, none of the occupants of the house were up at this hour apart from the servants. The children consumed breakfast quickly. Letty spent a few moments in front of a mirror pulling her hair this way and that and completely forgetting to eat. She tried in vain to find a conservative style, but there was so much of this hair at the moment that she could not hold it all safely together.

The parlour maid waved them off at the door, watching them wander through the park and down into the woodland. She admired the governess. She could see the lady was a quiet person, but intellectual, and she carried herself with such grace about the house. On humourous occasions, the governess would grin wickedly at the young maid, although that smile never lasted long and she was soon back to her usual melancholy demeanour.

When she was alone with the children, she became playful and humourous yet still commanded their respect with ease. That character disappeared, however, when she was in the company of adults—except, of course, for those brief twinkles in the eye when the governess could not seem to help herself.

The parlour maid did not understand why that side of Letty should be hidden in front of the adults, almost like the moon hiding half itself in the heavens, but she guessed it must be something in her past. Letty guarded herself so very completely, and that was something only a hurt woman would do. But whatever the hurt was, none of the servants could guess, and Letty never let her control slip enough to reveal anything of her past.

That control was perilously close to disappearing now, however, as Letty set forth with the children. She was panicked to get away from the house, and it was only when they started down the gravel path then crossed over the thick damp grass and into the mottled shade of the woodland that she felt some relief.

What did it matter what a nephew thought of her? Did not Lady Spencer and Sir Philip constantly thank her for her work with the children? Yes, she could handle the nephew. Besides, she would only have to bear with him until his convalescing was over, and he would only have to bear with *her* that long. She could keep her conversation polite if she tried her very best. If she managed to hold her tongue, they could get on well enough until he recovered. But that was only if he wanted to live amicably with her for the next few months. If it was his intention to catch her out, as she suspected and feared, then these next few months would only be another trial amongst many. She must bear it as she always did. She would carry on with the silent resolution that so clearly marked her.

As she opened her eyes to the summer woodland around her, all those trials faded into the distance. There was no need for silent resolution here. The children giggled and played about her, and their antics began to draw smiles and even chuckles from her. Frederick kept climbing on logs and falling off and then climbing on again. Cecile skipped along picking flowers and singing to herself. She was really very good at pretending there was a handsome prince coming for her through the woodland on his valiant steed.

Letty made them gasp and laugh and shout, "Yuck!" with all the curiosities she pointed out to them. The fungus on the trees was something of a favourite, and Cecile exclaimed that she never knew trees had their own parasols. Letty named each and every flower that Cecile picked and had her recite them back to her in a song they made up together. Then Frederick named the trees in the woodland: the oak, sycamore, and horse chestnut. He claimed rights to all the green conkers still growing on the horse chestnut trees and described his plan to bring a cart from the farm and collect them all in autumn.

After many hours of freedom and ease within the woods, Letty regretfully realised it was time to return and face the adults. She herded the reluctant children back toward the house, but when Frederick and Cecile demanded a game of tag, her mind was quickly distracted. Bounding through the woodland, they cornered and tapped each other until Frederick grew tired of chasing his sister and tagged Miss May instead.

Letty picked up her skirts, looked about her, and decided she would allow herself this freedom. She ran over the woodland floor and skipped over a small log to tag Cecile. The little girl huffed and puffed in anger.

"Freddy, I'm going to get you, you meany! You cannot tag Miss May!"

"Just because you couldn't have tagged her, Cici!" he taunted, dodging a small fist swiped in his direction.

"Yes, I can. I'm faster than you." The blonde curls bounced as she bounded forward in her cotton dress and boots.

"No, you can't!" yelled Letty triumphantly. She ran out of

the way and back out into view of the house. The sun was high in the sky and blazed over the green lawns. Lunch would be soon, she thought.

Her face broke into a magnificent smile as she ran forward away from Cecile's grasping hand. Then, taking pity, she allowed herself to be caught before chasing the children up the lawn and into the house. At least, they would not be late for lunch, she thought as she looked guiltily at Cecile's mud-spattered skirt and the grass stains on Frederick's shorts.

Letty was no picture of neatness herself. Her cheeks were bright red with exercise and her ill-contained hair had escaped in large tresses about her face. Yet when she reached a hand to her cheek, she felt a smile still upon her lips, and she realised that happiness and hope had been restored in her heart. Why couldn't adults be more like children?

Voices echoed in the hall. Smoothing the rumpled look of her dress, she prepared herself for meeting Mr. Bonville and her employers. A mirror hung in the entrance hall, and she turned quickly to try and make her hair presentable.

She was still pinning tresses back into place when a party, headed by a man, entered the hall. She turned, rather sheepishly, expecting to meet Mr. Bonville, but instead her hand dropped from her hair in shock. Her mouth dropped open several inches. Her fine brows puckered then raised, and without thinking she gasped the word, "Viscount!"

He stopped mid-stride, his driving coat with its many capes swaying and his head cocking to one side in curiosity and not a little surprise of his own.

"What the devil...." He took a small step forward. He blinked several times, wanting to make sure this woman would not disappear like a dream. When she did not, he resumed his speech, "Mrs. Burton, what the devil are you doing here?"

Letty's small feet stepped backward on the hall floor,

retreating from this intruder, but his tall form seemed to envelop the hall and she had nowhere to run.

He raised an aristocratic brow as he surveyed her appearance. It was such a contrast to his own immaculate one.

A few days' journey had had no effect on Beauford's dress whatsoever. His cravat was starched and perfectly folded as if he were about to attend a dinner party. His driving coat was of the best cut, showing his broad shoulders to full advantage. His trousers were like a second skin to his thighs, and his boots reflected every particle of light in the room.

Despite all this, Letty could see his face was different from the last time she had met him. It no longer held that slight humour and that arrogant disdain. Instead, his smile was strained and his face haggard with fatigue. She felt her own face crease with worry as she resisted the urge to cry.

It did not take more than a few seconds for him to cover his tired face with a mask of ease. Letty swallowed back her tears and did the same.

The rest of the family party, who were following closely behind him, had not heard the two exclamations. Now they waited expectantly beside the visitor, wondering at Miss May's expression before being distracted by Cecile.

"Miss May? Miss?" Cecile grabbed the governess' hand. "Freddy's got a frog! He brought a frog home from the woods. Come quickly!" The child was oblivious to the two grown-ups staring in fascination at each other. The only important thing was the amphibian in her dollhouse upstairs.

She tugged her governess' hand and Letty was dragged quite rapidly upstairs to examine the intruder and punish the smuggler. She had never been more grateful to Cecile in her life.

She reprimanded Frederick absentmindedly, still in shock from Viscount Beauford's sudden appearance. What on earth could he want here? Was he a friend of Mr. Bonville? Surely

Charles Bonville was a little too straight-laced for the outrageous Viscount!

With a thousand questions plaguing her—and the knowledge that her change in circumstance had undoubtedly shocked the Viscount to no end—Letty went down to lunch. Perhaps he had gone out shooting. Yes, that is what Mr. Bonville did in the afternoons. Surely they had gone together. She prayed and hoped they were out. Her worst fear, that the debts and bills she and Clarissa had run from would become public, plagued her mind immeasurably. At the same time, it took all her strength to suppress the previously buried feelings that had started to rise up inside her.

Her prayer for the Viscount's absence was not answered favourably. As she entered the room, she saw Mr. Bonville sitting at table while the Viscount rose to his feet and held out a chair for her. A wicked smile flashed across his face as she curtseyed and took her seat.

She felt the brush of his fingertips on her shoulder; it was the touch that broke the dam she had so carefully constructed, and against her will, all her suppressed emotions poured out in a flood. That briefest of touches brought everything back—their first meeting in Truro, the months in London, the arguments and debates, the satire and laughter, and the unwished for desires that had been so cruelly trampled upon during that night at his own ball. Her ill judgment stared her in the face once again. Would she never be able to discern character?

"Miss May, I hope you are well? You look quite pale." Lady Spencer studied the pinched mouth and drained complexion of her children's governess.

Letty nodded slightly.

Lady Spencer continued to chirp away, forever the anxious hostess. "I am so sorry that you were not introduced to the Viscount earlier, but I think Cecile was quite upset about that frog. This is the Viscount Beauford. He is staying at Grange Manor whilst inspecting his estate and Grange House."

If it had been a different situation Letty would have been filled with amusement at the polite introduction to a man she already knew. As it was, she found herself unable to speak.

"The delightful *Miss May* and I have already met, aunt." His gaze was not on his aunt; it was focused immovably on Letty.

Aunt! Lady Spencer was his aunt? But that would mean...no! Letty's thoughts raced to catch up with the new information.

"Indeed, we were great friends, though I am afraid I did offend her and rather foolishly lost her friendship. I must endeavour to gain it again." His brown eyes twinkled across the table at her but there was also a layer of gravity beneath the mischief. Did he mean it?

Even after all these months, the picture of his eyes had been so clear in her mind. Yet now, on seeing them again, there was something in them she did not remember—something darker and far more intense, something that remained unspoken. But she would not, or perhaps it was could not, match his gaze long enough to decipher it.

"Yes, I expect you did offend her," interjected the other gentleman present. "You really are so provoking sometimes, Beauford. I'm not surprised she wanted nothing to do with you."

"Now, now, Mr. Bonville," replied the Viscount to Mr. Bonville's clipped tone. "You may be my aunt's nephew, but I am not beyond shooting you if you irritate me with your reprimands."

Letty felt the corners of her mouth tweak; they were betraying her and trying to smile. For goodness sake, she thought, exclaiming mentally at herself. How could she smile at his banter after all the torment he had inflicted upon her?

Lady Spencer was definitely not amused. Her head shot up so quickly at this comment that it almost hit the ceiling. "Gentlemen, please! That is most improper conversation, especially in front of the children."

"Oh, I don't think so," said Beauford turning to little Frederick. "How'd you like to learn to shoot? I'll teach you."

"Yes!" said the boy, although it was more of a mumble than a shout since his mouth was full of sweetmeats.

"Firearms are detestable," said Bonville acidly.

"Not if you're the one holding them."

Letty hid a smile behind her napkin. Memories of laughter began to flow through her mind. It was a long time since anyone had made her laugh. She did, however, keep her head facing down, her eyes focused on eating. She would not be fooled by him twice.

"That is very fortuitous that you know my nephew, Miss May." Lady Spencer eyed her nephew who was staring at the young governess. "Though where you met him I cannot imagine?" It was posed as a question, one which Letty's quick wit, for once, had no clue how to answer.

"Oh, she was the daughter of my governess, weren't you, cherub?" Beauford carried on swiftly, not waiting for an answer. "Used to play in the garden all the time when we were little, though you were a tinker."

"As I recall, it was you who were the rather worse company." She was being drawn in again.

"Oh, no, I don't think so, though I remember you preferring the company of a certain dog."

Letty could not help but let him draw a small laugh from her as she took some more cold ham onto her plate and remembered her comments at the Grays' soiree.

"And how long do you intend to stay in the neighbourhood, O childhood friend of mine?" How long would she have to guard herself from him?

"A couple of days, though I haven't really decided yet." He shrugged with little care and then looked intently at her from across the table. His gaze was focused, judging her reaction, and her only response was avoidance. What he was playing at she did not know, but that was not the worst of it. His appearance had not only dredged up pain but also those feelings she thought she had extinguished months ago. She had denied them and ignored them until she thought they were gone, but she discovered now that they had returned, far stronger and far more terrifying.

Later, as the children were playing outside after completing their mathematics, Beauford strode languourously onto the lawn. He made his way slowly but steadily towards Letty who was sitting at a table in the centre of the lawn.

"And so, Mrs. Burton, we are alone at last."

"No, indeed. The children are here." She gestured to the brother and sister playing on the grass. But despite their presence, she felt her chest tighten and her heart gallop faster and faster. She had tried since lunch to avoid him, but now he had sought her out.

"How may I help you, my lord?" She placed her quill on the table and sat back in her chair slightly. She laid her ink-stained hands in her lap and tried to meet his gaze.

"Not at all, in fact. Though I did come to inquire after your mother-in-law—she is well, I trust?"

"Yes, I thank you."

Ah, so this is how it would be with her—answers that gave nothing away. She had constructed an impregnable wall while she had been away and seemed determined to keep him at arm's length. Could he blame her? After all, what she had heard at his ball, even if it was out of context, was incriminating. That was all there was to it. Had he not felt the burn of love's betrayal before himself?

He toyed with his quizzing glass before letting it drop on its ribbon. A different tack perhaps. "Pardon my impertinence, but what exactly are you doing here?"

"Marking papers," she said simply, not allowing her expression to falter. She would not tell him that when she had left Town, though it was for lack of money, she was happy to leave him and the pain he had caused her. The silence of the country was like a tonic, and he was upsetting the glass.

"No, you misunderstand me. What exactly are you doing staying here in this part of the country?"

"Why, filling a governess position, of course."

Her act of surprise would have been convincing to anyone less observant, anyone who did not know her as well as he had begun to.

In truth, he did not need her to tell him why she was no longer in the metropolis. No, indeed. She was not to know that he had searched the heights and depths of London for her after she had left. She was not to know that he had quit his own ball early, regardless of the social outrage, to search for her the last night he saw her. His aunt had been furious with him for abandoning his guests, and she would have rung him a fine peal had he not explained the whole. It was then that his faith in Lady Lincombe had proved justified. She had nodded calmly, patted his hand sagely, and said, "Well, go on then, find her!" Behind those wrinkled lids, her eyes had been smiling at the sight of her reckless nephew so distraught over a woman. And that was not a joy in his distress but rather a joy at the sight of him caring for another.

He had, of course, had no luck that night, discovering only that her party had taken the carriage home. He had gone to find her the next morning, only to find himself knocking on the door of an empty house. Letty and her mother-in-law had both disappeared!

It had taken him some time to find out who had rented them the house, and he had demanded answers from that man. Why had they left so suddenly? Where had they gone? When the businessman did not answer, Beauford had lost his temper and threatened him.

"My lord, I've told you all I know. They didn't leave a forwardin' address. All they did was pay part of what they owed and went—s'all I know, I swear!"

Not even realizing he had been holding the landlord up against the office wall by his shirt collars, Beauford suddenly dropped him on the floor. The Viscount did not know what madness had overcome him, but his blood boiled and he felt a total lack of control. Later, he would realise it was the knowledge of losing Letty resting its full weight upon him which had begun to drive him to a maddening despair.

He had left the office and spent the rest of that day brooding in his study, his brows knitted above uncertain eyes. Deveril came in at a late hour to pay him a visit. Beauford questioned where he had been, but the gentleman fenced off the question, driving it back round to Beauford's current state which was explained in bleak accents.

The next day they had made inquiries everywhere for the missing ladies, but to no avail. Beauford did not give up, however, keeping up the search for weeks and weeks before Deveril eventually stopped him. The only thing the Viscount succeeded in unearthing was a series of unpaid debts all across Town left by the two women's husbands and Letty's mother-in-law. What had happened he did not know, but he could make more than one educated guess. However, he had to admit defeat on not finding them, and it was Deveril's suggestion that made his mind up about his next move.

"Look, old man, I know you want to find this girl and her

mother-in-law, but the fact is they cannot be found and that suggests they don't want to be. You need to start accepting invitations again—don't want to be known as a recluse from Society!"

"Hang Society!" Even as he uttered them, those words had only reminded Beauford more of Letty, a woman who had been like no other.

At the urging of Deveril, the Viscount had begrudgingly taken up an invitation to a small private ball and resumed socializing at his clubs. Unfortunately, Deveril did not come to the Viscount's residence before going to the ball. If he had, he would most certainly have made sure the Viscount stayed home. As it was, the aristocrat arrived after the ball supper had been served, alone and rather foxed. He stumbled this way and that, a source of shock and consternation to the other guests. His intoxicated state and dishevelled appearance made it hard for some to even recognise him. If he had been in his right mind, Beauford would never have been seen in that awful toilette in public. But earlier in the evening, after yelling at his valet to, "Get the bloody hell out!" he had been left to his own drunken devices.

After the Viscount had wandered around the ballroom a few times and uttered more than one loud and disparaging comment, Deveril herded him into a private room. "What on earth are you playing at, man? You can't turn up to a place like this foxed. There's delicate ladies present." Deveril had found it hard to hide his disgust at the Viscount's state, but it did not matter anyway—the man in question would not have seen a horse standing three feet in front of him.

At first, Deveril assumed that it was some self-indulgent caper and sent the man home, making believable excuses to the hostess and her husband who sniffed with disapproval. On reflection, the Major could not help but wonder if his lordship's behaviour had something to do with Letty's disappearance, but he did not regard the situation as any more serious than a child losing his favourite toy.

A few days later, the Viscount had quit London with Deveril as his companion. Deveril would have done anything to stop the Viscount on his self-destructive quest in Town. Even if it was a self-indulgent phase, they were still friends, and friends protected one another.

They, therefore, began an extensive tour of Viscount Beauford's country estates. There were matters he had not attended to in months, and he could definitely stand to leave London Society for a while. Without Mrs. Burton, nothing seemed very entertaining anymore; the only purpose Society served was to remind him of her loss.

And now, after believing her lost to the world for so many months, here he was, and here she was sitting before him. It was as though some divine power had appointed their meeting again. He noticed everything about her as he looked upon her once again, drinking in all that he had been missing.

"And, how is it that wherever I go you seem to be there also?" He raised a brow at her and examined her through his quizzing glass.

"I assure you, my lord, it is not my intention." Whether he would choose to take offence at this comment she knew not.

He was, in fact, too busy admiring how she did not blush from his examination as most people did.

"That may be, but still, here you are, governess to my relatives and tenants. Here I was making a customary tour of my estates. I come to Grange Manor to visit my aunt and uncle who live in Grange House on my land, and suddenly, I discover that the woman who has eluded everyone has been residing on my own property these many months. What am I to think? Perhaps you missed my company, after all, and this is some elaborate ruse to throw yourself in my path?"

There was that twinkle. Would he be forever provoking her?

"Now, now, my lord. Let us not assume too much." She packed the lesson things away and called the children to her.

"No, indeed, let us not." It was spoken more to himself than to her. As Letty bowed, he believed he had won at least a little battle—she had spoken to him, and it was with humour in her voice. Now, however, she was leaving his presence as quickly as propriety allowed her.

At the Viscount's request, Letty was treated with even more kindness and care at Grange House. An increase in her wages helped her pay Clarissa's expenses more easily—and how was she to know it arrived from Beauford's pocket and not Sir Philip's?

A few days after the Viscount's arrival, Letty's walk to Clarissa's cottage was interrupted by her anonymous patron's appearance.

"Ah, governess!"

She disliked the way he called her that, and she was sure from his face that he knew it.

"My lord." Her cheeks were already flushed with walking and so she hoped her unbidden blushes would remain hidden.

"May I join you in your walk?"

What could she do but agree? He was, after all, her employer's landlord; he was clearly not a person to which no could be said.

"You are still fond of walks?" he questioned as they carried on together.

"Very. These woods are so beautiful at this time of year."

He observed the look of delight in her eyes as she surveyed

the forest. "If I may say so, you seem far more at home in the country."

Who was this man speaking to her? So quiet and amiable, not like the conceited and cynical man she had met in Town, not like the man who had hurt her.

"I confess I am. I love the country very much."

"And"—he paused, watching for her expression—"is that why you came away from London?"

Her face closed and the look of weariness and anxiety came back to haunt her eyes once again. "Why must you ask so many questions?"

"Oh come!" he cried, a flash of frustration bursting through his calm and languid façade. "Can you not let me a little way into your confidences? We are hardly strangers, *Miss May*."

"That does not mean I trust you." Her frankness only matched his own.

"Why? Because I am a gentleman with ungentlemanly habits? Because of a few ill-spoken words at a ball? Oh, come! Spare me that mocking blush!" Of all the conceited people he knew in London, there was not one he would lift a finger for. Yet this broken woman evoked a feeling of pity in him that he had not realised he had the capacity to feel anymore.

"It is no secret you have fallen on hard times. I wish to help if I can."

The heads of the bluebells quivered while silence descended again on the woodland.

"Well, I...." Letty was so taken aback by this outburst and offer of charity she knew not what to say.

He watched emotions flicker across her face, one after another like the seasons of the year. Would she still prove to be an enigma? Or would she finally allow him a full picture of the character of which he had only seen glimpses—a character that perplexed him to such an extent that not even a dozen glasses of port at White's evening after evening had been able to erase from his mind.

All the girls in society who had set their cap at him seemed dull, school-girl titterers. And then there was Corianna...but s'truth! He'd rather sit and be insulted by this widow than be fawned upon by all the others.

"Tell me what I can do." The silence between them grew so loud that neither of them heard the footsteps in the woods nearby—the footsteps of someone who could hear their every word, the footsteps of someone that both of them called friend.

Deveril had been no fool where the Viscount was concerned; his friend had developed another tendre, and this time for a widow. Sadly, Deveril also knew how quick Beauford was to lose interest in things once he had tired of them.

That is what had provoked the Major to encourage Beauford to go into the country—as well as the worry he would destroy his reputation in Town completely. Checking his estates and visiting his relatives were fine distractions for the Viscount. Unfortunately, Deveril could never have guessed Letty's current location. He had no idea that the cousin Clarissa had mentioned was, in fact, one of Beauford's tenants.

After Letty left London, Deveril had missed her advice on Miss Gray and her company most dreadfully. The ladies had not sent word to him besides a scrawled missive to say they had arrived safe at a relative's home. He had written back a number of times, but after several weeks of receiving no answer, he agreed to go with Beauford on his travels. He trusted that the two friends he had come to love were safe. But now, after all his effort to keep Beauford from going after her, he had brought him directly into her path.

By this point, Deveril knew enough of his dead friend, John Burton, to know exactly the sort of husband he had been. Seeing Letty's hardness and her numbness to everything had made his compassion for her overflow. He had vowed in his heart to protect her from any more harm.

The fact that Letty and Clarissa were on the estate on which both he and Beauford were currently staying had been kept from him since his arrival. Beauford had seen how Derveril had steered him away from Letty, and he was not about to have this opportunity taken from him.

It was a profound shock for Deveril to come upon Letty and Beauford conversing in the woods outside Grange House. After the initial surprise, he did what any self-respecting gentleman would do in this situation and promptly concealed himself close enough to ensure he could listen.

"I say again, I do not need any help."

"Because you are in no trouble or because it is offered by me?" Beauford was snarling, his temper already lost on account of this provoking woman.

"Both. You have shown yourself to be disagreeable, rude, ungentlemanly, and grossly inappropriate about my marriage. And I cannot"—she paused feeling the hurt rising to the surface—"I cannot be indebted to *you*, my lord."

All thoughts of being affable to her employer's landlord had been lost, first in fury and then in pain. His words at the ball that night were still clear in her mind. Besides, how did he know she needed help? Had he read the new bill that had arrived for her this morning? To be indebted to the man who had hurt her would mean some sort of tie to him, and that was one thing she would not be able to stand.

"Indeed?" he spat. "And I thought us friends! Two like minds adrift in this world."

"No, my lord, we are nothing of the sort." She did not trust him at all anymore.

"I see that now. I was wrong, for I thought you at home in male company. And perhaps you are, just in different company than mine. It's Deveril, is it?" He could not stop now, even if he was humiliating himself.

The Major, still listening, craned his neck further while trying to avoid a spiky branch.

"Major Deveril is a gentleman and friend of my late husband. Nothing more than a very dear friend at a hard time. And I thought you loved women's company, but perhaps the company of more compliant women than me?" She saw his colour change from the roots of his hair to his starched shirt points. He was crimson now. The words were out; she had challenged him, but she did not feel any the better for it.

"If you think that, then, indeed, you know me little." His voice was cold, but not for long. "And I find you surprisingly loyal to your husband's friends considering you had no love for the dead man."

Letty's shoulders stiffened and she felt light-headed. How had it come to this? With tight lips she straightened herself up to face him.

"How dare you." They were only three words, and yet whispered with such cold clarity he could not mistake the full meaning of them. She silently picked up her shawl, which had fallen on the ground during the argument, and turning, she walked into the woodland and disappeared behind the branches.

It did not take long for shame to burn hot in Beauford's cheeks. He felt his jaw clench convulsively as the words he had uttered tumbled back into his mind. After a moment he began pacing. He dragged a shaking hand through his hair, realizing he could not still himself. No human being had evoked such ferocious emotions in him before, not even Corianna.

He raked in a breath, then strode deliberately forwards. As he marched back to Grange Manor, he thrashed out at the undergrowth with his cane. He did not even school a countenance of calm for the servants. Entering the hall, he flung aside his greatcoat and let his cane fall on the marble floor.

Higgins had, on occasion, seen his master so wild-looking. Being a butler of the highest quality, he made no comment but merely picked up the scattered belongings and asked if tea was wanted.

A pair of wild, dark eyes landed on him. Beauford shook his head. He walked to the library door, flung it open, stalked inside, and slammed it shut behind him. He was just raising a glass of brandy to his lips when Deveril entered the sanctum.

CHAPTER SIXTEEN

Love will find a way through paths where wolves fear to prey.

– LORD BYRON

"Curse it all, Beauford!" Deveril marched in as if to take a swing at him. "What in the hell did you think you were doing?"

"What?" snapped his friend, looking up startled and slamming down his brandy glass.

"Don't give me that rubbish! You know darn well what I mean—not telling me Lettice Burton was here and then speaking to her as you just did. I've never been so ashamed to call you a friend."

Beauford stared at him but could not match his gaze for long. Picking up his glass he threw back the contents and refilled it before answering.

"And just how did you come upon this information?"

This time the usually relaxed Major bounded up to Beauford and grabbed him by his dishevelled cravat.

"I warn you, Beauford, if you're not straight with me, I

shall not be held responsible for my actions!" He did not remember having been this angry since he had left behind the horrors of Portugal.

"Unhand me, if you please, and I will tell you the whole." The Viscount spoke with a calm authority that contradicted his feelings and infuriated Deveril no end.

"Mrs. Burton, currently calling herself, Miss May, has recently taken up the post of governess at Grange House for my tenants, the Spencers."

"Your aunt and uncle?" The military man came out in Deveril as he checked the details.

"Quite." Beauford poured himself another glass and threw it back with scarce a delay. At this rate he would be three sheets to the wind by the time the story was finished.

"I happened upon her the other day, when I first paid my respects to my aunt and uncle. She was devilish flustered, made me want to shout with laughter. At least, I wanted to after the shock of seeing her again had worn off.

"I know you remember when I investigated their disappearance and found the debts left behind them in London. Well, she and that mother-in-law of hers are clearly in some degree of money trouble. I mean, governess indeed! It does not take a bluestocking to see they must have run into financial difficulties. Naturally, I offered my help. And do you know what that stubborn woman did?"

"Refused it."

"Yes, she darn well did! The cheek of her, after I offer my help." He was up and pacing once again.

"Sit down!" Deveril commanded, tired of watching the fevered walking and constant hand-raking through cropped hair. A little compassion filtered through the Major's anger after his friend obeyed. It was not a usual occurrence for Beauford to offer help to his own family, let alone anyone else.

"I overheard the whole of it, or at least a great deal. You

need to apologise, old boy." His voice was blunt, yet with a hint of gentleness.

"I know." Beauford allowed his head to fall into his hands. But how could he even begin to do that? He had disgraced himself so utterly. She would never accept his apology, not after all he had said, and he could not blame her.

Deveril studied the Viscount and seemed to read his thoughts. "What you said was cursed awful, even if it was true. It was no way to speak to a female, but Letty is a good girl. I'm sure she will forgive you. She knows you were trying to help— you just forced your hand a bit."

He slapped Beauford's broad shoulders and chuckled, but the other man would not join in. The use of her first name was so strange to his ears. It was soft and vulnerable. Still confused, he asked, "You knew her husband, did you not? She did not love him, did she?"

"How did you come to that conclusion?" Deveril cocked a brow, looking sideways at him.

"Something she once said, that night at the theatre. She proclaimed quite vehemently that love does not exist."

"Mmm, sounds about right. Though I am surprised she said it to you."

"I may have provoked her."

"You devil!" Deveril was laughing at his sheepish-looking friend. "Well, I have been finding out more about the character of her marriage since meeting her. I knew John, you remember? You may have met him once or twice at some hell or another. Anyway, I grew up with him, was the happiest of lads, but when he married Letty it was quite the opposite to advantageous."

Beauford's mind began to piece the information together.

"It was much the same with old Mrs. Burton's other son and his wife. Now, all was happy to begin with, but when John came up to Town a year later he was a changed man. All grave and 'hear my woes!' Of course, at the time I thought his wife was as bad as he described her. No breeding, little to recommend her. A right ol'...well, you get the idea." The Major coughed briskly and changed his tone.

"John would go on after he was drunk about all the opportunities he had missed, the fortunes he had lost. If only I had known Letty then...if only I'd heard the self-pity, the self-centredness of John's moaning! But it's of no use now." The Major shook his head. "When she came to Town with her mother-in-law and I saw the frail young girl she was, I could've shot myself. And then, when first speaking to her, to misjudge her so—it was a blot upon my name. For she has spirit enough for all of us. In fact, I almost said things as bad as you did, old boy, but that was before I saw...."

"Saw what?" Beauford raised his head from his hands and looked at Deveril questioningly.

"Nothing, well...if truth be told, it made me so mad I could not believe it. So, if I tell you, don't you go and do anything idiotic."

"Me? Never!" Beauford's mocking tone was belied by the curiosity and protectiveness he was trying hard to hide.

"Let's just say that when a man, in this case John Burton, is angry, something must bear the brunt of it. And though the marks might be gone, that something was still holding the fear of them when I made her acquaintance in London."

"Marks? Fear?" It took Beauford a few minutes to understand what was being said but only a few seconds for his blood to boil and shame to cover him once again. She had been beaten. She had been beaten, and still she had stood stronger than any other woman he had ever known in a Society that had plagued her without mercy. He remembered all the conversations he had had with her, all the provocation that she had taken so calmly. He could not believe it. With sudden clarity he understood her character intimately.

"I cannot see that she did anything wrong by John." Deveril was still talking. "Maybe she did love him despite himself. Even if she did not, that doesn't make her any the worse in my book."

Beauford looked up from his hands. His voice was no more than a hoarse whisper. "I think I love her, Deveril." His face was weary and tired, and, for once, Deveril saw the real Viscount Beauford—no satirical gleam in his eye, no wicked smile that was always at someone else's expense, no title or fortune, just a man. A man in love.

The Viscount leaned back in his chair and let a grim smile spread across his lips. "D'you hear what she said to me? I enjoy the company of compliant ladies, apparently! She has heard Society's dazzling version of mine and Corianna's story, no doubt."

"Yes, but how would she know otherwise? Not even I know the whole of it, and I like to think myself one of your closest friends."

"Aye, only a close friend could yell at me one minute and counsel me the next."

"Will you tell her the truth?"

"If she has been burdened with half as much pain as you describe, I do not see that I should add to it." How could he add to her confusion? How could he topple all of the troubles in her life which she was so carefully balancing by telling her he loved her?

"My dear, you have no idea what fortunate news I bring!" cried Clarissa, as a rather pale and shaken Letty ventured through her door. Not only was she distressed by her chance meeting with Viscount Beauford, but she also had the added burden of new merchants dunning them which she must conceal from Clarissa.

"Oh, my dear, you look ill. It is hot today, I shall give you some tea directly, no complaints! It will revive you—though I have already strained through it seven times." She bustled away to clink china and fill the teapot.

"Good afternoon, my dear," said Clarissa's friend and fellow gossiper, Miss Vince. She sat in one of the high winged chairs and was obviously joining them for afternoon tea today.

When Letty finished her first sip of the weak tea, Clarissa could wait no longer. "Guess who is in the neighbourhood? Oh, you will not, I daresay, for I would never have guessed myself." She laid a hand on Letty's, her eyes glowing with excitement. "It is none other than the Viscount Beauford and Major Deveril! Yes, you will be surprised, but there is better news. My friend here has just told me that the Viscount is visiting relatives!"

Oh no, thought Letty. There was no way out of Clarissa realizing the truth. This, on the heels of her encounter with the Viscount, was too much.

"Yes, and you may well ask who these relatives are." She stopped, allowing a pregnant pause. "None other than the Spencers! Sir Philip is his maternal uncle. Indeed, and you know that must mean"—she could not temper her excitement as the words tumbled out—"we are related by marriage at the very least!" The old lady clapped her hands together like a jolly child till Letty's unreadable expression caused her to question. "Are you not happy?"

"Very."

"And to think this whole time I could be oblivious to such a fact. But do you not see? If you go to him and present yourself again, but as his cousin by marriage, then he may look kindly on us. For you know how he favoured you a little in London."

Letty could not believe this was happening. Her breathing became more rapid.

"He may give us money to settle our debts. That could mean we might have some hope, in the future, of re-entering Society!" Clarissa clapped her hands together again in glee at the prospect of a London Season once again.

Only Letty could shatter this dream, and she almost did.

"Ma'am, forgive me, but I cannot ask him for financial help." Or any other help, she had made it all too clear. She could never face him after what she had said.

"Rubbish! He is family," Clarissa replied sharply, shaken by her usually compliant daughter-in-law's disobedience. The woman had been too happy, dreaming about this relative giving them money so they could come out of their worry-filled corner. Letty must go—that was that! And it would be good for her to go, for then she too could stop her sleepless nights if she knew all would be well.

"And though you have not mentioned it, I know more bills have followed us since London, for copies have been addressed to me as well. Will you truly be so cruel as to let your poor, caring mama-in-law die in a debtors' prison? Oh, the shame!"

A drawn-out bout of moaning and a fit of the vapors, followed by continuous arguments, resulted in Letty walking rather unsteadily towards Grange Manor, the Viscount's country residence.

If she only managed to put one foot in front of the other, then she would make it there. She stumbled several times—she was in too much of a daze to concentrate—but by the time Grange Manor came into sight in all its majestic beauty, she had become somewhat herself again.

It would be hard to judge whose eyes were wider as Letty was announced and the Viscount watched her enter his library, hers widening through fear and his through pure, unadulterated shock.

He may have seen the plain calling card, read and re-read the starkly printed name to himself, but truly, it was not until she entered his private sanctum that he believed it was really her.

"Miss May." He bowed quickly and strode rapidly across the room. Yet, as he halted in front of her, he felt his throat constrict. What could he say to right the wrongs his mouth had uttered?

"My lord." She curtseyed a little and eyed his proximity with an anxious expression.

He had not yet escaped his own raging mind to really look at her, but when he finally did, he did not approve of what he saw. Pinching at the sides of her mouth, a clear weariness overcame her face; she looked as brittle as bone china, draped in a gown too big with a shawl cast carelessly about her angular shoulders. She was the china, and he was the bull. He must tread carefully this time now that he knew how fragile she was.

Her eyes caught him with their distinct hopelessness, and seeing this, his heart ached for her. He saw in front of him no longer a strong and captivating woman, but a broken woman who still captivated him but also stirred in him compassion and a love that was strong and unbidden.

He kept her eyes for a moment longer. In the past they had always retained that satirical gleam, the hint of humour unspoken, and yet now they were just circles of dullest brown, numb to everything.

"Earlier...."

"Please, my lord. I have not come to speak to you about this afternoon." She put up a weak hand in protest. "That is to say...." She struggled with how to word the request. "I have come to ask for your assistance. It appears we have been burdened with another bill we cannot pay—my mother-in-law and I, I mean. This is why we left London. I believe that answers your earlier question?"

He inclined his head a little.

"Our husbands both ran up considerable debts, and it was not brought to my immediate attention—hence, interest mounted." She focused on the chair back on which her hand rested. "We have dealt well so far, renting out the Burton manor house. I keep my mother-in-law in a cottage on your land. But you see...." She carried on the monotone speech, knowing that if she stopped she would run, or worse, she would cry.

"This most recent of debts is beyond my power to mend. Clarissa—Mrs. Burton—has asked me to come to you, after learning of our connection by marriage." She could not let him think she had chosen to come herself.

He didn't.

"My husband was a distant cousin of yours."

He exhaled at this.

"And so, as family, I ask for your assistance if you would be so kind."

He watched her agitation. She did not wish to be here. It was not as he had hoped. That mother-in-law had no doubt coerced her.

"I thank you for asking me." He paused, deep in thought. Letty's pained face was almost enough of a persuasion for him to give her the money here and now. He could send a message to his banker; it would only take a few days for the debts to be cleared.

That would be simple, and he had already offered her help before. Now he had time to think upon it, however, he knew it would be easy for the loose mouths of Society to talk. Had he not brought Letty under intense scrutiny in London by his marked attention? He had heard talk at the clubs, jokes at his expense on the relationship between him and the widow. She had been the subject of gossip at the assemblies and a great deal of Society gatherings. Those people who talked were convinced that it did not stop at flirtation, that he had taken her to his bed.

What would their ever-ready tongues say if they were to find out Beauford had paid her debts too? Large sums of money from a titled man to a single woman—that did not look wholesome. Coupled with his attitude towards her in London, it would create a rumour that could not be easily refuted. In fact, Beauford knew the ton well enough to know that a refutation would be impossible.

His actions would provide fuel for the fire of gossip he had already lit in London. Society would sink its teeth into this and not let go of the story until it was well and truly dead, Letty's reputation along with it. He could not let that happen to Letty. While his title and fortune would eventually redeem him in the eyes of Society, she would be ruined forever.

"I cannot help you."

The blunt answer shocked Letty into a frown. Brown eyes stared at him, finally showing life and willing him to explain.

"We—no, *I* caused a great deal of attention to fall on you in London."

And a great deal of gossip.

"If it were heard that I also paid your debts, no matter if we are related or if the debts were your husband's, can you imagine the appearance of it?"

She slowly understood the path of his thoughts.

"I am sorry for it...." He looked again at the small woman before him, the epitome of vulnerability, and, inwardly cursing, he searched for alternatives. The one he struck upon was not ideal.

"There is, however, another man far closer to you in relation, whom I daresay you could ask without propriety being breached. It is the safest option for you."

"Who?"

"Charles Bonville. He must be first cousins with you or something similar. Asking him would be no oddity in others' eyes."

Letty had not even thought of him. Her mind was not working as it usually would; it was like a well-kept garden which had become wild. She could not think coherently, and it was clear at whose door she could lay that blame. She realised how silly her mother-in-law had been to think of asking the Viscount for money—and how silly she herself had been to agree to do so. Imagine the gossip it would cause and the subsequent embarrassment to her already degraded mother-in-law.

The darkness in his eyes when speaking of it brooked no argument or questioning from her. And yet, how odd that the Viscount was concerned about scandal touching himself! Was she that much lower than him? Had his words when they first met, about her low-breeding, been truly meant?

And why had they not already thought about Bonville and his relationship with them? Letty wondered whether the man, who so clearly did not like her, would do anything to help.

"Do not be anxious. I shall speak to him myself," carried on the Viscount, oblivious to Letty's thoughts. "I am headed that way this afternoon. I shall speak to him on behalf of you and your mother-in-law. I hope he answers favourably."

"Thank you." She curtseyed, unable to fully take in what he had just said and the honour in it. Instead, she turned swiftly to leave.

Before she travelled two steps, she felt the strong grasp of a hand on her wrist. It was firm but not painful, and it would not let her go until he had spoken.

"I was wrong in what I said this afternoon. I apologise, Mrs. Burton." He used her real name, her married name, and she could hear the honest regret in his voice. It was almost as though the use of her name showed his resolve to build back the boundaries of trust.

She saw the honesty in his eyes and heard no sarcastic tone, saw no teasing gleam, and knew he played no charades with her. She gave a watery smile—it was all she was able to do without losing her composure completely—and she answered in the quietest voice, "You were not wrong."

CHAPTER SEVENTEEN

Rather fail with honour than succeed by fraud.
  – SOPHOCLES

B eauford could have been entering White's gaming rooms certain of winning a fortune, so confident was his appearance and manner when he entered Lady Spencer's drawing room. The dinner invitation had been issued at a rather late hour, but, nevertheless, Beauford and Deveril were pleased to accept.

The latter was dressed in evening wear, an elegant but simple cravat encircling his throat. A blue and silver patterned waistcoat and fitted jacket showed off his military physique to advantage. He came in with his easy smile, and it was not long before his eyes alighted on the governess.

The effect of this old friend's appearance on Letty was indistinct to the others in the room who did not know her well—the curve of her full mouth, the relaxing of her shoulders, and the glimmer in her eyes—but all of these reactions were caught by both the visiting gentlemen. The look Deveril gave her, as he bent over her outstretched hand, held all the greeting she could have wanted.

"Major Deveril."

He was happy to hear the warmth in her voice and to know that at least yesterday's problems had not destroyed her calm. He did not realise to what lengths she had gone in order to create this perfect countenance for the benefit of everyone else.

"It has been too long, my dear. And how well you look! No doubt thanks to these good people's care." He turned to be presented to her employers. Greetings and pleasantries were exchanged, and with the subject turned to hunting, Spencer and Deveril struck up an easy conversation.

Beauford made his bows, greeted Lady Spencer with his effortless charm, and began speaking with her on the matter of the rhododendrons which seemed to be causing trouble on the lawn. When the mood took him and the company was to his liking, Beauford was rather a benefit to social gatherings, mused Deveril as he heard the Viscount's amiable conversation with their hostess.

After greeting the Major, Letty excused herself for a few moments to put the children to bed. For once they were happy to go to sleep, thanks to a tiring day outside. She read to them a little and when she left them, only half a story later, they were both dozing happily beneath the bed covers. She re-entered the drawing room silently, but the Major was watching for her return. He took her hand, tucking it firmly in his arm, and walked her through to dinner.

"You are looking a little tired, my dear. You know you *are* allowed to sleep. Beauford's on top of the ol' financial situation."

His careful whisper extracted a surprised look.

"Come now, Mrs. B., I am nobody's fool." He grinned

down at her as he pushed her chair in, careful that no one should overhear the name he called her by.

"Bar, of course, Miss Gray's!" she replied with a quickness she had not used in many weeks.

There was that twinkle he had hoped to see in her eyes. This was the Mrs. B. he knew, and if she still existed, then there was hope for her yet.

The Viscount Beauford came to sit on Letty's right. When he took his seat, she felt a distinct prickling sensation as his arm brushed hers. She could see his figure from the corner of her eye, but she dared not turn and look upon him directly.

"I hope I find you in good spirits this evening, Miss May?" Nothing to cause suspicion—that was his aim when he asked the mundane question.

"Yes, I thank you, my lord." She paused while a servant placed a napkin over her knees.

"And, you are well too, I hope?" Still she did not look at him.

"Physically, yes. Though I believe my character is in need of some mending." He spoke in a quieter voice now, meant only for her to hear.

"Isn't everybody's?" she replied lightly, bestowing a smile on no one in particular. She was too weary to be drawn into any heavy conversation tonight. Though it might be inevitable due to the company, she wished to postpone it as long as possible.

Deveril, watching her from the other side of a wonderful table decoration, was happy to hear her bright banter. At least so far, Beauford had managed not to harm her.

Their discussion, thankfully, moved on to walking. "Yes, that's it, by the mill-pond, a delightful little path. I remember the roses one year seemed to be as tall as me, though I own I must have only been eight."

"Ha! You at eight!"

"And, why do you laugh so, madam?" Amusement played in his eyes.

"Just the thought of you at eight. What a monster you must have been for your governess."

"I shall have you know I was exceptionally well behaved, when I wanted to be. You must remember?" said Beauford, aware that their earlier ruse was still in play.

"Of course, I do. I specifically remember the 'when I wanted to be'." She replied to the provoking gleam in his eyes, allowing the fabrication to slip easily from her lips and thankful that he had his wits about him in front of the Spencers.

When exactly was it in his childhood that he gained the satirical edge to his humour? The almost cynical outlook on life? These were both questions that ran through her mind, but Society's dictates and her own weariness refused to let her ask them.

Aware that the rest of the table was listening in on their conversation, Beauford decided to engage the others. "Bonville, you grew up around here. Would you know the walk I spoke of? Or better, would you be able to direct Miss May to a good ramble?"

The cousin was startled at being called so casually into conversation with this man—a man who but four hours ago had called upon him to ask for finance for a mere governess, a non-relation. The prospect of speaking to Letty after realizing her debts repulsed him. He had found the weak link in her armour he had been searching for, and yet her marriage into his family, even after her husband's decease, prevented him from telling Lady Spencer about her debts and causing the scandal she undoubtedly deserved.

Debts. He should have known. Her extravagance had almost brought her into ruin, and now she was on the brink of it, she asked for his help. And not even in person! His thoughts drifted back to this afternoon.

"I thought, as you are a near relation, that you may be able to provide assistance. It is, I believe, some four thousand pounds."

Mr. Bonville blanched as he comprehended Beauford's words and that terrific sum.

"Will you help her? I can, of course, but I would not take your place before her in the family."

"Well, of course, this is a shock indeed...." Bonville played for time while deciding upon his answer.

Beauford had borne the self-righteous, self-loving character of his cousin on every occasion they had seen each other since they were boys. He already feared the answer Bonville would give, but propriety bade him take this route. What other options were there? He could not settle Letty's debts himself and allow her to suffer the consequences, could he?

He listened to the monologue of various excuses spoken in that pompous tone, none of which mattered a jot in the Viscount's opinion. When it ended, he raised his quizzing glass, forcing his cousin to heighten in colour under the scrutiny. "Sometimes I cannot comprehend why I haven't shot you yet."

Bonville smarted at these coldly spoken words and then took a foolish step. "Oh, do not be so dashed...well, there simply isn't a word for it! Why should I help some puffed-up governess out of her debts? She's not even a blood relation. Probably a tradesman's daughter or worse." Bonville's voice was pregnant with malice. "How can even the virtue of a woman like that be trusted?"

The Viscount was not a man to shout when overcome with fury. Instead, his mouth became an uncompromising line, his eyes deadly. He seemed to double in size when he stood up square. His shoulders uncurled and his chin leveled.

He did not just outmatch his cousin physically, however, but rose above him in honour as well.

"Another crass word about her on your lips and I'll lay you down where you stand."

Bonville, petrified, watched as his better flicked open a snuffbox and inhaled a few particles.

A look of disgusted amusement entered the Viscount's eyes. "Y'know, it's clear you're not related to me by blood, Bonville." He went to the door, but before exiting, turned and looked the other gentleman straight in the eye. "There's no cursed honour in you."

Bonville could not stop reliving the scene all that afternoon. And now here they were, at the dinner table, talking about walks. Did Beauford intend to kill him? He did not know, but whatever his cousin did intend, silence was Charles' motto this evening.

"I have never been a walker. I would not know."

And so the evening flowed on like a stream, with a soft, unbroken ripple on the surface covering the wild currents that jostled and tumbled over obstacles on the streambed beneath.

"Now, no lies, my dear, only the truth. How are you? Really?" Deveril had found Letty outside after dinner on the large, flag-stone-paved area which lay just beyond the dining room doors. Her lonely figure was silhouetted in the half-light of a forgotten sun. She rested slightly against a stone wall, her eyes fixed somewhere in the distance.

"Really?" her voice sounded far off. "I feel...I could not give you an accurate answer."

He watched the profile of her worry-ridden face. Her hair floated about it in the evening breeze with ethereal beauty. Her too large mouth quivered then closed. Her lips twitched. One of her hands wrapped farther around her small frame, warding off the cold which was creeping closer with every decrease of the sun's light.

"I wish I could do more." It was the almost-begging plea of a friend.

"My dear Major, your company this evening has been enough. You made me laugh." Her eyes misted when she turned to look on him. Instinctively, he had taken her hand into his own. She squeezed it once gently. "Thank you," she whispered. She let go his grip and instead put her hand in the crook of his arm. "Shall we play some cards? Else it shall be thought you were having a lover's tryst with a reckless widow."

"Scandalous," he replied, smiling down at her.

"Indeed." Her eyes, almost clear, beamed up at him as they re-entered the room.

"Ah," said their host. "I was wondering where you had gotten to, Major. Now tell me about this bitch you have—has she got a good nose on her?—because I'd be very interested in her pups." And so her friend was taken from her again and drawn into conversation with the merry-faced Spencer.

Letty read for a time while the rest of the party conversed, but upon finishing her volume she found herself in need of the sequel. She excused herself from the room and came into the library. Footsteps sounded behind her, and for a moment her heart began to beat wildly. Then she turned and her hopes were dashed. There stood Mr. Bonville, his stern countenance beholding her.

He bowed stiffly. "I was wondering whether I might solicit a few words with you in private, madam."

"Of course." What choice did she have? He had already followed her here. She could not turn him away. She spoke in monotones, not knowing what to think, and then curtseyed in dumb acceptance, waiting for him to close the door and begin.

"Mrs. Burton—that is your real name, is it not?" He did

not wait for an answer. "I wish to speak to you on the matter of your finances."

So it would be him to whom she would be indebted. Despite his abrasive character she felt relieved.

"It has been brought to my attention that some serious troubles have befallen you. Or rather, you have brought some serious troubles upon yourself. I was reading sermons only the other day which discouraged the lavish spending of money. It said to indulge in such spending makes those possessions a god: 'What folly is this that I should give up the salvation of God for those material possessions I crave.'"

Letty could only listen in shock as he carried on. He took some time chastising her for spending that which was not hers, gambling too high at card parties, and buying frivolous things. She opened her mouth in utter astonishment and then shut it again in anger.

The arrogance of a man such as this she could not have even dreamt of. She listened in tight-lipped silence as rage ignited like a small fire, growing and gripping her whole body in its uncontrollable heat. Apparently, the debts in London were hers. Apparently, she had been the cause of Clarissa's downfall. To this man, she was the sinner who had drawn her husband John into terrible circumstances. So, this was his true opinion of her. This was what his scrutinizing eyes had ascertained in those long-gone months. Now she knew for certain how much she disgusted him.

She managed her silence until he had finished his speech, though the entire time her hand was on the chair, gripping the back of it for support. She watched as he stood preening his feathers, pleased with the lecture he had delivered and feeling far superior to and morally better than her. He was looking down on her physically and figuratively, and she held herself very still, knowing she was capable of stabbing him with the letter opener on the desk if she even moved. Never once had she uttered a cross word on John's account, not even since his death. But this was too much; even she could not sit idly by.

She turned the words over in her mind. "Should your loving husband be alive...he would be ashamed...his honest character and name...."

"Sir," she began, taking her hands together, leveling him with her gaze. "I presumed on your kindness when I agreed to let the Viscount speak on my behalf. And you presume on mine, to twist the facts and think so wrongly of me."

"Madam!" he cried in shock, his frank countenance quite put out of turn.

"Sir, please let me finish."

This stricture only incensed his anger. He would not stay silent while a penniless, gambling widow censured him—a gentleman. "I shall hear no more, bar your apology to me!" He squared himself up as though he had taken the high ground, looking down his bulbous nose at her.

"Apology?" It was her turn to be shocked.

"Yes, for the way you have just spoken to me."

"I could well say the same to you, sir, presuming to know so much about a cousin you cut upon his marriage to me."

"Yes, well, he was above you. It was to be expected."

"No, sir." A new voice entered the conversation, one that commanded instant respect. "I believe her above your cousin infinitely, as she is clearly above you at this moment. No, do not speak. You have done enough damage with that serpent tongue of yours." Beauford stepped over the threshold, dominating the room. Then, producing his snuffbox, he slowly, methodically took a pinch.

"But, sir, I heard it from your very lips." Bonville's face was agitated and his tone a worried squeak.

"Do not drag my name through the dirt with yours, you oaf! I merely said she had to pay debts. It was your inferior mind that assumed this blameless creature was the cause of them."

"Well, who was, then?"

"Quite obviously her husband, *your* relative." He subjected Bonville to a look of intense dislike.

"No, no, I will not hear you speak ill of my own relations, my own blood. It must be her. Those of low breeding regularly indulge in—"

The snuffbox snapped shut. "Speak ill of her again and, law or no, I will call you out. You should make closer inspections of your relations before you besmirch a good lady's name."

"But it cannot be."

"I most thoroughly assure you it can! I have already been informed of her husband's barbaric propensities. To leave her encumbered with debt was by far one of his mildest actions."

Letty stood there, dumb as a mule, while the gentlemen stood each other off. Beauford overshadowed his cousin by a generous four inches, and the undeniable menace of his unflappable fury was something Letty found herself admiring.

Even Beauford's mention of her dead husband's character did not shock her at first. She was simply happy to see Charles Bonville finally taking the thrashing his up-turned nose deserved. There he was, knowing himself beaten, backing down, mumbling some excuse but, as could be expected, no apology. And as she saw her defender staring him down, even out of the room, she felt an overwhelming gratitude.

"Infernal man! Are you all right?" Beauford's fury dissolved in an instant, and now his aristocratic face held nothing but compassion. "Here, sit, please. You look quite shaken."

She accepted the kindness.

Once she was seated he quickly answered the curiosity in her eyes. "I saw that buffoon follow you out and had a feeling he wasn't coming in here to woo you. I stood in the hallway for a good five minutes just to make sure I was needed."

"Oh, thank you! To own the truth, I almost felt compelled to strike him! It was good you came."

"Believe me, I have wanted to do the same almost every time I've met him. He's an absolute ass—" He saw her flinch. "Sorry, carried away there. He's an absolute *fool*—that any better?"

She nodded, smiling. "I can hear such words from others' lips but they should not cross your own." She reached up, but then paused—what was she doing? About to touch a finger to his lips?

She dropped her hand away and managed a half smile. It had seemed the right thing to do; she had even wanted to do it. She smiled again, looking him in the eye to dispel the tension she felt.

He had stilled when she raised her hand, but once she retracted it, he broke out of his trance. Reluctantly, he stepped away from her to lead her to the door and back to a world in which other people and events stood in their way.

She stopped at the doorway. "My lord?" He looked down at her as he held open the door. "I know I should not ask, but how did you know about my husband?"

How could he lie to those frank brown eyes? "Major Deveril. I am afraid he knew both sides of your late spouse."

"Ah! Of course," she said, as if finishing a puzzle. And then she passed through the door, as though her violent husband were nothing, and carried on.

They entered the drawing room without the book she had originally left to procure, but no one was the wiser. When the Viscount and his friend eventually left, Letty allowed a smile to creep onto her lips for the Viscount's benefit. He saw and replied in turn, inclining his head to her.

The Major took her hand and, leaning close for a moment,

dared to whisper. "Heard you took the cousin on—*brava*!" He kissed her hand. "You are quite a woman, my dear."

"Major, I think you missed the vital part about my saviour stepping in."

"Indeed? Yes, I believe he left that part out."

Beauford saw them both look in his direction.

"Sleep well, my dear."

"And you, dear Major."

It took time for Letty to blow out her candle that night. Too many minutes were wasted staring into nothingness, trying to grasp everything that had happened, everything that would happen in the future. Bonville had refused to pay her or her mother-in-law's debts. The creditors' letters had been arriving in a steady stream over the past few weeks, each with a threat worse than the last. Would they be bound for a debtors' prison and a debtor's death? She shivered, the thoughts too morbid for even her practical mind to think on.

They truly did have no other way out of it, unless the Viscount could be persuaded to lend his aid. He had been so adamant in his refusal—but perhaps she could ask again? She would beg if she needed to. He had seemed so kind this evening, so fierce in his protection and so compassionate in his care of her.

As she thought upon his gentlemanly actions, however, she realised her heart would not allow her to make the same request anew. He may have been thinking of her reputation in his refusal of help, and she would be thinking of his when she did not ask again.

It left her mother-in-law and herself in the same place— without a permanent home, indebted to strange men, and facing a future that was nothing else but bleak. They were not hopeless; that word implied they only had less hope, that they could find more. No, rather, they were without hope entirely.

But, at least, when their doom arrived in all its fullness, she would have that moment with the Viscount, that smile which had overcome status for the briefest of moments to create something which, however transient, she would keep within herself forever.

Locking that moment away like a treasure, she thought again on the future. How would they survive? Mercifully, she finally came to the realization that the answer to that question was beyond her, and only then did she allow herself to sleep well and deeply, leaving the wonders and the worries for another day.

For Beauford, however, it was not so easy to fall asleep. He stayed awake far longer. No logical reason could claim the cause for his insomnia. The bed in which he lay was almost new, stuffed with feathers, and very comfortable. The covers draped over his long, relaxed frame were of the finest quality, smooth to the touch, and warm to his tired limbs.

He was surrounded by all the luxuries his immense wealth had privileged him with. Yet, no matter his possessions, sleep still eluded him. The vision of Lettice Burton smiling at him was playing constantly on his mind. It was as though she had spoken to him through that look, a secret conversation, a look of knowing and of trust—the trust which had at first eluded him, and which he had found himself desperately seeking ever since.

His mind wandered here and there, thinking over Bonville's refusal to assist Letty, his subsequent attack on her, and her brilliant defence. She had been formidable in that moment; her strength had come to the shining fore, and he had seen all her inner beauty so clearly before him, a beauty laced with the vulnerability and pain of her past, but a beauty that had overcome those things with its bravery.

Truly, she captivated him like no other. His brow furrowed. She was in trouble and he could not help, yet he loved her. Oh, how he loved her. He loved her enough to spend the remainder of his life with her.

Would he? Would he marry her? The objections to her status surfaced. He did not even think upon them before casting them aside, acknowledging but choosing to ignore the useless vetoes. It was like a business decision in his head, and despite the disadvantages, his heart was set on accepting the transaction.

It would solve two problems: Letty and her mother-in-law's debts and Beauford's desire to make her his own. What evil could the world say if he were to give money to his own wife? It would be no scandal to pay her debts if she bore his name.

He would happily avert the scandal of giving money to a single widow if he could create another by marrying a woman with no title or fortune! He had caused scandals before, and he had said himself he had no intention of stopping now. This would be the best yet. He smiled to himself, stretching a long arm behind his head.

She was good and honest—had she not looked after that dratted mother-in-law of hers for months? Had she not put up with all of Society's mocking taunts with that quiet dignity which framed her?

She would be his wife, and to hell with everyone else! Besides, had not his relatives—his aunt, mostly—been harping on at him to get married? His family and Society would simply have to accept the disparity in the match.

He had come so close to offering for her in London. If those ill-spoken words at the ball had never been said, he could not begin to imagine where they might be at this moment. So, he had conceived the ambition of taking her as his wife, and he intended to follow it through to the end.

But wait! What about Deveril? Would he approve? He must speak to him soon—tomorrow. After all, how can you get to the lady without persuading her faithful watchdog to allow you?

He smiled again. He had almost been jealous of Deveril, of his familiarity with Mrs. Burton. It was not until he caught him writing some dashed awful poetry to that Gray chit that he had realised Deveril really did hold Letty in almost sisterly affection.

Deveril would surely approve once he knew it was *marriage* the Viscount intended. That was what he hoped, for he would hate to have to marry Letty without Deveril's blessing. But with or without it, he *would* marry her—he was resolved on that at least. The thought of her alone, or worse as someone else's, was unbearable to Beauford. She would be his. As he lay in the bed looking up at the canopy, he realised how much he wanted and desired her. Yes, he would marry her.

Then again, perhaps he was assuming too much. Would she take him? He had all the earthly possessions she could want and a grand title in the bargain. But then, she had said herself she would never marry again—was that still true? How could he blame her after that husband of hers had mistreated her so abominably? It was the same rash vow that Beauford had made himself when in the depths of despair after Corianna...but never mind that. He had not known Letty then, and that changed everything.

Letty would only marry for love, and the only hint she had given of it was that one smile, that one look. Could he really trust so much to a fleeting expression on her face? She did not even believe in love, or so she said. Would she take him if he asked? He did not know, and as the morning calls of birds filled his ears, there was still no answer to his question.

CHAPTER EIGHTEEN

Love is composed of a single soul inhabiting two bodies.
– ARISTOTLE

"I say, I hope I am not interrupting? You look deadly serious, old man." The Major had sauntered into the library, and he was staring at his friend's more than usually tired face.

"Hmm? Ah, yes, Deveril, I need to speak to you. Sit down, will you?"

"If this is about me sending your lad out again with a letter, I'm sorry, but I simply had to send it." He looked like a naughty schoolboy.

"Ha! No, but you certainly are moonstruck, you daft scoundrel! And I'll wager you have not had the courage to talk to Mr. Gray yet about his daughter's hand? You have simply been writing her awful poetry instead?"

"Oh, thank heaven you're not angry about me sending letters! And, of course, I haven't asked yet. I've been attending to you, haven't I? What's the matter then?"

"Well, you know what I said concerning Lettice Burton?"

"No, what was that?"

"You know, when we spoke the other day?"

"Not ringing a bell, old boy." The Major's face was innocent, his eyes wide with expectation.

"Oh, curse it, Deveril! I said I loved her, didn't I?"

The Major chuckled. "Yes, you did. I just wanted to hear you say it again."

"Devil!" Beauford flashed a pair of rueful eyes at his friend before continuing. "Well, I resolved last night to make her an offer."

"What? Not a mistress? She would slap you if you asked her."

"I know—besides, it's not fitting for her. She's not a mistress, she's a wife."

Deveril broke into a generous smile. He had finally realised over the last few days that it was not lust that tormented his friend but real, true love. He had never seen him like this before, and now he was happy to encourage him. "She'll make you an honest man, Beauford. About time, too. So, what's the problem? Worried about where to ask her? Want to get your wording right?"

"Not exactly. You see, now that Bonville's refused to help her, I'm the only one left to settle the debts those wretched Burtons have heaped upon her. I'm more than happy to help her. I have the money, and what better use could I put it to? But as things stand, if I settle her debts now, I will send Society into an uproar. You can imagine the things they will say of her —the reasons why I give her money. But if I marry her, who can say anything about how much money a man settles on his wife?

"The trouble is, I have a sort of worry she will refuse me. I spoke to her in London once, when we watched that surprisingly well-acted play by whatshisname."

"Oh, I know the one you mean. It was there that you stole

Letty away. First time I was worried you had any dishon-ourable intentions concerning her. Mind you, I soon lost the worry when I saw the fury you had put her in. Is that what this is about? What did you say to upset her so?"

"Oh, it was foolish banter—I was trying to draw her out, to study her. When I asked her about her marriage, I saw her defences fly up. It's clear to me now why. That husband of hers was a beast. I half wish I hadn't said it, but, you see, because I knew I'd hit a nerve I carried on, asking her if she would ever marry again. She told me she would never marry and that she did not think love exists." Beauford finished on rather a desperate note and sat back in his armchair, his eyes closed, awaiting the response of his friend.

Deveril, however, was not close to responding. He was far too deep in thought. To give up on love, well, that was to give up on a part of life so integral to a human's being. He had not really taken it seriously when Beauford had repeated Letty's sad words the other day, but now it seemed they could actually affect her happiness. Love is the tie that connects human beings to all things in one form or another. Yet, it was the cruelty and abuse of Letty's husband that had violated that most sacred of emotions and actions. He had broken Letty's trust in love and all that that word entailed. How could one rescue a broken woman when she had no belief in rescue? How could one save her when she had almost no ability to trust another? Curse John Burton! If he had never lived, Letty might now be unscathed. "Curse him!"

"I know." Beauford opened his eyes sadly, his own thoughts having followed the same route as his friend's, and his mind fully aware of whom Deveril cursed.

"So," he said softly.

"Well, I cannot see any other way but to go for it, come what may. I mean, dash it all, if I wasn't lovelorn for Miss Gray, I would make Letty an offer. She is quite a woman, the sort that you would rather find out the answer, be it bad or good, than regret not asking at all."

Beauford murmured agreement.

"Has she given you any indication?"

The Viscount's skin gained a rosy tinge as he thought of her smile the other night. What a ridiculous thing to rely on— a small smile directed at him. Yet, it was trust that he had glimpsed, the most important thing for Lettice Burton to give away.

"I believe so, but I don't want to force her into marriage if I can help it. I will not coerce her by using her money troubles or any other means for that matter." It was as though he were telling himself.

"I doubt that she could be forced. She's stronger than she looks."

"Yes, she is." Beauford spoke softly once again, and his sight drifted from the room as his mind thought of her.

"Today, then—best get it over with." The Major made it sound like some terrifying ordeal. Perhaps it would be. Then again, perhaps not. The Major watched his friend with amusement. The aristocrat first rubbed his palms together, then ran a hand through his dishevelled hair, and finally fiddled aimlessly with his wilted cravat.

"I say, Beauford, got it bad, don't you? What made you change your mind so suddenly? First time you met her you despised her."

The dark eyes of his friend looked up curiously at him. "Did I say that?" He took snuff subconsciously before continuing. "Bizarre! I confess I was never expecting her to be so... full of spirit. I was waiting for the usual insipid conversation of a Society miss—but she instantly disliked *me* for my manners, and who could blame her?

"I never expected her to take such offence and make it known to me, to be so lacking in propriety and timidity. She was not afraid of me or my title. Rather, she was bold and willing to take a stand for what was right. No, in truth Deveril, I do not think I despised her. She confused me, yes, but I believe...I believe I was captivated by her from the very first."

Deveril smiled genially down at his friend, amused that the Viscount's feelings were only just becoming fully known to himself. The Major's thoughts flitted back to his worry over Letty and her relationship with the Viscount. How could he ever have guessed Beauford would actually fall in love with the girl?

"She is the best of women," continued the love-struck man. "She truly is one of the strongest creatures I have ever met."

"To endure Clarissa, one must be!" Deveril emitted a low chuckle.

"Yes, exactly," replied his friend in a deadly serious tone. "That woman! I can hardly abide her and the way she treats Letty."

"Indeed, though Clarissa has her saving points. She is a sort of rough diamond you see, gem underneath and all that." Deveril had a fondness for the old lady despite her faults and felt obliged to defend her.

"I'll believe that when I see it. I mean, for Letty to leave the countryside which she loved and endure the Society in London all in the name of saving her spendthrift mother-in-law from herself! Dash it all, Deveril, she is such a good creature and I...will she have me? No, do not answer! I shall find out soon enough."

Giving his friend the briefest of handshakes and bestowing upon him a look of gratitude, he headed for the door.

Letty was slightly startled by the Viscount's visit, though it did not show beneath her calm control. When he saw her, he stopped a moment on the threshold. She was dressed simply in lilac with rose-tinged cheeks. Her hair had been fastened back carefully, yet still, a few tresses fell gently against the skin of her neck and lay over her shoulders. The smooth, continuous line from forehead to nose-tip, the quick up-turn of her lips, the grace of her slight figure, and the light contained in those all-engaging eyes—every one of these things was absorbed by him.

She encapsulated everything he would ever want, ever need, in a woman—things he had not even known he needed before meeting her, and yet things it now seemed he could not live without. And here she stood before him, in all her God-given beauty, her frank brown eyes asking expectantly why he was here.

Why had he come? Oh, yes! Of course, he had come to offer for her. His mind was in a shambles and, for once, the quick-witted Viscount struggled for words.

"Good afternoon, my lord." She inclined her head formally. He closed the distance between them, striding forward and taking her hand.

The warm roughness of his fingers brushed against her own tired hands. His lips hovered above, and then, taking her by surprise, rested for a second on her skin before being whisked away. This time she did not snatch back her hand; she let him kiss it.

"Good afternoon, Miss May." He seemed peculiarly awkward. His relaxed languor had been replaced by an exacting stiffness. His mouth did not utter a single humourous or scandalous comment, and this behaviour shocked her even more than one of his comments would have.

She offered him a seat in the small, sunny morning room, but he did not take it. Perhaps this was about what had happened last night. Did he mean to bring up the unpleasant scene with Bonville?

She could see a furrow disrupting his dark brow, and those deep, delving eyes of his furtively examining the room, then her, then the room again. She quelled the anxiety of being in a room alone with him. He was such an enigma to her, and it was as though some force drew her to him constantly.

She could still feel where his warm breath had run over the back of her hand. The prickling his lips had left on her skin had not subsided. While her hands were hidden behind her back, she brushed her thumb over the place he had kissed.

"Am I to understand you have come about Mr. Bonville? I am sorry for my impropriety last evening." She bowed her head, believing that he had perhaps rethought his actions.

"Never mind that!" he snapped, his grip tightening on the gloves he held. Then looking up and viewing her again, his brow cleared. "I beg your pardon." He came and took her hand once again, and the look on his face made her long to clasp it tightly to herself. "I meant that you should not fear. Never stand on ceremony with me, please?"

She nodded, relieved, and yet, as she looked in his eyes, her heart was disquieted; its usual steady beat was increasing.

"I did come about your situation, however." He let her hand go and turned away for a moment.

"Yes?" The softness in her voice made him turn and look at her again.

"I wish to help you." He could see rather than hear the sigh of relief; it was in her eyes. "I wish to help you with all your debts now and hereafter, Mrs. Burton." Her old name slipped easily from his lips, and his long legs brought him swiftly back to her side. His face was within inches of her own.

"Letty,"—his voice softened—"I wish to make you my wife, to protect you and care for you...for all of my life."

Her heart was beating furiously now. Her hand lay quivering in his, and her eyes could not leave the floor. She could not describe the feelings that raged like a channel storm inside her.

"I came to your house the night after my ball to apologise for what you heard. I came to offer for you then, but you were already gone. I thought I had lost my chance, dearest Letty, but fate gave me another and you are here."

Two opposing forces of emotion fought against each other, her heart and mind the battlefield. She could not decipher her feelings, or perhaps she did not want to, knowing she would have to make the decision she was dreading. Why did he have to come here now and say these things? What was she to say in return? What could she possibly give him?

She could see her plain gown opposite his gleaming hessians, and suddenly, it was simple. A tear rolled down her pale cheek.

Beauford brushed it gently away with his thumb and, putting a finger beneath her chin, he slowly raised her head until her eyes met his. "I have upset you." His voice was deep and mournful, as though her wound afflicted him also.

Her courage came back a little, and she prayed for strength before speaking. "I cannot marry you." She turned her head as another tear fell. "I will not make you happy."

"Letty, Letty. You are the only woman who could. Before I met you I was bored, reckless, hopeless, but you—you challenged me, made me want to better myself." He chuckled. "And besides, you are the only woman I can stand conversing with for more than five minutes."

It could not make her smile. "My lord." She stepped away from him and took back her hand. "It is easy to think nothing of our differences now, but one day you shall regret your decision. You cannot ally yourself with me. I have no title, no fortune to offer."

"What of it? I have plenty of both. What could I gain by

marrying wealth and titles? And yet if I married you, I would gain something of far more worth. You are the soul of sweet kindness and faithfulness, and I know for all your goodness you have been repaid naught. Rather, you have received burden upon burden, things too heavy for you to bear. I wish to protect you from it, from it all."

He touched her arm and she flinched.

"And as for that," he said bitterly, "I know very well Deveril would put a bullet in me for even thinking of laying a finger on you without your consent. He wanted to protect you from me, until he realised how desperately I love you."

She looked at him then.

"Yes, I am in love with you," he repeated, tenderly cupping her face with his hands. "Letty, let me take you away from these people, away from hurt and pain. I won't promise it shall be perfect."

That is what John had promised. He had said that it did not matter that she was below him. He had told her it would be perfect when they were together. He had lied.

"I am human. I have faults—you already know that."

This drew from her a small, unbidden smile as she remembered their first encounter.

"Letty, come and be my wife."

It sounded like such a simple request. "And your family?" she asked desperately.

"My mother and father are dead, and my aunt, well, she likes anyone with spirit. In fact, she has already told me to go after you on more than one occasion." He smiled longingly at her.

She was not convinced—could she be? Did she love him?

"I...no...no, I cannot. Please,"—her voice wavered—"please leave."

He almost stayed, but the tears in her eyes became his persuasion. He could not cause her pain despite how much he wanted her. He picked up the gloves and hat that he had discarded and bowed, his face grim. And then, he left her.

After the Viscount had gone, Letty almost collapsed. Her hand searched through the midair, desperate to find anything to support it. It found a chair back which she clutched tightly to steady herself. The air that entered her lungs came in ragged gasps. Her mind spun, and she felt as though she were not in control at all.

She landed heavily in the chair. She wanted to cry, and then she wanted to scream. She wanted to disappear. To not exist would be sublime at this moment. At least if she did not exist, then the unbearable pain in her chest would not be hurting her as it was now.

"Lettice May!" she whispered to herself. If she lost control now, if she forfeited her wisdom in this moment of upset, then all of what she had been so strong for would be in vain.

She rose as if someone outside of her was controlling her body and pulled the chair to a large writing desk in the corner of the room. She drew out some paper, dipped her quill, and began to write across the page.

After several minutes she dusted and blotted the sheet and laid it on the mahogany desk. Had it only been moments ago that he had proposed? It seemed like an age since, and yet the feelings were fresh—feelings of pain, of uncertainty in the face of an improbable, if not impossible situation.

She did not know how their debts would be paid now. They were again without hope, and she was the cause. They had been offered a way out but she could not take it if it meant marrying Beauford.

She had done the right thing. Her answer could not be changed. The assurance of that gradually became a foundation beneath her unsteady feet. So, she was certain, no more questioning. She was resolved in her refusal and with this realization came a feeling of sickness, not of the stomach but higher in her chest cavity.

It was accompanied by a feeling of grief, a grief of something lost, something necessary but unattainable. Would she mourn it as she had mourned another? No, it would not be the same. Things would be different now.

She stared into space in silent contemplation, trying to imagine the life she had now decided upon. Thoughts of the past brought sadness to her—thoughts of conversations never again to be undertaken, of jokes left unsaid, of deep feelings that would now be buried deeper still. The ticking of the clock was loud to her ears, the distant thumping as a servant beat out a rug, the clatter of silverware being polished in the kitchen, and that clock forever ticking.

With quick precision she came to life, folded the fine paper, sealed it with the last of the wax she had managed to find, and placed it in the hands of a young chambermaid whose eyes belied her mind's twitching curiosity. Instructions were pronounced for it to be given to a trustworthy footman who should deliver it to Grange Manor. The letter travelled down the large staircase, through a small door, down narrow, soot-stained passages, and into the rough hands of the footman in question. The name written upon the front caused a flurry of gossip in the lower floors: "The Viscount Beauford."

Letty stood in the middle of the frugally furnished room, her letter taken from her. It was over. She felt her stomach hollow and her legs weak, but no matter! She smoothed the creases of her muslin dress, allowing only one tear to trace the line of her smooth cheek. Once it had reached her jaw, she brushed it away, a moment of weakness. Now she had to be strong for Clarissa.

She glanced at her reflection in the looking glass before donning her bonnet and cloak. The same dull brown curls hung about her face in a ruffled fashion, and she tweaked a rather outlandish one into submission. Avoiding looking into her own eyes, she pinched her milky cheeks and turned to leave. Setting off for Clarissa's cottage, she began schooling composure onto her unwilling countenance. She had bitter news to tell her mother-in-law about the debts which must still go unpaid.

CHAPTER NINETEEN

Many waters cannot quench love, neither can the floods drown it.

Deveril did not have to ask the outcome of Beauford's offer when he returned a few hours later. The Major looked his pained friend in the eye, his own face turning grave, and handed him a letter that had just arrived for him. The writing was not familiar to the Viscount, but there was some part of him that knew it could be from her. His heart ached as he read his name across its front.

He held a hand up for Deveril to leave him be and retreated to his library and solitude. Once he was surrounded by the dark, paneled walls and the door was closed to the world, he felt secure. He was able to flick the pathetically small seal easily and in painful silence read the following:

Lord Beauford,
    In regard to the offer of marriage you were so kind as to

honour me with earlier this morning, I have come to a definite decision and wish to confirm it with this letter. I must decline your generous offer respectfully.

As I will not be accepting your offer of marriage, it would be wrong of me to accept your financial help. I ask that you do not become anxious over me and my mother-in-law; we shall survive the situation, I am sure.

I thank you for your kind and devoted care of me and my mother-in-law. For this we shall be forever grateful. We shall remember you.

Lettice May

At first, Deveril did not fully comprehend the effect of Letty's negative answer to the Viscount's offer. By the afternoon, however, he could see that it was nothing short of disastrous. The Viscount had barely spoken, and just before dinnertime he left Deveril to his own devices and went out for a ride, presumably to clear his head. Deveril could have forgiven him his solitude, except that the Viscount disappeared for nearly two days!

As the second afternoon rapidly slipped away and there was still no sign of the wayward Viscount, Deveril, tired of feeling useless, went to the Spencers' home. The Major wished to speak to Letty, not just to see if she was well but to see if she was also insane! Ever since Beauford had returned with his offer rejected, the Major could not, for the life of him, understand why she had said no. What had happened between them for her to turn down an offer that thousands of other girls would leap at? Did she not realise he loved her?

Lady Spencer informed him that Miss May was feeling poorly and had requested a day or two of respite from her duties. She was staying at her mother-in-law's cottage while she recovered her health. The sun was setting fast when Deveril walked across the dusky landscape to Clarissa's cottage. It was somewhat of an unsocial time, but his errand was essential.

"Mrs. B., you do not look well." He took her hand upon entering the room.

"I confess I feel a little under the weather. I am probably just tired." She eyed him as shrewdly as exhaustion allowed and guessed correctly the reason for his visit.

Deveril dropped her hand and paced the room before swinging round wildly. "Do you not love him?"

Shocked, she merely looked on, a little pain showing in her eyes. Several seconds ticked by before she returned an answer. "Major!" Her reprimand was hardly above a whisper. How could she explain to him?

"Now, now, my girl, I am only trying to make sense of why you have refused a man who not only loves you but can care for you in ways you can only imagine. Both are things John never offered."

The mention of her late husband's name still caused painful recollections; it probably always would. The guilt she felt at Deveril's words for refusing the Viscount made her speak. "He is a man of the world. He does not realise the damage it would do to marry me." But she knew the damage. She knew what it had cost her first husband. She knew what her low relations and lower origins would do to Beauford's reputation. She had already lived through it.

"Oh, yes, he bally well does!" returned the Major with fervor. "Do not be blind, Letty, and give the man a little credit." He paused, judging how best to word what he would say next. "You may not know it, but he was very much in love once, about three years ago, when he was just a younger son. It was about that time that his elder brother Edward died, making him the heir. Well, he chased after this chit who was, let's just say, the toast of the Season."

Letty's stomach twisted uncomfortably, she had a feeling she knew who this woman was.

"She accepted his offer. I've known him for a long time, and I've never seen him happier than when this woman said yes. Then, quite suddenly she cried off. It wasn't until a few months later that he realised it was so she would be free to marry a duke who had fallen under her spell."

At the title, duke, Letty knew exactly whom the Major was talking about. It was undoubtedly Corianna, Duchess of Bedford. That explained the anger and pain she had seen in his face when the Duchess had been in close proximity, like the evening at the concert they had attended. He had given the most precious part of himself to her, his heart, and all she had done was trample it underfoot.

"I cannot explain completely what a dark man he was after that. Disappeared almost completely from Society, lost himself in the country for a few years. I think he could not come to terms with the fact she had never loved him, that she had just been in search of a title and found a better one than his. When he finally came back to Town, he never spoke of her or of what had happened, but it was clear to me he did not intend to settle down again. It only made it worse when that old love of his started having affairs all over Town. Even attempted a meeting with him. And in return he threatened to call out her husband for not controlling his wife! Caused quite a scandal, his second scandal, I believe, and as you've seen, not his last."

Letty's heart was racing. She had accused Beauford of being a libertine without understanding the blow that had pushed him down that path. Oh, if only she had known! If only she had used her brain and realised! She felt foolish, and worse, she felt cruel. How much pain had she inflicted on the Viscount unwittingly? At the library in Truro, that was after he had seen Corianna for what she was. It was no longer a mystery why he had appeared such a dark and distressed man.

And those words at the ball she had heard him speak to Corianna? As she traced back over the memory, she had to question her own facts. Had she jumped to conclusions? She had blamed him and caused herself pain for no reason when he had, in fact, taken the honourable route throughout the situation, no matter the scandal that followed him for it.

The Major, who had been watching Letty, spoke again, his voice soft. "So, you see, my dear, him offering for you, it ain't just anything. He really has fallen in love with you. The fact that he wants to clear your name of debts is certain proof. You brought back his old self, his caring side. Y'know," the Major mused, "I believe that is what he is trying to do for you, bring you back." He smiled as fresh tears rolled down her face.

The Major came to her side, laying a warm hand on her shoulder. "Who knew I'd be giving you advice, m'dear? It's usually me taking all your advice for the delightful Miss Gray." His wry mouth curved up into a boyish smile.

Letty looked up through tear-filled eyes at the Major and rested a hand over his. "Thank you," she whispered.

"Now, girlie, I am not about to insult your intelligence by telling you what to do, certainly not. And it is, of course, your choice and will not be an easy one to make, that I know. But you will realise, Beauford is one of the most decent men I know, though he would not have you think it." He chuckled. "I mean it though, he is. And if I were to pick a husband for you who I know would care for you as you deserve—apart from my handsome self, of course—it would be Beauford."

She was studying her hands in her lap now and nodded in understanding as he vouched for his friend. The gap between Viscount and governess seemed to be closing up, and that scared her more than anything.

"Now,"—Deveril spoke in lighter tones—"I do not expect

you have told any of these goings-on to your mother-in-law."
As he came round to face her again, he saw her raise a comical
eyebrow. "Yes, so I will speak to her for you. She will understand all and not become silly if I tell her."

Letty was doubtful, but her heart and mind were in such
turmoil she barely noticed him leaving. Before she knew it
Clarissa was in the room, coming towards her with arms
outstretched, and for once she did not utter one word! The
Major was more capable than Letty had given him credit for.

The last she saw of the Major was his figure in the doorway
with a smile on his face and—was that a nod of satisfaction?

Letty, left in Clarissa's care, was hugged and petted and
comforted for hours. The older woman never once
mentioned herself, showing the same devotion for Letty as
Letty had shown for her. It seemed Clarissa had had some
supernatural revelation filling her with empathy for her
daughter-in-law; either that, or it had arisen during the stern
talk with Major Deveril. Letty did not know which was the
case, and to be frank, at this point, it was the least of her
thoughts.

She was crying. She was crying over the marriage that had
left her damaged, she was crying over Society's taunts that had
cut her deeper than she had known or realised, and she was
crying over a man she had refused because of her fear that she
might have fallen in love again. She was like a shaken and jolted
bottle of champagne, and somebody had just popped the cork.
She felt relief as she finally grieved.

Her mother-in-law continued to hold her tightly. After
years in Society, mixing with every person of quality and
enjoying the finest goods money could buy, Clarissa would
never have guessed she would be here now. She had had everything she wanted, and in a few meagre years had lost it all. Yet,
despite all her reversals of fortune, this small wisp of a girl had
stayed beside her. She had been there when Clarissa had lost all

hope. She had listened patiently to all the bitter old woman had moaned and groaned over.

Despite her constant thoughts about herself, Clarissa had not been blind to the character and work of her loyal daughter-in-law. She had watched as Letty had navigated Society. She had seen the girl turn the heads of many, few without admiration on their faces. But not once had she seen this frailty in her. Clarissa had shown her pain and suffering openly, but Letty had taken everything life had given her quietly.

In spite of all of her failings, Clarissa was not stupid. Though she had chosen to ignore it, she had seen John's handiwork upon Letty. She had been a mother who had watched her son become something no mother wishes to see. And, as much as she wished to lay the blame at another door besides her own, she could not. She knew that decisions made, long ago, by her and Percy had affected their sons very negatively. Despite wanting the best for their sons, they had valued things which now held no value, and they had neglected the things which were priceless.

Well, Clarissa was not able to change the past, but she would certainly change the future. She could see her failings more clearly now, and she did not intend to moan over them in self-pity. She intended to learn from them.

"I know John was not always a good husband, my dear, but...well, it seems to me that it should not stop you from loving again." Dawn's sharp colours began to pierce the night sky as Clarissa finally spoke. "I know it seems like you may not have what a viscount's bride should have in the way of connections and fortune, but he has enough for both of you. Letty, he can give you a home, a name to cover your past, and a family." She swallowed hard to keep from mentioning the debts that hung over her own head. "Why pass that up, my child? For you cannot wait for me to have more sons! Heaven knows that will not be happening soon." The old widow chuckled, rubbing Letty's back again and again like she would a babe's.

Letty did not look up, but she had been listening. How many hours had passed or what time it was now she did not know. The tears were dried on her face. "But I refused him."

"And? So what? Go to him. It is true you cannot ask, but, well, you can stand in front of him until he asks you again, can you not? My child, you should not be afraid of the past. This man, you love him; he can bring you out of the past. You will always regret not taking this opportunity that God Almighty has given you for a fresh start if you do not grasp it, my dear." Clarissa was back in all her imperious form, and yet she still cradled Letty to her. She rocked her as one would a child, until strength and courage returned.

That burst of forcefulness was what Letty had needed. She felt her strength returning to her. Clarissa was right—did not God give chances in order for one to take them?

Once the sun was risen in the morning sky, the young woman, wrapped in a cloak, her hair down and quite forgotten, walked out the door of Clarissa's cottage, Grange Manor her destination.

The sky was white, yellow, and blue, a canvas blurred by the cool colours of the dawn. Letty shivered as she looked up at the warm sun that had not yet worked its wonders upon the cold landscape surrounding her. A low-hanging mist floated above the grass, its lazy tendrils rolling over the small hills and shrubs.

She softly stepped on moss and twigs, all damp with the morning dew. Her footsteps were steady though her body was quaking. Birds called out early morning songs from the heady heights of the oaks and sycamores. They heralded the birth of a new day, all different songs joining together in chorus.

And, up ahead, beyond the swathes of well-cut, grassy banks, stood Grange Manor. Its soft yellow stone was shaking off the morning dew, readying itself for the warmth of full daybreak.

Beauford had spent a restless night yet again. He had arrived back from his ride a few hours before dawn and tried to gain a little sleep. It was two days since Letty had turned him down and in that time, although his mind had been in pieces, his body had been to London and back. The room was too cold, then too hot—too cluttered and then ghostly in its emptiness. He stared into the darkness of the room and traced the outline of the phantom objects it contained. Maybe he was looking for answers, answers to the feelings inside him which would not let him rest.

Had he not done what was right and honourable? He had stood before that woman and asked her to give him the right to love her. He felt angry and betrayed. But at the same time, his heart still overflowed with a deep love for that woman which he could not banish from his being. He had wanted to bring her out of the life she was leading and give her something new, but she had not wanted it. He looked at the situation from every angle, and still he could find no answer, he could see no solutions, and worse, he could do nothing.

Finally, rising before the rest of the house, he dressed himself again in riding clothes. He pulled the garments on roughly, as though causing himself physical pain would staunch the emotional pain he felt in the rest of his body. In his viciousness, he ripped a seam beneath the arm on his shirt. He ignored it—what did it matter? What did anything matter anymore? He did not bother with the collar or a cravat. One did not have to impress the woodland with fine attire. Better still, one did not have to worry what the woodland would think of him dressed like this. He reached for the familiar leather of his riding boots and drew them over his calves.

Finally, with a riding coat slung clumsily over his shoulders, he headed for the stables. The door of his bedroom opened without a sound, and he slipped into the faintly lit corridor. As he came to the wooden banister of the great stairs which led to the hall, he paused. The wall paintings and portraits which lined the hall's walls were all cast in half shadows. The sparse furniture of this grand entrance was lost to the dark edges, and the room looked more hollow than it ever had before. It was like him, dark and empty inside. He moved on. His wooden heels clicked on the stairs, on the hall's marble floor, and then outside, on the wide flagstones of the stable yard.

He knew where he was going. He crossed over the straw-strewn yard and ignored the inquisitive heads of the carriage horses in their stalls. His hand nearly drew back a bolt, but before he entered his favourite horse's box, he noticed something with the corner of his eye.

There, just beyond the gravel path which wound around the outside of the stable yard, stood a figure. At first, he ignored the intruder. It was probably an under gardener or grounds-man, but when the figure did not move and kept standing there, silent and still, he turned to face it. He was in no mood for a disturbance of any kind; his temper would not stand for it. He looked squarely in the interloper's direction, determined to scare the servant back to work. But when he took sight of the figure, there was no mistaking her.

She saw recognition in his eyes and dropped the hood of her cloak. The fabric fell back onto her shoulders and exposed her face, framed only by her unbound hair. She watched his eyes taking her in, she watched his body turn towards her, but she still simply stood, waiting for him to move, to say something to her.

He was walking towards her now. His buckskin breeches whisked together as his determined stride led him ever closer. He stopped before her. She could smell him and see the roughness of his unshaven chin. She could see the dark shadows beneath his eyes which told of little sleep, and she could see those dark brown eyes which held a deep longing which he no longer hid from her. Her heart had felt like the hoof beats of a racing horse, and now he was before her it stopped in her chest.

"I...." She breathed in. She could not do this, she was sure, but then it came, as though the words were gushing from her like a fountain. "I am in love with you."

It was only whispered, but he heard. There was a moment in which they stood, their eyes interlocked, unsure if this was dream or reality. Then the hard set of his face crumbled, and his lips drew into a crooked half-smile while light dawned in his dark eyes.

"Is this a new answer for me?" The smile invaded his husky voice. He saw her nod shyly once.

"But what about Clarissa?" she said suddenly. The truth was out, and now she was worried about so many things, so many people.

"She'll be taken care of, do not worry." He moved closer to her; dew flecked his boots as they stepped through the grass.

"And what will people say?"

"Does it matter?" He took another step.

"And Frederick and Cecile? How will they get on without me?"

"Lettice?" He tipped her chin up as he came closer than he had ever been to her.

She could feel him, his presence, his heat.

"They can find someone else." He finally stood so close his coat was touching her cloak and his chest was mere inches from her own. "I however, cannot." His hand encircled her waist. "You are safe now," he said, planting one soft kiss on her forehead.

She relaxed against him for a moment, feeling the firmness of his body, the strength of his arms about her, and then, realizing what was happening, she stiffened slightly.

He released her immediately and looked into her eyes, reassuring her. "It's all right, you are safe." He embraced her gently again. He would have to be patient, very patient. And then, tentatively, he dropped a kiss upon her lips. But it would be worth it, of that he was sure.

CHAPTER TWENTY

Re-deem - to fulfil; to set free, rescue, or ransom; to make up for; to restore the honour, worth, or reputation.

The door opened and light flooded the dim world within. The warmth of the sun swam into the chapel, breathing life into the cold stone floor and near-empty pews. When the door swung wide, more of the sun's light shone in, illuminating the pure white of the bride's wedding gown, outlining the intricacies of the lace, and radiating through the gossamer veil.

The bride was ready for her bridegroom. She stood waiting in the archway, silhouetted by the morning sun, her face hidden for a moment. A handful of the simplest and yet most beautiful flowers were clasped in her small hands, chosen for him—chosen for him to delight in.

The sound of music drew her through the doors where the few churchgoers sitting in the pews could see her, her beauty, and her grace—all of which had been seen by the groom long ago, in his first meetings with her. These were her gifts to him, but what was he giving her in return?

He was giving her hope.

And it was clear, as she walked down the aisle toward her waiting groom, that the hope which he had caused to flower inside her was now enabling her to blossom. She no longer wore the dark clothes she had once donned. She would no longer be associated with her past. She had been given a dress of the purest white, and it was more than just a bridal day tradition.

Every step which drew her closer to him drew her out of her old life. She was discarding the name she had once borne; she was discarding who she was before she had met him. From this day forward she would be somebody different, shaped and molded by her past and yet beautifully new to her groom.

He had rescued her. He had fulfilled her debts. He was restoring her honour with his name. He would set her free from her past and release her into her new future.

And there, now she could see it, the face of her groom. She looked upon the face which held compassion, gentleness, and love. She looked upon the face which had looked upon her first. She looked him in his tender eyes and felt the assurance and certainty of her future.

No more would she worry. No more would she cry at night, not knowing what the next day would bring. No more was she alone in this world.

The journey had been long and hard. She had been scarred and pained. But now she stood restored, loved, and ready for her groom. There had been trials, there had been days when she thought she could not go on. She had stumbled and lost her way before finding it again. And now, here she was, before him.

He looked upon his bride. He looked and drank in the sight he had waited and longed for. His heart had broken over her. He had worked and toiled for this bride and at last she was here. Where she lacked, he had excess, and yet, she was everything he wanted. He had waited to cherish her, to live with her and love her.

What was she to him? She was the obscurer of past sins. No longer would they mark him, nor the bitterness that came before. Where wounds ran deep, she would be the balm. She would bring him back to his former self. Betrayal had left its scars, but with her faithfulness she would erase them. Where he had looked for fulfillment in debauchery, he would now find it in her. She would hold him captivated by her strength, by her purity of mind and spirit, and by her compassion. And he would hold her with his hands.

Now he could see her face. The veil lifted slowly, and her radiant beauty shone upon him. He could see the joy in his bride, the peace and the happiness. Beneath this joy, he could see her longing for him. Her heart burned for him as his did for her. They were here, they were ready.

They took hands and stood beside one another to make their vows before God.

EPILOGUE

I am my beloved's and my beloved is mine.

THE GOOD OLD BOOK

A SERIES OF LETTERS SENT BETWEEN
1816 AND 1817:

D*ear Sophie,*
     It has been such an age since we last spoke and more still has happened, except this, I think, you will not believe at all. I only hope you are not angry with me, for you were not there on the day that made me the happiest of women. Yes, you must have guessed correctly, I am married. To whom, will be slightly harder for you to guess, I expect, but here it is: you are currently corresponding with the new Viscountess Beauford! I do not say it to boast; no indeed, I think I hardly can comprehend it myself. But you see, he thought it only best to elope, for we would be so covered by scandal anyway it would be better to just be wed

before God and forget the peering eyes of Society. In fact, we have both decided that the best thing to do is to stay in the country for a good while until London forgets about us and our unusual love story.

I would still have loved it, however, if you could have been there, my dearest friend. It was so wonderful, and my only regret was that you could not share the day with me. Still, no need to be moping for I am writing to you now, and within this letter I am sending an invitation for you to come and stay. Acceptance is mandatory!

Have no fear for old Mrs. Burton. She is quite happily installed in the gatehouse here. It may seem a little cruel to put her there alone, but she has with her a friend whom she made while I was a governess. I believe they discuss the village's goings-on quite incessantly while they are together, which is almost every day. In fact, it has become such a ritual that I was dismissed from Clarissa's presence when I came to visit her the other day, for I would be interrupting her conversation with her friend. I believe it was very important, something about a scullery maid stealing table linens at a nearby residence! She is quite happy living where she is, and, if I am honest, which I can be with you if with anyone, my husband told me quite firmly that he would rather live in the stables than share a house with "that bossy and loud woman". I confess it quite made me laugh how serious his face was when he spoke those words. I have been gracious with him, for I know Clarissa's company is sometimes an acquired taste.

I beg your pardon for talking about myself for several sheets, and I beg you, please write soon and tell me what has been happening with you.

Your selfish but very interested friend,

Lettice

(Although I have a title now I do not wish to use it—it makes me sound old and rather fearsome.)

Dear Major,

I wanted to write to you briefly to tell you how much I am in your debt. You were right—I have married a man who loves me, and it was you who encouraged me to do so. I do not know how to thank you enough.

You would not believe what he did for me and Clarissa. He has cleared our debts—all of them! The very day I refused his offer of marriage he still rode to London and settled the debts we owed. That was when he thought me unloving, or at least indifferent towards him. What you knew then, I know now—how wonderful a man he is!

You need not reply, for your answer is not needed. I know the answer already in my heart.

From a friend you helped,

Lady B.

(You may call me by that initial once again!)

Dearest Letty,

I can, in fact, well believe that you are wed to the Viscount Beauford. I have been praying for a good long while that you two would finally see each other's worth! And you would not believe it, but I also have news of my own—I am soon to be married to Mr. Simpkin! I do not know if you remember me speaking to you of him, but he is the red haired gentleman who laughs a lot (whether at me or not I will never know!). I understand that you could not have a wedding to which everyone was invited, and, from the sounds of it, it was a wedding that suited both you and the Viscount utterly! However, I hope to see you both at my own wedding. Please bring along dear old Mrs.

Burton, and if the Major comes too, it will be like old friends reunited once again.

As you can see, I have returned Maria to you. I shall indeed miss her plaiting my hair at night, but I told you I would return her to you when you could keep her again. It thrills me to be able to even say that. Although, I have to say, I do not know if I shall ever overcome my fear of the Viscount. He is such a dominating man; I shall always feel as though I am an ant to him!

In other matchmaking news, have you heard whether the Major has proposed and been accepted by the darling Miss Gray? They go so well together, do you not think? One with all the common sense and the other with none—I shall leave you to choose which. What has come over me? I do apologise. I am afraid that the delight of receiving a letter from you is making me say things you would say. I only hope my dear Mr. Simpkin will not mind. Indeed, he may laugh. That is him now at the door! I shall seal this letter before he can see it—it is not that I do not trust he will still love me, I just do not wish to disappoint....

Love,
Sophie.

Dearest Sophie,

I have good news! You must swear to keep it a secret, but it seems the Major has told my dear husband that he intends to propose to Miss Gray next week! Oh, how exciting, and how very satisfying, for it seems the Major has been making quite the fool of himself while he's been wooing the dear girl. He sends her endless poetry and lots more nonsense far worse with which I will not offend your ears.

But how rude of me to begin a letter to you starting with the Major—indeed, I am so silly! I wanted to say how much Beauford and I enjoyed your wedding. It was very beautiful and you looked a vision. I even heard the Major whisper to my husband how lovely you looked as you took your place before the altar. I hope you are well and have had a wonderful honeymoon; you went to Kent, I believe? How was it? Was the weather good while you were away?

And I need most to thank you for returning Maria to me. It is so wonderful to see her, and I am happy to say our reunion was marked by tears! She was shocked, as you can imagine, on arriving at the Viscount's country seat. I doubt she has ever seen anything so grand. Well, I have not, in any event!

When you come and visit you will see it for yourself, but let me just tell you, you are in for an architectural treat! Both the interiors and exteriors of the house are stunning. I have never seen so much marble and mahogany used in one dwelling place.

The Viscount has given me a suite of rooms he said used to belong to his mother. They are so very beautiful, Sophie, and when you come to visit I shall take you through them. They are known as the duck egg blue chambers.

I am so looking forward to seeing you, hearing you, and embracing you once again, my friend! Four weeks is far too long a wait to see your sweet face again.

Waiting most improperly impatiently,
Your friend,
Lettice

Dear Lady Beauford,

How queer to be calling you a "lady", Letty. I never would have thought it! Well, congratulations, I am sure. You have caught yourself a Viscount! I still remember seeing him at the library in Truro when I was with you—how very long ago that seems! I only hope he is not as odious now as he was then.

Now, for my news: I have been settled in my parents' resi-

dence for almost a year, and how very dull it has been too. There have only been as many as five single gentlemen come this way in the last six months. At least, that was until a Regiment came into town. Oh, Letty, their scarlet coats and tall black hats—I declare that they are the finest looking men in all of England!

I would love to see you again. I know we parted on bad terms and for that I am sorry. I was just so unhappy in not going to Town, and look, I have been proved right by you marrying so advantageously! If my parents had allowed me to come, why then I might be the one signing my name Lady Beauford on this letter. But it's no use dwelling on it. I should still be delighted to see you if you could find it in your heart to invite me to stay.

Your former sister,
Theodora Burton

Deveril,

You would not believe the uproar my new wife has made in my house. Dash it all, I thought the woman a quiet thing, but it seems she has grown more into her voice since we wed!

The other day was yet another example when Letty's former maid arrived from somewhere or other. I have no idea what all the fuss was about, but when my wife received her, she was positively gushing over the girl, though I have to say for her size the maid is a surprisingly efficient little thing.

Congratulations on getting yourself engaged. I confess I am slightly surprised the girl said yes, but life always surprises one immeasurably. For instance, I am surprising myself as I write now to invite you to come and stay with us for a few weeks—I have little idea as to how I shall stand your lovesick swooning, but no matter, the invite is written now.

Come when you will.

Beauford

Beauford,
    I will be up tomorrow.
    Deveril

Dear Lady Beauford (Lettice),

I thank you from the bottom of my heart for a most enjoyable few weeks. Apart from the lack of my darling Miss Gray, I wanted nothing. It was such a pleasure to be around friends once again. I have missed you two terribly in London, but I think staying away from Society was definitely for the best. Beauford seems far happier, and so do you. I love to think it was by my fair hand that you are both now so happily situated—and now I am far away I can say so without the likelihood of being swatted for it!

Sophie seems happy too. I was glad you invited her down at the same time. We shall have to do it again, for I was the only one without a spouse. That Simpkin fellow is rather a good sort, though a trifle serious at times. I think that must be why Miss Egleton, or rather Mrs. Simpkin now, looks upon him with such awe in her eyes! Oh, it is love indeed!

Now, last arrangements for the wedding: I wish for Beauford to be my best man, but he is dashed awful at organizing things, as I guess you are realizing. So if you could only make sure he is there on time that would be a godsend.

I must dash now—I have to go for tea with my future father and mother-in-law. I daresay they know more about the wedding details than I do, for my dear Miss Gray has left me completely and utterly in the dark about the whole thing. Thank you again, and I shall see you soon.

Your faithful friend,
Major Deveril

My Dear,

I am writing to you, as I believe this is the only way to get your attention away from your writing desk despite the fact I am seated merely feet away. Would you do me the honour of taking a turn with me in the garden before lunch? No need to reply—you simply cannot resist my charms.

B.

Letty picked up the piece of paper pushed at her by her husband and leant back in the chair to read it.

"Oh, I see, I am just to obey you, am I?" she chuckled.

"Most certainly. Come, we must leave this dark morning room for the brightness of the outdoors. It will do you both good."

"Very well." She allowed a coy smile to play about her lips. "Let me just finish writing this letter to Sophie."

The Viscount made a face filled with mock horror before dropping a hand gently onto his wife's shoulder and playing with a tendril of her hair. She sat forward again and picked up the quill. Before she resumed writing, she rested a tentative hand upon the swelling of her stomach and read through the beginning of her letter—

Dear Sophie,

I am writing so soon after you have just visited because I have some wonderful news....

The End

AUTHOR'S NOTE

I hope you have enjoyed reading *The Widow's Redeemer* as much as I have loved writing it. One thing rather interesting about the plot of the book is that it is actually based on the book of Ruth in the Bible.

Ruth is one of my favourite biblical characters. She is a young, non-Jewish woman who marries a Jewish man and begins to believe in God. Her husband dies while she is still young, and instead of staying in her native land, she travels with her Jewish mother-in-law Naomi to Bethlehem in Israel. Naomi and her family had abandoned Israel during a famine many years earlier, but when she returns with Ruth, the land is bountiful. This is in stark contrast to Naomi who has lost her family, her land, and her home. Naomi renames herself Mara (meaning "bitter"), and the two women live in a cave in Bethlehem.

To provide for her mother-in-law, Ruth leaves during the day to find food. She goes to a nearby field, and, after the harvesters have made their bushels, she goes around and picks up the leftover ears of grain to take back to Naomi. One day, while she is working in the fields, Boaz, the owner of the land, sees her and asks his foreman who she is. The foreman tells his master that she is a foreigner who returned to Israel with her mother-in-law. Intrigued, Boaz instructs his foreman to tell the harvesters to leave more grain on the ground so that she will have enough and to give her a drink if she needs it.

When Naomi finds out it is Boaz's field in which Ruth has been gleaning, she tells Ruth that Boaz is a far relation of her family. Naomi then tells Ruth that she must go to Boaz and ask him for help. Ruth listens to her mother-in-law, and as night falls she goes to the threshing floor, a place reserved for men. Weary after their work in the fields, the men are all sleeping soundly. Ruth finds Boaz and lies at his feet while he sleeps. Startled, Boaz awakes and asks Ruth why she has come to him. Her answer? So that he can redeem them by buying back the land which had once belonged to Naomi and by taking Ruth as his wife.

Boaz is eager to help, but there is another relative who is more closely connected to Ruth and Naomi, and in Jewish law, the other man must be given the chance to help first. Boaz goes to the closer relative and asks the man whether he will redeem Naomi's family's land. The man replies that he will. But when Boaz tells him he will also have to marry the foreigner Ruth if he redeems the land, the man immediately declines. He does not wish to marry a non-Jewish woman. I imagine Boaz must have been pretty happy at that reply since I believe he wanted to marry Ruth himself!

Boaz returned to Ruth and told her that he would marry her. They married and had sons together. Naomi's family land was redeemed, and Boaz and Ruth looked after her in her old age.

It is a simple story, but it is also one of the great romantic stories of the Bible—a story of real love, compassion, and courage. Ruth shows herself to possess great character and strength. She leaves her homeland to follow her mother-in-law and a God she has only just come to know. She travels to a land and people completely alien and then, even though she is a woman, takes it upon herself to go out and provide food for herself and Naomi. She shows courage again when she goes to Boaz in the middle of the night. Her actions would have been just as scandalous then as they would have been in Regency England! She showed such bravery, and that is one of the reasons I admire her so much.

Then there is Boaz, a man moved to compassion when he sees a young, foreign widow working so hard. He is honourable in his actions, and he ultimately falls in love with a good woman and marries her.

When I was younger, I read books by Francine Rivers, one of which was *Redeeming Love*, a story based on the book of Hosea set in the Wild West. I loved the idea of writing a Bible story in the Regency period, and I was inspired to write the story of Ruth.

I have always loved Regencies; there is something about the etiquette, the richness of the period, and the wonderfully witty word-sparring which made me want to write in the genre. Not all of the story of *The Widow's Redeemer* is completely true to the book of Ruth since I had to change a few parts to fit into the Regency time period. However, I hope you can see the main story is still there, a story of God's love for us and the redemption He can give. Again, I hope you enjoyed the book!

With love,
Philippa Jane Keyworth

REVIEW THIS BOOK

Thank you for reading *The Widow's Redeemer*.

If you enjoyed it, please share your review on Amazon, BookBub or Goodreads to help other readers find my book.

FREE CHAPTER
THE UNEXPECTED EARL

"It was a letter..."

BLACK HOOVES STRUCK THE COBBLESTONES IN rapid succession, the sound echoing into the London night. Torch-light caught the well-polished flanks of the pair pulling the carriage, their ebony coats stained even darker with sweat and their heads bobbing up and down as they made quick work of the streets. On either side of the travelling carriage, the Town houses climbed high into the midnight, an avenue of sleeping giants. Tucked away inside the buildings, the owners were either entertaining guests or else enjoying a breath of quiet before the bustling London Season truly began.

On went the carriage. The houses and squares disappeared into darkness while bright lights illuminated the destination ahead.

The driver headed towards the lights as fast as the cobbled streets would allow. The autumn had begun mild, but tonight was proof of the progression towards deep winter. The horses' breath escaped in plumes from their nostrils. The heavy great-coat that the driver had donned in place of his summer livery warded off the majority of the cold, but fingers of icy air still managed to find their way around his neck. Blast it! How could he have forgotten his woolen scarf on a night like this?

The occupants of the carriage fared slightly better. Protected from the cold wind, two gentlemen sat across from each other on the cushioned seats, both in evening attire. One lounged comfortably, but the taller, darker of the two kept his arms crossed over his chest and threw frequent glances out of the window.

"Curse it all, Courtenay! How long does it take to get to Almack's?"

The ill-natured question only served to make the other gentleman smile, his rounded cheeks bulging on either side of his mouth. "Oh, you are in a sour mood tonight, Wolversley."

The taller man scowled in return. "You would be too if you had travelled all the way from Sussex only to have your best friend cart you off to the most boring charade of polite Society."

"You're lucky there is no one to hear you say so. I declare, if one of the patronesses heard your description of their hallowed rooms, your voucher would be revoked!"

A jolt on the near side of the carriage upset the occupants for a moment until the vehicle settled into its regular motion again.

"Besides," Courtenay continued after repositioning himself, "how can you be in a bad mood? You have been away from Society all this time, not even bothering to come back to Town for Viscount Beauford's ball, and now you are back to civilization and dinner parties and masquerades and all things marvelous, and you're miserable! I tell you, I do not understand you."

That last bit was a barefaced lie. Lord Courtenay understood his old university friend very well—which is exactly why he had refrained from telling him that their destination for the evening was not, in fact, Almack's. They were en route to a private ball, the sort of event that Wolversley rarely attended, preferring his estate and account books to most kinds of social engagements. Part of Courtenay did not blame him. After all, it was not an easy thing to mix with your peers when you had a past like Earl Wolversley's.

"You make a mistake in thinking my misery is connected to being in London. Rather it's connected to you whisking me away from a large bottle of Burgundy I had at home. It could have kept me far better company than you will this evening."

"Oh, a dagger to the heart! I am so hurt." Courtenay's lips gave an affected pout. "But in truth, you did surprise me. I half thought you'd refuse to come out, even at *my* invitation."

Wolversley snorted, muttering something about rather being under the table at home, and then finally mustered up some kind of civility. "I suppose I *am* pleased to see you again. My sister, though pleasant company, is somewhat exhausting when she assumes I am her sole entertainment on the estate."

"Ah, the lovely Selina, I wish I could see her again." Courtenay's eyes went misty in the dim light of the carriage and his tone turned wistful.

"I expect you do," said Wolversley dryly, "but I shall not let you near her until she is out and until some of that naïvety is rubbed off. You are far too much of a scoundrel for her company at present."

"Well, no matter, we shall have plenty of schoolroom misses where we're going."

"Almack's? It's all rather staid don't you think? Hardly the place for you to make young chits swoon."

"Ah, well...that is the thing...." Courtenay looked down at his black silk breeches moulded tightly over his podgy thighs and below those to his astonishingly elegant feet encased in evening pumps. The thing was—although he was dressed in the requisite uniform of Almack's, one of the most exclusive assembly rooms in London, he had never intended to go there.

Now came the sticky part.

"I actually thought we could take advantage of an invita-

tion I received. It's to a somewhat better place than Almack's."
He was trying his best to seem nonchalant while revealing his
deception. "It's a coming-out ball. I know your distaste for this
kind of thing, but it will be a splendid evening. I was assured
by the father of the debutante that his wife was sparing no
expense. All the beauties of Society will be present, and I
daresay one might even catch your eye, despite your habitual
insistence on prolonging your bachelorhood."

Wolversley's anger had been growing steadily as Courtenay
unfolded their new plans for the evening, and due to that last
comment, he was positively seething. "You ass! How dare you
lie to me?"

"It's for your own good, my friend, I promise." Courtenay
shifted a little farther away from the Earl who looked ready to
round on him. "You know, since you've been away from
Town, there have been plenty of young bachelors trying to
usurp your place as the most eligible gentleman this side of
thirty. I had to take it upon myself to hold that position until
you came back."

Wolversley's lips curved up into a crooked smile, "You did,
did you?" If there had been more light in the carriage,
Courtenay would have seen Wolversley's pale gray eyes begin
to dance.

"Yes, because I am a dear, dear friend."

"And a dear, dear liar." Wolversley sighed. "How on earth
could you be deemed an eligible bachelor with your estate
teetering precariously between dun territory and utter ruin?"

Courtenay could hear the Earl's anger turning to amusement, and he took advantage of his friend's improved temper.
"Ah, it's all about wording it right, my good man." He leaned
forward and waggled his finger under the Earl's nose. "But
since I am a faithful friend who cannot help but see to your
best interests, I will allow you to reclaim your position. You

need to come out into Society again somewhat, reclaim at least a semblance of a figure in the best circles, if only to ensure you can someday get yourself betrothed and all that."

Wolversley grimaced, but his face was obscured by the shadows in the carriage. He had been betrothed once. He did not have any intention of finding himself in that position again.

"Besides," continued Courtenay, "I have it on good authority that Jonny Odd is attending Almack's tonight."

Wolversley grimaced again. Courtenay was adept at stirring up unpleasant memories. The two of them—or rather, the three of them—had attended university during the same period. Jonny Odd had never liked the Earl, making him the object of many of his taunts and practical jokes. Graduation and the intervening years had done nothing to improve their acquaintance. The man was an ass and Wolversley quite agreed with Courtenay that he was best avoided.

"So, I thought the ball the better invitation of the two. And of course, if you should manage to find a little amusement there to entice you back into Society, then all the better."

Before the Earl could question Courtenay about their actual destination, their journey was over. The horses ceased their spanking trot, the hoof beats slowed from two to four beats, and the carriage came to a dignified halt.

"Ah, we are arrived. Excellent." Courtenay peered out of the window at the Palladian Town house lit up by hanging lanterns.

Outside, the driver relinquished his tight hold on the reins, giving the slack back to his horses. He pulled the collar of his greatcoat up about his ears and blew on his hands. The groom was not long in performing his duties, and soon the steps were down. The door swung wide, and Lord Courtenay's elegant foot and shapely calf descended, followed by his rather larger upper half.

Courtenay's countenance was now lit by the lanterns held by the servants either side of the door. His avid consumption of wine showed in his pinkish face, and he had a rosy tint to the end of his nose. That being said, it could not be denied that Lord Courtenay was a good-looking man with a good-natured face. As he reached the ground, he swung round to await his friend.

"A coming-out ball, you said?" Wolversley called, descending the carriage steps. He glanced up at the house, not waiting to listen to Courtenay's response. He was too intent on stifling the unpleasant memories that his friend had dredged up. As he caught sight of the building, however, a sickly feeling began to invade his body. He glanced up and down the street, trying to ascertain if they were in fact standing where he suspected—and feared—they might be.

"It is indeed, and in honour of a beautiful young girl I'm told." Courtenay slapped a hand on the Earl's athletic shoulders, ignoring the unsettled look that had painted itself across his face. "I am jolly glad you're back in Town. It's been dashed dull without you, believe it or not. Despite your moods, you do make a man much better company than these jumped-up young scamps running about the clubs and balls these days."

Wolversley neither felt umbrage at the insult nor gratitude at the compliment. It was all quite lost on him as he kept looking up at the house, determined to believe he was anywhere other than where his mind told him he must be.

"Where are we exactly?" he managed at last.

"Wiltshire Square."

Wolversley cursed.

"I say!" exclaimed Courtenay, looking around uncomfortably. "Bad form, old man."

Fortunately, there were no ladies in earshot, but two young bucks who had just alighted from a nearby carriage ceased their jocular conversation to raise eyebrows at Wolversley's uncouth remark. One of them looked the Earl up and down and snorted unfavourably.

The Earl, who took no pleasure in being so brazenly measured, felt a stab of annoyance as the young man's appraising gaze fell fearfully short of impressed. It was not just the crude language the Earl had used that caused his disdain; it was the Earl's jacket. Wolversley could feel the young man's eyes on his shoulders and lapels as his lips curled up in scorn.

Wolversley had been in the country too long. His jacket was outdated—he had known that when he had put it on this evening, having already seen several gentlemen walking the streets of Town in far more modish creations. He enjoyed a well-cut jacket, though he would not claim the careful eye of a dandy where his appearance was concerned, but his extended trip to the country had left him no opportunity to ensure that his wardrobe was full of the current fashions, nor to cut his hair for that matter. The luxuriously dark lengths were tickling his collar, unlike Courtenay's sandy locks which were swept up into a form of the Brutus, a style far too ostentatious to be attractive. Wolversley looked back to the young men. Those scrutinizing eyes that would not forgive his outdated clothing were one reason he disliked Society gatherings so much, and yet, thanks to the cajoling—and chicanery—of a particular friend, he was back.

The Earl glared at the young buck who did not approve of him, but it seemed that he had already forgotten the Earl's existence as he turned to go up the stairs to the house. Wolversley looked back at his friend. His jacket was a very minor problem compared to the one presented by his location.

He knew exactly where he was. He knew exactly whose house this was. And if his exacting knowledge was correct, he was in quite a deal of hot water.

Courtenay, having missed most of this unvoiced exchange

thanks to a beautiful young woman stepping out of a carriage four spaces down—waved his hand at their waiting vehicle and ordered his driver to come back later.

The driver tipped his hat and then took this last chance to pull his collar up. After his neck was protected as well as it could be from the elements, he whipped up the horses and returned the way they had come.

The Earl stared at the departing carriage, his only method of retreat disappearing into the foggy London evening. Several more people emerged from carriages and chairs along the length of the street. Mothers and fathers shepherded young daughters past the two men towards the open door of the house.

Courtenay smiled at his friend. "Shall we go in?"

"A moment." Wolversley held up a hand. "It would perhaps be best for me to know who the hosts of this ball are, seeing as I am arriving on their doorstep uninvited." He struggled to maintain an even tone.

"Oh, well, the funny thing is, someone I was talking to the other day seemed to think you might know them. It is the delightful Miss Annabelle we are welcoming into the affectionate arms of Society this evening, but the family name is Rotherham."

Wolversley cursed again, this time under his breath. "You should have told me where you were taking me this evening."

"Oh, I know, I know—my deception was inexcusable. But it can hardly be helped, and besides we are here now."

"Courtenay?" Another male voice entered the conversation. The gentleman walking towards them presented a fine sight, his long legs encased in some very fine and very tight silk breeches, his stockings showing off a set of fine calves and his evening jacket, made of superfine, mirroring his form with a closeness some might think impossible. The subtlety and taste of his clothes denoted his status as a dandy, and the fine cut indicated he was a man of considerable fortune. His countenance gave nothing of his age away with its high cheekbones, well-cut jaw, and lack of wrinkles. He could have been anywhere between one-and-twenty and thirty years of age.

"I say, is it Highsmith?"

"Yes, Courtenay, how'd you do?" The gentleman was upon the two now and bowed to both.

Courtenay presented the Earl. "A fine friend, Wolversley, and quite the ladies' man!" He winked at Highsmith. "I can vouch for him."

Wolversley hardly cared. He was far too distracted by the confirmation of his fears. This was the Rotherham house, the house he had avoided since their taking it. The family he had avoided for six years. He was hardly in the mood to make new acquaintances. He mumbled a perfunctory greeting to Highsmith and was so distracted that, before he knew it, Courtenay had taken his arm and led him into the house he so much wanted to flee.

They walked through the crowded hallway, discarding their coats and hats and, in Courtenay's case, a cane. All the while the colour was draining from Wolversley's face. Courtenay reached the top of the stairs beside Highsmith, oblivious to the Earl's deteriorating state of calm. Wolversley drew level with them at the end of the landing where a small set of stairs led down to a ballroom. The high ceilings of the large room had filled with the heat from the energetic crowd of people, and below, the guests were dressed in their finest gowns or breeches and eagerly chatting to their neighbours.

"I say, a splendid affair, just as I was told it would be." Courtenay turned to Wolversley for agreement, but his look of pleasure was soon changed to one of slight concern. "You're looking a trifle peaked." The concern turned to funning as he nudged his friend's arm. "Perhaps a glimpse of our beautiful debutante will restore your colour. Come, it's high time we greeted our hostess."

Courtenay descended the stairs and left Wolversley to do the same. The Earl did so with a mind full of foreboding and a set of particularly unsure feet. Courtenay's earlier words concerning Wolversley finding a betrothed were about to become shockingly true.

WHEN JULIA ROTHERHAM caught sight of Lucius Wolversley at her sister's coming-out ball, her jaw shot downwards, her fan fell to the floor, and her feet stumbled backwards in an unladylike fashion. She blinked, but rather than the Earl's presence being a trick of the mind, as it so often had been, he remained. She felt her fan pressed back into her hand by one of the servants, but her gaze could not be shaken from the man who had just entered the ballroom. He had not seen her yet, and she prayed that it would remain that way. If only the priceless crystal chandelier would fall down and break a hole in the ballroom floor through which she could be swallowed.

At any moment, according to decorum, he would come to greet the hostess, her mother, the woman next to whom Julia was standing. She absolutely could *not* speak to him. Why on earth was he here? Had he been invited? How dare he invade her home in this manner!

Julia's wide green eyes flashed around the room, in the hopes that Peter Highsmith, who had greeted her mother just before Lord Courtenay, was still in the vicinity. Surely, he would lend her his arm and support her through this nightmare? They were friends, after all, despite the proposal he had offered and she had declined last year. Where was he? It was no use, thought Julia. He had already dissolved into the crowds.

The shock Julia felt at once again seeing the dark hair and cool eyes of Earl Wolversley gave way to sheer panic. He was closing in on her. She glanced about again. How could she escape speaking to him?

Her darting eyes found a path through the crowd. Perhaps if she ran now.... She looked back at her mother and father and knew in an instant she could not run. It was quite simply the most scandalous thing for a lady to do in the midst of a ball, and her mother would not forgive her for it.

The middle-aged woman, dressed in dark blue, began sending her eldest daughter excited looks. Julia could sense that her mother had spotted Earl Wolversley, and her panic increased.

No, she could not run, but if she managed an athletic leap, she might dive under the seats lined up against the wall just to the side of her. A whisper of reason told her that this plan was also no good. Even if she managed to fit through the chair legs, she would most probably upset the occupants of said chairs, not to mention that it would be far more improper than merely running away.

Botheration! Why was it so difficult to form a devious, last-minute departure plan in the midst of a ball? One would think that, owing to the large amount of people, it would be easy to dissolve into the melee. Not for Julia Rotherham it seemed. There was a spacious gap between the Rotherham welcoming party and their guests, and her mother's watchful eyes would catch and put a stop to her flight in seconds. Julia glanced again at the chairs next to her and huffed in frustration.

In mere seconds she would come face to face with the man who had broken her heart six years ago, and not one decent plan of escape would materialise in her mind. Fiddlesticks! If only she had worn a better dress. She had not wanted to steal attention from her sister this evening—as if she *could* steal attention from her golden haired, Greek goddess of a younger sister—but the determination not to do so had led her to wear a plain evening gown with very little decoration and a rather high neckline. If only she had taken up her mama's offer to buy her a new dress. She could have chosen a ravishing one. She would have had it made up in green silk to pick up her eyes and set off her rich brown hair. She would have asked Madame Trouleux to cut it daringly low. Oh, the preparations she would have made if she had known that Lucius Wolversley would be in attendance. She would have looked so enchanting that Earl Wolversley would have fallen on his knees and begged for her to take him back.

Ridiculous! She reprimanded herself silently. Her daydreams were even more foolish than her plan of running through a crowded ballroom or diving under a set of chairs. She closed her eyes and shook her head a little just to be sure she had rid herself of the ludicrous notions her panicked mind was manufacturing.

She opened her eyes again to see a much larger hand taking hold of her own. Before she could look up, she felt the briefest press of lips on her silk glove.

"Your servant, Miss Rotherham."

After presenting her hand with a perfunctory kiss, the face before her rose steadily, its eyes intentionally evading her own. Her hand froze into position, and it was just as well that the Earl's larger hand let go of it, for she would not—could not—have made the conscious effort to take it back.

After the first jolt of recognition, her lips became an uncompromising line and her eyes widened with anger. It took all her will power to keep her from laying a stinging slap across Earl Wolversley's falsely smiling face. Fortunately for him, the gentleman had turned back to her mother almost immediately after greeting her, thus avoiding the blow to the cheek that he richly deserved.

How dare he! She cast a look of fury in his direction. She could still feel the heat of his fingers where they had touched her silk gloves. She clenched her hand, pressing all her finger-tips savagely into her palm, obliterating the sensation of his hand holding hers.

She watched his face as he spoke to her mother. It still contained many of the features of the youth that she remembered, and yet now she could see small lines at the side of his mouth and eyes. The latter were still the pale, engaging gray they had always been, but now they seemed less open, with a sharpness she had never seen. His face also seemed stiff and guarded. He appeared old—well, not old, but certainly aged. She remembered the boyish side of his character with the mischievous tendencies that she had found so amusing in youth, but now he looked world-worn. If she had been on good terms with him, she might even have accused him of being in the sulks. Then again, she was fairly sure her own face did not hold any affability at this present moment, and besides, she was most certainly *not* on good terms with this man.

He glanced at her then, as if to include her in the conversation he was having with her mother. She stared back at him as though she were a statue, wondering what had paralysed her, wondering why she could not react. Then realisation struck— the one thing that was missing from his face was a recognition of their past. There was no spark or knowing look when his eyes met hers. There was only the presence of controlled bad flavour underlying a false smile of civility. Julia could not but wonder if it was really an act or—heaven forbid!—had he really forgotten?

She certainly had not forgotten. It was not every day that an engaged girl was thrown over. It was not every day that a betrothed young man tasted the sinful fruits the world had to offer and developed a decided preference for them over his intended. A saint turned rake. Well, that was a slight stretch— he had never been, exactly, a saint, and she did not have any proof that he was a rake, just a suspicion.

All those years ago she had been in love and had thought herself loved in return. In the end it had all been for nothing, leaving her with a deep, aching loss which time had only been able to numb but not completely heal. Now he was here and she had no idea what to say. She was, in fact, for the first time in her extremely talkative life, completely lost for words. There were no words large enough or furious enough to express what she was feeling. Nor were there any words subtle enough to convey the cutting remarks that wanted to fly through the air like knives at this very public occasion. And since the right words were not available to her, Julia could only stare, her mouth poised to open but refusing to do more.

Mrs. Rotherham, seeing her daughter's verbal ineptitude, fanned her pink face in an attempt at charm and then leapt into the conversational void as Julia still remained silent. "Do not mind my eldest, my lord. I suppose you will remember her." She fanned herself slightly faster as she glided over the allusion to Julia and Wolversley's youthful betrothal. "She was a shy girl always."

Julia could hear her mother's voice babbling away and, despite her frozen state, she was sensible of the fact that her mother was telling outrageous lies. If Wolversley remembered their first meeting, he would most certainly know the truth that she was not now, nor had ever been, a shy girl.

She had been introduced to the Earl when he was still in shortcoats at a garden party. Much to her mother's distress, Julia had run amok, engaging in rowdy horseplay with Wolversley and another neighbour's son. The real gem in this memory was when Julia dared Wolversley to paddle in the lake, and then called him a coward when he refused. There was a supposed man-eating fish lurking in the algae-infested waters. Julia had then decided to brave the beastly deep herself in order to prove Wolversley's cowardice. Annoyed by such slurs being cast upon his character, Wolversley had raced ahead of Julia and knocked into her as he ran past. This rude bump she had taken to heart, and when they both finally stood in the shallow waters, Julia discreetly put a neat foot behind Wolversley's right leg and gave him a sturdy kick. He landed on his backside in the muddy shallows and promptly pulled her down after him. It had ended in a quarrelling match, a bout of splashing, and finally a fit of the giggles.

Whilst Julia dallied in the waters of nostalgia, her mother continued to talk to the Earl, asking after his family. "I was sad to hear of your uncle's passing, though it is some years ago now—so sorry that your family has suffered so much loss, first with your parents and now your guardian." Mrs. Rotherham's most winning trait, as anyone of her acquaintance would tell you, was her compassionate heart. Her soft brown eyes grew wide with sympathy. "I suppose you miss him greatly."

The object of said sympathy, however, did not seem to receive it in an appreciative light. His eyelids narrowed, the muscles at the corner of his mouth twitched, and his lips compressed themselves into a firm line. It seemed that his uncle, the guardian of his deceased father's estate until Wolversley had come of age, was someone he did not care to discuss.

Mrs. Rotherham did not notice the displeasure manifesting itself in Wolversley's manner. She carried on, assuming it was grief that kept Wolversley from speaking. "How have you been getting on since?"

Wolversley, seemingly pleased that the topic had changed, spoke again, but his conversation was now stilted and abrupt. "Well enough, thank you, Mrs. Rotherham."

"And your poor, dear sister, Lady Selina. How is she?"

"Well, I thank you, and much grown since you last saw her, I am sure."

"Does she accompany you for the Season?"

"As simple observation can show you, madam, she does not."

This curt remark, unlike Wolversley's previous change of countenance, did not go unnoticed by Mrs. Rotherham. But once again, she simply attributed his abrupt manner to grief at the references to his departed uncle. Knowing that gentlemen in general disliked showing sensibility of any kind, especially in public, she smiled and accepted that the conversation was coming to an end. A queue of guests was forming behind the Earl and, not wanting to be disagreeable to them or detain the Earl against his will, Mrs. Rotherham decided it best to release him.

"Well, it has been a pleasure to renew our acquaintance." Her voice softened. "I am sure you are also pleased to re-acquaint yourself with my daughter."

Julia, still frozen with shock and unable to deliver the set-down she so desired, cringed inwardly at her mother's mention of her.

"Indeed," responded the Earl flatly.

Julia did not miss the slight.

"I do hope you enjoy the ball, Wolversley!" said Julia's father, who had hitherto been caught up with another guest and was just now turning to shake hands with the Earl. "I am sure you remember most of the faces—a good many of our neighbours from Sussex are in attendance." Mr. Rotherham's good-natured voice seemed to soften Wolversley's reserve, at least for the moment.

"Good to see you again, Mr. Rotherham. I must apologise for not calling previously, and also for darkening your doors at such an event without an invitation. My friend, Lord Courtenay, insisted that I come along with him. I only arrived back in

Town today." Wolversley's guarded tones had changed to honest ones as he conversed with the country squire.

"Think nothing of it. It's just jolly good to see you again, my lad." Mr. Rotherham pumped his guest's hand with genuine warmth. "It's been too long since we've had you under our roof."

At this comment Wolversley's clouded countenance cleared a little.

"Thank you, sir."

"Yes, indeed!" Julia's mother would not let the chance slip by, especially as the Earl's mood had become affable once again. As her daughter shot her a despairing look, knowing what was about to take place, Mrs. Rotherham proceeded on her motherly course. "So much dancing to be done this evening." She lifted her eyebrows helpfully at her daughter, but Julia only shot venomous looks back.

Oh, goodness! Julia felt sick. How was this happening? How could he simply barge back into her life again? It was true she was situated in the busy hub of London at the start of the Season—certainly not the place and time to avoid seeing another member of the ton—but still! This was *her* social circle, *her* life, *her* part of the world—and he was like a bull, coming in and crashing everything about. She felt the crushing misery of six years ago come bubbling back to the surface.

"Indeed," said Wolversley, once again without much enthusiasm. He bowed with ingrained courtesy and took his leave of his host and hostess.

Julia stared after him like a lost pup, completely ignoring the guests who attempted to greet her. It was a letter—that is how he had broken their engagement. One single sheet of paper, that's all it was, and that insignificant object had broken her heart. She forced her eyes away from his shoulders melting into the crowd and turned her attention to the boards on the floor.

"Daughter, you do not look yourself," Mr. Rotherham whispered in Julia's ear. "I think you had best go and find some refreshment, my child."

Julia grasped for an excuse to explain away her pale face, but one look at her father told her she did not have to. She nodded and left the greeting line.

Mr. Rotherham turned back to his wife. "Now, my dear, that was a little hard on poor Julia."

"What was?"

"You know very well what I mean, my dear, and although I admire your knowledge of the marriage mart and your matchmaking ways, that was not one of your finest moments."

Mrs. Rotherham coloured at her husband's reprimand. She fluttered her fan for a few moments before speaking. "It's all very well her wanting to be unmarried now, but the years are passing faster than she knows. I simply thought that perhaps, since he has come tonight and since so much time has passed since the…unfortunate event, there may still be hope for them."

Mr. Rotherham, who knew the anxiety his wife suffered over their eldest daughter's future, could understand her path of logic, but he could hardly concur with it. He sighed. "Do you remember how low our Julia was after Wolversley cried off? That same look she used to wear was on her face again just now. I doubt there is any hope for them until her heart is mended."

"It's been six years, George!"

"Yes, and just imagine if it were you and I."

Mrs. Rotherham smiled at that. "Well, I don't believe you would have been foolish enough to cry off."

"And suffer your wrath? I think not!" He let out a practised cough and shook his head.

"George!" She swatted his shoulder with her fan. "Behave

yourself. We have guests to greet, and you will paint an awful picture of me if you carry on so."

"Your wish is my command, O Wrathful One!" Mr. Rotherham grinned mischievously at his wife, winked, and then nodded to signal that the next guest could approach.

philippajanekeyworth.com/TUE

WANT TO BE IN THE KNOW?

Be the first to know about freebies, sales and when Philippa's next book releases by signing up to her newsletter.

Sign up below:

philippajanekeyworth.com/newsletter

ALSO BY
PHILIPPA JANE KEYWORTH

LADIES OF WORTH

From the gaming hells of 18th century London to Bath's fashionable Pump Room, the Ladies of Worth series opens up a world of romance, wit and scandal to its readers. With formidable heroines and honourable heroes who match each other wit for wit you'll find yourself falling in love with the Ladies of Worth.

philippajanekeyworth.com/FMT

philippajanekeyworth.com/ADD

philippajanekeyworth.com/LOW

REGENCY ROMANCES

philippajanekeyworth.com/TWR

philippajanekeyworth.com/TUE

FANTASY

philippajanekeyworth.com/TE

ABOUT THE AUTHOR

Philippa Jane Keyworth, also known as P. J. Keyworth, writes historical romance and fantasy novels you'll want to escape into.

She loves strong heroines, challenging heroes and backdrops that read like you're watching a movie. She creates complex, believable characters you want to get to know and worlds that are as dramatic as they are beautiful.

Keyworth's historical romance novels include Regency and Georgian romances that trace the steps of indomitable heroes and heroines through historic British streets. From London's glittering ballrooms to its dark gaming hells, characters experience the hopes and joys of love while avoiding a coil or two! Travel with them through London, Bath, Cornwall and beyond and you'll find yourself falling in love.

Keyworth's fantasy series The Emrilion Trilogy follows strong love stories and epic adventure. Unveiling a world of nomadic warrior tribes and peaceful forest-dwelling folk, you can explore the hills, deserts and cities of Emrilion and the history that is woven through them. With so many different races in the same kingdom it's become a melting pot of drama and intrigue where the ultimate struggle between good and evil will bring it all to the brink of destruction.

facebook.com/philippajane.keyworth

twitter.com/PJKeyworth

instagram.com/pjkeyworth

amazon.com/author/philippakeyworth

bookbub.com/authors/philippa-jane-keyworth

goodreads.com/philippajanekeyworth